FATHER JUNIPER AND THE GENERAL

"What? Miracles in my diocese, and without my permission? I forbid them. . . ."
—Unamuno, quoting a Spanish bishop.

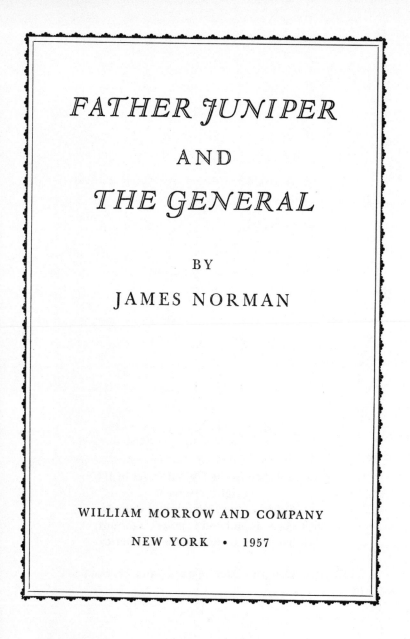

FATHER JUNIPER
AND
THE GENERAL

BY

JAMES NORMAN

WILLIAM MORROW AND COMPANY

NEW YORK • 1957

For
JUDITH
—Haec olim meminisse juvabit.

CONTENTS

THERE is a time of the year when people in the town of Santiago de Gante make a festival, an event involving a wooden saint who stands by while a pair of young angels soar through the warm Mexican sky, making fine speeches in Latin, and showering tiny colored confetti prayers upon the crowd below. Most years the angels are ordinary children, washed up somewhat, outfitted with cardboard wings, and launched out over the festive street by means of cables and pullies. The matter of cables is mentioned because on one occasion they were not used, yet somehow a great number of people saw the angels flying.

THE COMING OF JUNIPER

The fierce scarecrow of an old man who had once been a notorious bandit, but was now retired, led his small gray donkey to the crest of the hill overlooking the town. This Don Vasco, as he was called, had a long lean face and iron-gray hair. For a man of a hundred years he was wiry and durable. He had saturnine eyebrows and not many teeth. He wore the garments of the region: flyless white cambric trousers folded around the waist, a buttonless shirt knotted at his scrawny belly, sandals and a frayed straw sombrero. Attached somehow to his beltless middle was a murderous machete which gave him the airs of a pirate.

As he came to the hill-crest he saw a stranger sitting there upon a trunk that was shaped like a small frivolous coffin. The box was pale blue and narrow at the bottom. Old Vasco stared suspiciously at the man and his trunk, then he coughed. The stranger turned, and for a long moment each man measured the other.

The stranger was plump, with round fingers and very round, slightly protruding eyes. He did not seem the sort who took comfort in his roundness, but just accepted it as

13

one accepts legs and arms. He had the appearance of a man with some Indian blood, noticeable mostly in the gradual peaked shape of his head and in the largeness of his brown thumbprint eyes. He was not a dark man, however. In contrast to his eyes, the skin covering his round cheeks was so smooth and pink it glowed like that of a child.

With a bandit's knack of evaluating others, Old Vasco took in every point: the dusty black suit the man wore, his soiled collarless shirt, and the frieze of grayish silver hair peeking out like a tarnished halo from beneath the brim of a black clerical fedora.

Old Vasco hitched up his pants, his machete and shirt in one motion, and pronounced a greeting. The stranger returned it with a happy nod.

"Are you going down into Santiago de Gante?" the ex-bandit added, sweeping his arm toward the town below.

"The town is Santiago, then?" asked the stranger.

"Santiago de Gante. But how is it you come by foot?" Don Vasco glared searchingly at the stranger's possessions lying about on the rust red earth. Beside the blue trunk stood a cheap brass bird cage housing a tattered green parrot. A pair of scuffed shoes were tied to the outside of the cage like lifeboats.

The stranger stood up. "I was given a ride by truck," he said. "It turned off a little ways back. Nevertheless, I am going to Santiago."

Vasco eyed the trunk again. It was a sign that the stranger intended a long visit in Santiago. Although he resented this, Vasco did not reveal it.

"Are you from the town?" asked the stranger.

Vasco simply nodded. He had been away from Santiago for a week, hiding in the hills, and he was not anxious to talk.

"Perhaps, then, you know General Braga?" asked the man with the parrot. "Or would you know Señor Policarpio Flores?"

Old Vasco shrugged defensively. "Yes, Policarpio," he grunted.

The stranger sensed the old bandit's caution. He realized that he ought to identify himself. He should say, "I am Father Juniper. I've come to take Father Caldo's place." But it was embarrassing to present himself, thus, without his cassock. Furthermore, he did not want to reveal himself yet. He was looking forward to the pleasure of arriving in Santiago de Gante unannounced, of being able to feel out the town before anyone recognized him. It would be like being invisible.

"You plan to stay in Santiago?" Vasco asked.

"For a while, señor."

The priest turned to gaze down upon the town. From the hill-crest there was a view of the houses below, of the undulating valley beyond, and the distant pleated mountains. Between himself and the town lay a deep gorge spanned by an ancient suspension bridge.

The town was pleasant to look upon. Bathed by the mid-January sunlight, its houses were all lavender, lemon colored, brown or pink. There were several churches, each decomposing with charm, but decomposing nevertheless. The largest among them, a thing of pale green stone and lofty twin towers, faced upon a plaza where stone fountains, a red-roofed bandstand and iron grillwork benches were shaded by trees and splotches of red hibiscus flowers. The plaza was encircled by fine old colonial buildings with cool arched passages. This was Santiago de Gante, a very historic town, and somewhat troublesome for its size.

A sudden nerve shattering hawing startled the priest. It

had come from the mouse-gray donkey belonging to the bandit. Old Vasco pulled the small animal toward him and rubbed its furry ears affectionately.

"This is El Primitivo," said the old man. "He is very talkative, but it is limited to telling the time."

"He tells the time?"

"And why not? Each haw is for the hour. In Santiago de Gante all the burros tell time. But he is more intelligent than the others. He has learned to roll over and play dead." The old man glanced toward the caged parrot, adding, "Does your bird speak a civilized language, too?"

Father Juniper nodded and held up the cage to present the parrot. "I call him El Furioso," he said. "He is a native of Huaxtec. He is angry because there are eighty centavos of buckshot in the gizzard so that he does not fly."

The bird glared at the old man and the priest with an orange-eyed fury.

"How many words does he have?"

"Ten, I think."

"As a favor, would you get him to say one?"

Father Juniper spread his round fingers apologetically. "He is always so furious, he forgets, then he can say nothing."

The two men observed the parrot thoughtfully, as though they were devising some plan to appease its anger. Finally Old Vasco shrugged, murmuring, "If you are going to town El Primitivo can carry your box?"

"That is very kind."

When the blue trunk and the bird cage had been secured upon the donkey's wooden packsaddle, Vasco whacked the animal and they set out. The footpath, which had once been Santiago de Gante's main link with the regular state road that skirted the town, led down toward the gorge and the suspension bridge. When they reached the edge of the chasm the ex-bandit halted and motioned toward the bridge which was nothing more than a narrow wooden walk hung from a lacework of hemp ropes. It spanned the deep ravine where, far below, a pale ribbon of water bordered by green *palo blanco* bushes threaded among huge bone-white rocks.

"It is strange that you come by this route," Vasco observed.

"This is the road I knew about."

Vasco shrugged. "Most visitors come by the new auto road and the concrete bridge." The old man waved a hand vaguely to the south. "Here the bridge is useful only for burros, and it isn't safe. I shall go across alone. Then the animal will come. Afterwards, you may follow."

"Why isn't the bridge fixed?" asked the priest. "This is still a useful route."

"General Braga is against it."

"Is he one who likes danger?"

Old Vasco frowned. He might have explained that General Braga, as *presidente* or chairman of the town council, was against renovating the bridge because it was picturesque and therefore had a certain value. This footbridge had become the most painted and photographed bridge in all of Mexico, and was one of the things that attracted many tourists to Santiago de Gante. Don Vasco, and others in Santiago who found the bridge useful as a bridge, disagreed violently with the general. Old Vasco glanced suspiciously at the stranger and decided it was best not to discuss delicate town politics with him. He gave an indifferent grunt and started across the fragile bridge. His donkey followed at a safe distance.

"Now, you come," Vasco shouted to the priest. "But beware. Do not look down. It is dangerous to look down."

The priest moved cautiously across the nervously swaying span. He had noticed that the old man had carefully avoided looking down. He did likewise, though he was not aware of the reason for this precaution.

In the region around Santiago de Gante everyone avoided looking down into the ravine because of La Yegua—the Mare Lady. Santiagans were quite certain that La Yegua frequented the gorge just below the bridge where she often brought disaster upon men. Although few living people seemed to have seen her, it was known that La Yegua was an extraordinary woman blessed with a figure far lovelier than anything the other girls in town could flaunt. Her head, however, was that of a horse. It was this that made her so dangerous for she was attractive not only in the eyes of ordinary men, but also to ranchers who had a passion for horses. The women of Santiago feared her because she could entice their husbands and lovers into the ravine, and the next morning they would be found dead. On windy nights La Yegua's winsome whinnying could often be heard, and there was scarcely a man in the region who could resist it if he were near the bridge.

When the priest finally joined Old Vasco on the other side of the bridge, he pulled out a huge handkerchief and mopped his brow. "That is indeed a dangerous crossing," he murmured.

"Only when it collapses," Vasco answered waspishly.

A steep cobbled street slanted down from the bridge into the town. As the priest and the old man came opposite the first houses, Vasco remarked that there must be some sort of fiesta in progress. On every side paper flags fluttered from balconies and the red tiled roofs. Sounds of firecrackers and an occasional hissing of rockets could be heard bursting above the tangle of narrow streets.

"Is it the feast of one of the churches?" the priest asked.

The ex-bandit frowned in a forbidding way. "A church

fiesta? No. Such feast days I never forget. But this thing today? Who knows? Perhaps it is someone's saint's day?"

They entered the plaza. The clatter of El Primitivo's tiny hoofs upon the cobbles made a positively prim sort of commotion, especially since the plaza was almost deserted. A few people could be seen hurrying toward a side street where the sound of fireworks was noisiest.

"Shall we look to the fiesta?" Don Vasco asked.

The priest did not answer. He had stopped, and was now staring across the plaza, fascinated by the pale green church of Santiago de Gante.

The church was truly an edifice capable of intriguing anyone. It was modeled after the Spanish fashion, being about twice the size it ought to be. Across its façade, in addition to the carved romanesque forms, there were little touches of gothic, of baroque, a pinch here and there of plateresque and of lesser architectural devices which were purely Mexican florentine. Still, for all its hodgepodge, there was something soaringly impressive about the church. The twin bell towers were delicate and magnificent. They were like pale filigree extending its tracery into the sky.

Father Juniper sighed. "It is a very suitable church for Santiago," he said aloud. "This must be the *parroquia,* the parish church, eh?"

Old Vasco squinted at the belfries. "Last week I almost blew it up," he announced as though this were an everyday activity. He shook his head sadly. "But I missed."

The priest's mouth opened in awe. "You almost blew it up? But how?"

"Dynamite. But I missed."

2

OF VARIOUS FIESTAS

The events leading up to Old Vasco's attempted bombing of church property were very complicated. They had to do with a miraculous saint made of wood, a finger-general, some American canapé eaters, a foolishly ambitious priest, a saloonkeeper named Policarpio, and in fact, just about everybody in Santiago de Gante.

The trouble began because of a difference of opinion about Santiago, the patron saint of the town, and concerning the fiesta celebrated in his honor.

In Mexico, where the celebrating of fiestas is a profound national occupation, there are very few towns that take their celebrations as seriously as does Santiago de Gante. During the warm months it is gospel in the region that if a Santiagan so much as thinks about a fiesta, or murmurs the word, everyone knocks off work until the next day. And, of all the celebrations, the July fête for Santiago, or Saint James, is the most important. On Santiago's day the people exert themselves to the maximum: there are splendid fireworks, a violent battle in the streets between the saint and some Moors; there are also bullfights, rodeos, and two small children flying overhead like angels. All this fervor is simply an expression of the townsmen's love for their saint, who is very old and is known to be miraculous.

The feast of Santiago had been celebrated in the town of the green church for more than two hundred years, and it was only during the Revolution of 1910, when the wooden saint mysteriously disappeared, that the trouble over the fiesta began. No one in town knew where the saint had gone, though it was suspected that one or two of his partisans had removed him from the church, intending to hide him until the violence of the Revolution had passed. Undoubtedly these friends, holding to the old Mexican custom of dying without leaving word of where valuables are hidden, had passed away with the secret of the saint's whereabouts.

After the Revolution had frittered itself out, the fiesta was resumed. But much of the old fervor was gone because the townspeople had to use a counterfeit saint made of plaster. Then, one day, the real Santiago reappeared. He was found within a sealed room in the old Gante monastery at the edge of town. This monastery, abandoned for many years and in disrepair, had been bought by General Hamilcar Braga.

Although the Santiagans were overjoyed by the rediscovery of their saint, General Braga, a newcomer in town, did not turn the saint over to the church and the people. Being a business man, he added the saint to his staff.

Hamilcar Braga had not always been a business man. Many years ago, while just a lad, he had ridden with Pancho Villa's revolutionary forces in the North. One day when the guerrilla army happened to be short of officers, Pancho Villa himself had pointed his pistol finger at young Hamilcar, saying, *"Hombre,* now you're a general." Thus Braga had become one of Mexico's first revolutionary finger-generals.

A little later, while in the region of Uruapan, Hamilcar had gone into the guerrilla business for himself and he had been quite successful. He had acquired several ranches, a Ford Motor Agency and a small Italian tank. Thanks to an American journalist who had followed him about, the general had also absorbed some culture. The journalist, a former Harvard man, never got the stories he had wanted out of the general, but he left his mark on him. General Braga learned to speak English with a broad A, and he developed a taste for fine paintings and poetesses. For a number of years he collected both without always paying for them. Then, during the 1930's, sensing that the era of brigandage was over, he went into the next best thing—business. He bought and built apartment houses in Mexico City, cornered cotton and weaving factories in Toluca as well as shoe factories in León. Within a short time he was so wealthy that he retired.

A few years before the coming of Father Juniper to Santiago de Gante, the general had purchased the old monastery, planning to make it over into a luxurious private estate. In the course of the restoration the wooden saint was discovered, along with a set of rare vellum-bound books, the *Annals of Santiago de Gante,* which identified the saint and told something of his history.

Braga knew a good thing when he saw it. He promptly gave up the idea of retirement. He had the monastery restored to all its ancient colonial charm, and he turned it into a fashionable resort for tourists. To attract visitors he began staging his own fiesta of Santiago, complete with hired Indian dancers and performers to enact the traditional battle of the Moors.

The people of Santiago de Gante did not so much mind the general putting on his own fiesta in opposition to theirs, but they resented the fact that their wooden saint was being exploited. They wanted Santiago returned to his niche in the pale green church. When General Braga disregarded their demands, they then petitioned the town council.

Now, a curious thing had already begun to happen to the town council. The councilmen, mostly well-to-do merchants, were impressed by the money General Braga's tourists had begun to drop behind them. Likewise, a certain number of them had rubbed off on the town and had become the nucleus of an American colony. These gringos came to be known as the canapé eaters because they did a great deal of drinking and they seemed to limit their eating to little open-faced sandwiches. Some of the councilmen attended all the cocktail parties given by the visitors, and they catered to them generally. Naturally, instead of acting upon the petition of the people, they rejected it. To make matters worse, they installed General Braga as the *presidente* of the council.

The people in Santiago began taking sides. On the one hand there were the merchants who dealt in liquors and canned food, and the landlords who could demand higher rents because now houses had to have bathtubs. On the other side stood the less powerful Santiagans who made no profit from the gringos, and who felt their town and customs were being taken over and changed for the benefit of the tourists. For these people, the saint became a symbol.

When the council did nothing about General Braga's refusal to return Santiago to the church, the plain citizens directed a petition to the bishop who lived some distance away in the state capital. The bishop ordered Father Caldo, the pastor of Santiago de Gante, to look into the matter and negotiate with General Braga. Caldo was the wrong man for this, as anyone could have told the bishop.

For many years the Santiagans had endured a succession

of pastors who were not at all to their liking. It was as if the bishop and the monsignors in the chancery office of the diocese knew nothing about the town, and figured—since it was in Mexico—any Spanish speaking priest would do.

Father Caldo, the last of this disastrous line, was entirely too strict to be accepted by the Santiagans. The people preferred that their priest be a little on the indolent and good-natured side: a priest should be a friend, and something of a pagan. Caldo was none of these. He was a man who knew his breviaries by heart, was sound on the Trinity, and he expected his parishioners to toe a similar theological line. The Santiagans did not mind the Church having rules and regulations, but they always thought of these things as one should think of a limit on a poker game—something to be observed for an hour, then broken. There were some Santiagans who believed in the saint, but not in God. And there were times, especially when rain was needed, that the image of a friendly old Aztec god such as Tlaloc, if slipped into the church, worked wonders.

The Santiagans could put up with Father Caldo's frowning attitude toward their little schisms and their pagan love for Santiago, but the one thing they could not stand was any indifference on the part of a parish priest regarding their saint's role in town. Caldo was foolishly indifferent. He had his mind on other things than wooden saints, and eventually, these things scandalized the townsmen.

It was Policarpio Flores who uncovered Father Caldo's most serious transgressions.

Policarpio was a man fitted for such deeds. He was a natural leader of the people, because, in the same breath, he was a Catholic, a saloonkeeper and the leading anticlerical spirit in town. On the occasions when he attended Mass with his wife, he always put clay plugs in his ears during the sermon. Although he was not an imposing man in build, he was memorable. People were attracted by the sardonic twinkle in his eyes as well as by his brilliant tattoos: a Campeche shrimp on his right forearm, a lavender dancing octopus upon the other arm. He had acquired these decorations many years before when he had run off to enlist in the Mexican Navy, only to discover that even though there were pictures of ships in the daily papers, still, there was no navy. The shrimp and octopus were a reminder for Policarpio that things are not always as they appear to be.

Part of Policarpio's anticlericalism had to do with the bar he had inherited from his father. This *cantina* had been scandalizing the more proper citizens in Santiago de Gante ever since it began leaning against the church in about 1904. Most people, however, did not object very seriously to the leaning, for they understood that the saloon's foundations were a little weak on the church side. The only person who really objected in a positive way was Policarpio. He leaned the other way to make up for it.

His bar, called *El Parlamento Inglés,* had been named by his father who had a vague notion that some important drinking and talking was done in the English Parliament. It was a good name and a good place. There were swinging doors, a long bar made of oiled mesquite wood, a handy open urinal in one corner, and upon the wall behind the bar, there was a huge mural painting of a fighting bull. This bull was Policarpio's pride and joy. No other saloon south-of-the-border possessed such elaborate art.

One day, from behind his mesquite bar, Policarpio informed a few close friends of Father Caldo's sin.

"It is a useful thing to know what has happened to our saint," he said. "Caldo doesn't want Santiago in the church. I tell you, the priest has been bought off by General Braga.

Caldo has betrayed our saint; not just for thirty pieces of silver, but for a bathtub."

Then the story came out. Father Caldo had built a beautiful American-style bathroom in the rectory, and he had gone into debt over it. General Braga had had to rescue the priest from this embarrassing situation by giving an exceptionally large contribution to the church. Since that day, the padre had taken no interest in suing for the return of the wooden saint.

That evening, after the news had gotten around, a handful of Santiagans met again with Policarpio.

"The priest has gone bad from hanging around with the Americans," shouted Zapopan, the sexton and bell ringer for the church.

Zapopan had reason to know Father Caldo and to dislike him. For years he had worked high in the belfry of the pale green church, ringing in all the services, tolling in the fiestas and ringing the hours of the day without need of a clock. He shrewdly judged the time from the sun, or if the day were overcast, he got the correct time from the donkeys. If, by chance, a donkey happened to be an hour or two awry, no one really minded. Even a donkey wasn't expected to know the exact time on a cloudy day. However, when Father Caldo became the senior pastor of the town, a clock was installed in the belfry. This was, in a sense, an insult to Zapopan. But Caldo had demanded American efficiency.

Now, Zapopan hunched his sloping shoulders, glanced down briefly at his immensely strong, coarse hands, then he glared about at the other men and added, "We ought to drive the gringos out!"

Policarpio shook his head sagely. He knew the law, so he offered another plan. "The Americans are too important and strong. Remember the Marines at Vera Cruz," he said.

"Although it is true that prices have gone up because of the gringos; although the town is no longer ours; even the saint no longer belongs to us—we must fight in another way. The thing is, we should show our disapproval by making an example of the priest."

Old Vasco, who was present at the meeting, chuckled waspishly. He was not normally a talkative man when it involved town gossip. Even when he was drunk he was prone to laugh and grin, or carry on reproachful conversations with himself in Basque and Spanish, yet he seldom concerned himself with gossip. When he did talk at any length, it was with his good friend Señor Tzintzuntzan, the maker of fireworks. The two could be seen sitting together in the plaza or at the *Parlamento Inglés,* whispering in turn, glancing about furtively or sighing angrily. No one ever knew what they talked about.

Now, however, Don Vasco had something to say. Although he was nearing his hundredth birthday, he still believed in direct action. As a former highwayman who had spread terror through the region, he did not like to see such atmosphere die out.

"We make a protest," he grimaced fiercely. "Something simple, like assassination. Then we bomb out the gringos!"

"No assassinations," Policarpio objected.

"Ah . . . a bombing!" Tzintzuntzan murmured thoughtfully. He smiled at Vasco.

"Bombs?" Policarpio looked dubiously at the others.

The idea took root. It called for very little discussion; simply a matter of who should be bombed.

Much later that night Don Vasco's gangling figure might have been seen stealing from the side door of the *Parlamento Inglés.* His movements as he made his way through the network of narrow streets were covered by the gray fog sifting into the valley. He halted for a moment at the house of Tzintzuntzan where he picked up a package, then vanished again. Somewhere in the shrouded night a guitar sang a love song. From the town jail there came the mournful notes of a flute. At midnight, instead of one of the smaller bells in the church tower tolling the hour, the town was startled to hear the giant bell, *El Temblor,* which was usually rung only on important occasions. Then, a moment later, a thunderous blast shook the town.

Perhaps it was because Old Vasco had drunk a bit too much *pulque* before setting out, thus getting mixed in his bearings, that the mistake was made. Whatever it was, the thing that occurred was unforgivable. A gaping hole had been blown through one wall of the *Parlamento Inglés.* Policarpio was as mad as a bull.

"If you were going to make a mistake," he shouted at Vasco, "you didn't have to use so much dynamite."

Old Vasco refused to take the blame. "I think like you," he shouted back at his friends. "Three sticks make a bigger noise than one. I put them under the window of the priest's house. That is on the other side of the church. I think Caldo moved them."

He repeated this loudly, and in public. His friends had to send him into the hills for a while.

Meanwhile, in the state capital, Bishop Sierra began to understand at last that Santiago de Gante was no ordinary town, and that the saint who was at the bottom of the trouble was no ordinary image of a saint. "Evidently, what the Church needs there," he explained to his monsignors, "is a priest who can be something of a conciliator. He should be one who has had some experience with minority problems, that is to say, with Americans. And he must be unselfishly loyal to the Church."

Father Caldo was transferred out of the parish. At the same time tracers were put out to locate a new pastor who might fit the bishop's qualifications. Such a man was finally found, a man who seemed to be just the right one for a troublesome post.

His name was Juniper. He was Mexican. He had recently been returned to his country from the United States where he had rescued a very shaky monastery in Wisconsin from financial ruin simply by making cheese.

WELCOME

The expected arrival of the new pastor by bus was the principal cause of the fireworks and celebration in the side street beyond the plaza. Unaware of this, Father Juniper and Old Vasco joined the crowd which had gathered before the bus terminal. No one there so much as noticed the priest.

There is some good, Father Juniper thought, in this Mexican law which forbids the clergy the right to wear cassocks and Roman collars in public. In a way, he felt almost invisible, and it gave him an opportunity to become acquainted with his parish without being noticed.

While watching the people he began to sense the marked rivalry in the air. There were really two crowds. On the shaded side of the street in front of the grocery store which served as the bus station, there were a number of polished automobiles decorated with pink and blue bunting. On one of the cars was a sign: *BIENVENIDA*. The important people of Santiago de Gante sat in the cars or clustered around them. Father Juniper saw a general in full uniform, a large number of men who made a point of wearing French berets, and with them there were some fashionably dressed women

30

who smoked cigarettes. Meanwhile, on the far side of the
street a larger crowd milled about in the glaring sun. These
were the humble, a poorer quality citizen, who, according
to the canapé eaters, were useful mainly for heavy work, and
to be photographed. Except for a few small shopkeepers
among them, the men wore white cottons, big straw hats
and crude sandals. Buried somewhere deeply in this group
was the town band: the individual musicians had lost sight
of one another and each man was playing a different tune
with great fervor.

Old Vasco vanished for several minutes. On returning to
Juniper, he said, "They're all waiting for the new pastor
who comes in on the noon bus. General Braga—you see him
there in the uniform—and his friends want to get him on
their side."

"To get who?"

"The new pastor."

Father Juniper's brows creased in a troubled frown. So it
begins already, he thought. His bishop had warned him of
the trouble in Santiago de Gante. Now, he stared shyly at
the crowd and he was glad he had not taken the bus.

"Who are the men who wear the berets?" he asked Vasco.

"Those with the funny little cloth hats? Ayi, some are
from the town council. Others are gringos. The gringos
began it, so the councilmen copy them. You will notice the
women wearing the pink bullfighter stockings. They are
the gringas. For some reason they wear such things."

Juniper nodded and listened to the band which played
from time to time. Fireworks were set off. The general's
people waited and grew impatient when noon came and
went. The crowd in the sun waited, as did Father Juniper
and Old Vasco. The priest began to feel embarrassed that

so many people should be waiting for him. Still, he found it impossible to announce himself.

A donkey somewhere up the street brayed the hour. Father Juniper pulled out his watch, a large, turnip-like brass timepiece which had only an hour hand and was limited to marking out the day in broad generalities. He shook his head. The donkey was at least two hours fast. Finally, when a little more time had slipped by, a man came out of the grocery store and announced that the bus had broken down on the highway. It would arrive the next day.

Father Juniper breathed a sigh of relief. He turned to Old Vasco, saying, "I shall go now. I'm hungry. Undoubtedly, I shall see you again."

"You have a place to eat?" Vasco asked.

The priest nodded. "I have my house here," he said. "Soon, when I am settled, you will have dinner with me, yes?"

Old Vasco watched with wonder when he saw the stranger carry his blue trunk and the bird cage across the plaza toward the pink parish house that stood next to the church. He finally shook his head and swore at El Primitivo.

Father Juniper knocked upon the rectory door. A moment later an old woman who was totally bald and quite toothless opened the door and peered out.

"I am Padre Junipero," the priest said, smiling at her. "I suppose you are Doña Maria, the housekeeper?"

The woman stared at him, then beyond him, as though she were expecting more than one man.

"This is El Furioso," the priest went on, offering her the bird and its cage. "If there is a patio, you can let him out. He's never in the cage except for traveling."

The old woman gulped and found her voice. "You're the new *cura?* But they are waiting for you at the bus station."

"Yes. I know it. I'll go there tomorrow when the bus comes in, if that is necessary. But at this moment I am hungry."

Doña Maria frowned forbiddingly. It was as if she had no love for priests and felt that they did not belong in church rectories. "There is a banquet for you at the hotel," she said. "They're waiting. Here in the rectory, I have nothing prepared."

Father Juniper smiled. "Perhaps you have beans and a little cheese?"

4

A SHORT HISTORY
OF CHEESE

Maria watched the new pastor with an unyielding suspicion
as he faced the plate of beans she had placed before him.
One good thing about him, she thought, was that he had not
demanded a formal dinner at the dining room table. He
seemed satisfied with eating on a bench in the patio.

"Padre Caldo did not eat here often," she said accusingly.
"He ate at the hotel, or with the general."

Father Juniper nodded. He tore off a piece from the flat
leathery tortilla and made a little spoon of it so as to scoop
up the beans. "I am not one who cares for fancy food," he
murmured. "Beans, such as these, I like. And perhaps a
good soup, perhaps a stew of *chicharrón,* or an *enchilada*
made of yellow squash flowers."

Maria's expression began to change. "Do you really like
such food?" she asked. "Such things are what I make best."

"Tomorrow, if you could get some *chicharrón?*"

The old woman's eyes widened with wonder. She stared at

34

the padre's round fingers as they manipulated the tortilla and beans. It was so long since the parish had had a priest who did not put on airs, demanding a fork with which to eat the beans, or even refusing beans, that it made her nervous.

Father Juniper set his empty plate on the wooden bench and beamed at her. "Doña Maria," he said. "You're a wonderful cook. I hope Padre Caldo appreciated it."

The old woman blushed furiously so that even her bald head looked like a rosy baked squash. Nothing like this had happened to her in years. She became so flustered that she fled to the kitchen and did not reappear.

After saying thanksgiving and reading his office, Father Juniper inspected the rectory. The pink parish house was old and partly in ruin, but it was comfortable. Like all Santiagan houses it was built around a patio that had a central fountain and lush growths of flowers. The rooms that were still in use were high and rather empty; each had a doorway opening into the next room, and a doorway facing toward the patio. The most interesting room, however, was the bathroom which the previous pastor, Caldo, had gone into debt over. Caldo had installed the bath after consulting a great number of movie magazines. The room was built like a church oratory: there were fluted columns, a series of marble steps leading up to a cream and pink porcelain tub. Next to the tub was a shower that resembled a baldachino; beside it, instead of a stoup for Holy Water, there was one of those little stainless steel basins for cleaning teeth, such as are furnished in American Pullman cars.

From the rectory, Juniper went on to look at his church.

Although the church was somewhat dark, it filled him with pride that he had been given such a fine place of worship. Here was a long narrow vista that reflected a coolness of at-

mosphere and an air of restful isolation. In the small alcoves
along the side walls of the church there were altars with the
customary saints and images: a statue of God the Father,
whose face had a purely accidental expression of ferocity; a
dark-skinned Madonna with blue and gilt robes of real silk;
a likeness of Saint Joseph and the Child. In a niche to the
right of the main altar, Father Juniper finally came upon a
thin plaster saint with painted robes. This was the counterfeit Santiago. The saint carried no sword in his hand, so it
was indeed difficult to think of him as Santiago.

Nevertheless, Father Juniper offered a prayer in his honor,
then added another for the Virgin, and one for God the Father. When this was done he returned to the rectory and
changed into his dusty, much-mended cassock. He put on his
biretta and went outside to sit on one of the uncomfortable
iron-grill benches in the plaza. He had been invisible long
enough.

From the bench he could marvel at the church and its
lime-colored towers thumbing the sky. He could see the
Parlamento Inglés leaning against the church as though anxious to get in. He sighed uncertainly, for he had not made
up his mind yet what to think about this phenomenon. Beyond the saloon, across a narrow street and behind high gray
walls, was the fortress-like convent and parochial school run
by the Dominican nuns. From where he sat, Juniper had
only to turn slightly to glimpse the other buildings surrounding the plaza. On one side there was the City Hall with a
stone Mexican eagle poised upon the roof. Next to it was a
billiard parlor, while beyond this, in a building of burnt-
colored stone was the police station. The *Inspección de la
Policía* also housed the town jail. The remaining two sides
of the plaza were occupied by several curio shops, a small

hotel, a grocery store patronized by the canapé eaters, a bank and the telephone office.

While he sat there serenely observing the flower-scented plaza and its surrounding buildings, two cars with colored bunting streaming over their hoods careened from a side street, raced around the plaza, then pulled up before his bench. Someone had telephoned to General Braga and his welcoming committee, informing them that there was a strange priest in town.

Father Juniper stood up to meet the delegation. He had no trouble picking out General Braga from the others. The general was a big man. He weighed two hundred and fifty pounds, without fat. He also looked like a person accustomed to maneuvering heavy tactical equipment, such as elephants, around a battlefield. His large, high-domed head was closely shaven, giving him a monastic appearance.

"Padre Junipero?" A small Mexican with overbright button eyes asked.

"I am Junipero."

"We were expecting—" said the man. "May I present the general." He turned, permitting General Braga, who appeared tightly corseted in his military uniform, to come forward.

"Braga. General Hamilcar Braga, your servant." The general introduced himself with vigor. He gave Father Juniper an *abrazo,* crushing him in his arms like a wrestler.

The general then turned, and with a Mexican's genius for stringing words upon a flashing chain of smiles and shrugs, he flicked his riding crop toward the five other members of the committee, introducing them. Juniper caught only one name, that of a young woman, a Miss Goldengrove.

The padre smiled at her politely. Miss Goldengrove was

quite young. She was an absurd, yet attractive, thing, who stared back with an expression of passionate celibacy.

"Definitely, you were expected in on the bus, padre," the general made a veiled accusation.

Father Juniper nodded. "I came by truck."

"Precisely. And we waited."

"I am very sorry."

The general studied the new pastor shrewdly. Although he did not find the priest very impressive, he realized that first impressions could be deceptive. He noted the dusty, tattered cassock, and interpreted this favorably. That a priest should be wearing his cassock in public, when it was illegal, could only mean that this Father Juniper had heard of the anticlericalism rampant in town, and he meant to fight it.

Pointing his whip at the button-eyed councilman, the general said to the priest, "He is our banker, Señor Ibarra. He has a speech of welcome. Do you wish to hear it?"

"*Pues—*" Juniper murmured in embarrassment. "But I am here already."

"Precisely," replied the general. "We'll dispense with it." The general grinned expansively because the priest showed every sign of being agreeable.

"Is not . . . ah . . . Señor Flores with you?" Father Juniper asked.

"Policarpio Flores?"

"Yes. The bishop mentioned him."

General Braga grunted. Then with startling frankness, he said, "Padre, this Flores is a man to avoid. Troublemaker. Definitely." His glance flicked darkly across the plaza toward the leaning saloon. "Troublemaker," he went on. "Policarpio Flores resists change. Our town is growing. Now, the Church recognizes this. It changes, too. Cooperates."

Father Juniper inclined his head. "Yes, cooperation," he answered agreeably.

General Braga shot him a broad smile. "Good, padre. Now if there is anything you need—new car, contributions, new altar—? let me know."

Juniper stared at the anxious-to-please faces of the welcoming party arrayed behind the general. "There is something," he said at last. "Should I ask for it now?"

"Definitely," replied Braga.

The priest shifted his glance to the general's huge thumbs that were thrust into his polished Sam Browne belt like sausages. "It is the bishop's wish," he explained, "that the wooden statue of Santiago should be returned to the church. Perhaps you'll do this tomorrow?"

Braga's heavy mouth tightened, yet he smiled. "I've a great respect for the bishop," he said. "Definitely. We'll arrange something in a friendly manner."

"Yes, it should be friendly."

"We'll talk it over later, eh?"

"I do not mind."

"There's no hurry then, padre?"

Father Juniper nodded his head in agreement.

"Bravo!" the general exclaimed with abrupt gusto. Once again he gave the priest a crushing hug. He winked broadly at the councilmen as if to say that this new pastor would be as easy to get along with as Father Caldo had been.

"We've heard of the monastery that you saved from ruin," the general went on. "Cheese, wasn't it, padre? Dairy? A man who can make a success of a dairy business in the United States must be a clever man. Competition is strong there."

Father Juniper shrugged shyly. When the welcoming committee returned to their waiting cars, the general waved back cheerfully, calling to the priest loudly so everyone in the plaza could hear, "Someday, padre, we'll set up a cheese business ourselves, eh?"

Had the general known more about Father Juniper he might not have ridden off so confidently.

Father Juniper was not made from the same mold as other priests. He lacked the worldly ambitions of a Father Caldo, and unlike his bishop, who was wise in the ways of the Church, Juniper was apt to be a little careless regarding such things as ritual and theology. This was partially due to his upbringing, and in part the fault of his nature. Juniper had been orphaned young. He had always been taken care of by the Church, living in various seminaries, studying and doing odd jobs, until he had been ordained. He had never had his own parish because his ordination had occurred during a time of strain, when Church and civil authorities had been at odds, when churches had been closed or abandoned, and in some states, there had been persecution. Along with other of the clergy, Juniper had been sent to the United States as a kind of refugee, a wanderer housed in whatever monastery had a spare room. It was in the last of such stopping places that he had achieved some note by inventing a cheese.

This particular monastery was maintained by an order of philosophic monks, profound men who spent their lives thinking up theological and moral problems but not always solving them. In order to do such work, an atmosphere of quiet was essential; thus the abbey had been located in Wisconsin, a place where no harsher sounds than the distant lowing of cows ever jarred a philosophic thought.

Although the brothers tried hard, they were never able to fashion Juniper into a professional thinker. Some of the trouble may have been because, whereas the monks were lean and bald in the manner of good philosophers, Juniper remained short and plump. When he wandered about the sunlit cloister, his round belly always looked disturbingly like a baker's dough bowl hidden beneath his habit. And his ways of thinking and doing things utterly dismayed the others.

At times he was found alone in his cell with a cut of strong cheese on his lap and a bottle of mild red wine at his side. This caused a raising of eyebrows and a scratching of tonsures. In the monastery there was but one place where Juniper might have gotten the wine; it had to disappear from the sacristy of the chapel at night.

The brothers did not resent their wine disappearing, but the thing that troubled them was the number of moral problems it presented. Juniper was sinning—not one sin, but many. No one could agree on the actual count. There were, obviously, sins of avarice, of theft, of borrowing from consecrated ground, sins of indulgence, potential sins of— The number was endless.

Father Juniper shook his head over the vivid catalogue of sins the brothers showed him. He studied each one carefully, and then scratched his head. This gesture in itself upset the brothers because of the ring of tarnished silvery hair which grew so easily around the rim of Juniper's head; when he scratched, it looked as if he were tipping his halo-shaped tonsure, almost as though it were an old hat. Then he would offer his opinion regarding the sins.

The wine, he reasoned, was very good. Anything so good could not be evil. It was his impression that a bit of wine always separated the soul from the body, helping him to think more about God and the Blessed Virgin. What could be better?

The brothers fumed and worried, until one of them, Father Conlan, came down with ulcers of the stomach. The stricken brother had to be put on a milk diet, so the monastery invested in a cow. In not too long a time, the brothers were startled when their cow had a calf. This began occurring with some regularity, and in a span of not too many years there was an entire Holstein herd. Although the brothers tried to keep up with the cows by drinking quantities of milk, this proved a strain. Monks just aren't built for milkdrinking.

Events finally forced the brothers into the dairy business and they began devoting all their time to milking, pasteurizing, barn-cleaning, bottle-washing and marketing, until none of them had a moment left for philosophizing.

When it was noticed that the production of philosophy books and tracts had fallen off, and at the same time there was no real increase in revenue from the milk business, the father general of this order made a journey to Wisconsin to inquire into the problem. While making his inspection he happened to approach Father Juniper's cell just when the latter was indulging in a bit of cheese and wine. Hearing the footsteps of the father general, and not wanting to embarrass the monastery, Juniper hastily shoved the wine bottle under his pallet and stuffed the wedge of cheese into an old shoe.

A week later the odor from the shoe grew so strong it was noticeable in the chapel on the other side of the cloister. When the guilty shoe was found, Juniper was ordered to seal it in a large metal milk container and bury it. By chance, while the can stood outside near the barns, one of the lay brothers whose sense of smell had been dimmed by a cold, poured a batch of fresh milk into the container. In a short while it was noticed that the contents of the can had turned into a vigorous cheese. Naturally, Juniper was the first to test it.

It was good cheese. It had fine color and texture, and it had, in fact, so rare an aroma that an adventurous cardinal archbishop in Chicago began serving it at his table. Thus the fame of the cheese spread. Using the first batch, with the shoe in it, as a mother-culture, the monks began producing their now famous *Shoecheese*. Today, this cheese is marketed in little lead-lined boxes, like fissionable stuff. On the printed label there is a picture of a philosophic cow, and beneath it, the motto: *Haec olim meminisse juvabit,* which is to say, it will be pleasant to remember these things in the hereafter.

POLICARPIO'S BULL

A moment or so after the general and his committee had driven away, Father Juniper strode purposefully past the front of the church and into the *Parlamento Inglés.* He was met at the swinging doors by Policarpio, who had watched the meeting between the priest and General Braga with suspicion.

"I am Junipero," said the priest. "I'm your neighbor, the other side of the church."

Policarpio nodded coolly, implying that this was obvious. For several seconds the two men exchanged stares, Father Juniper studying the bartender with a direct candidness, while Policarpio judged the priest with a shrewdness that comes from tending bar. The latter was perplexed by what he saw. He found the padre's face kindly enough, but the way the man's hair grew, like a lopsided halo, was quite disconcerting. Furthermore, the black cassock which the priest wore so brazenly aroused his suspicions.

Father Juniper withdrew his glance from Policarpio and let his brown thumbprint eyes take a hasty impression of the barroom. He took in the red tile floor, the mesquite

44

bar, the big mural painting of a bull and the open urinal in one corner. There were no other patrons in the room and the place seemed forlorn.

"Do you mind if I visit?" Juniper asked the barkeeper. "You are the one who is against priests, yes? For this, I am anxious to know you."

Policarpio shrugged without politeness. It was well known that when people were in trouble and needed money, Policarpio always had a five or ten peso bill waiting for them. He had never known a priest to do likewise, so he resented this newcomer questioning his anticlericalism. He also took it for granted that the priest was already attacking, therefore he was prepared to fight back.

Glancing scornfully at Juniper's cassock, the bartender said, "It might be useful for you to remember that the clergy do not wear such garments in the streets. It has been a law since the Revolution. Did you know that?"

"Yes, it is the law," the priest answered.

"Yet, you wear it?" Policarpio frowned disapprovingly at the other's Roman collar which was soiled, worn and ill-fitting.

"I am not against the law," replied the priest. "But I thought it would do no harm here in Santiago de Gante. I have just seen Señor Braga wearing the uniform of a General of the Division, yet I know he is no more than a finger-general. And I have noticed the American women in their pink stockings, and the councilmen wearing berets in the manner of tourists. I did not think the cassock would be noticed."

Policarpio stirred the cup of his ear thoughtfully. The priest's logic was indeed curious, yet it made sense. At this point Policarpio took note that the padre, unlike Father Caldo, wore no fine leather shoes. The priest's stubby feet were encased in the cheap, sturdy, cross-woven leather sandals of the region.

When Father Juniper moved from the doorway and planted himself before the bar, gazing up at the mural of the bull, Policarpio followed him. The bartender edged around so he could better observe the priest's face, for he felt that the padre's first reaction to the mural would be an important test of his character.

The bull in the mural was somewhat special. The *cojones* on the animal were monumental: there was enough maleness to do for twenty bulls. This painting of the bull and its oversized parts had figured in the long feud between Policarpio and the former pastor, Father Caldo. The trouble between the two men had originally started because, in the room directly behind the bar, Policarpio had a *tinacale,* a brewery where the milky, sourish *pulque* was made. At times, when this amusing alcoholic beverage was being nursed to maturity, the odor grew so powerful it often penetrated the walls into the church next door. Even during Benediction, when incense was used, the smell was noticeable. The first time that Father Caldo had come to protest about the odor he had noticed the bull and had objected because its parts were so visible. Policarpio had promised to do something about it. The next time that Caldo came to check, the bull's parts were larger. They kept growing from time to time.

Now, Father Juniper glanced from the bull to the barkeeper. There was no expression of shock on the priest's round face. Instead, he seemed sympathetically distressed, as though he were touched by the suffering and agony of a helpless animal. "The bull, is he sick?" he asked.

Policarpio's eyes filled with their usual sardonic twinkle. "Do you like bullfights?" he asked.

"I saw one when I was young."

"In Mexico?"

"Yes."

"You are Mexican? Or are you Spanish?"

"Mexican."

"From the capital? From Mexico City?"

Father Juniper shook his head. "My father, I think, was part Tarascan," he explained. "My mother, she came from this town as a child. The Candelaria parish." He motioned toward the lower part of town where the poor lived.

"From the *barrio?*" Policarpio's expression lost some of its suspicion. "Do you know the district?"

"No. But I plan to go down there to look for Padre Mérida. He is the priest there. And I shall look for Don Vasco, who has become my friend."

"Old Vasco? You know him?" Policarpio raised his brows. Then he pointed to the bar, asking, "You want a drink, padre? What do you want? Coke? Orange?"

The priest shook his head politely. "I have no taste for sweetened water," he said. "It is for children. But sometimes I take a little wine or *pulque,* just enough to wet the tongue."

"*Pulque?* I have that."

The priest hesitated, glancing toward the swinging doors. "Perhaps it isn't right to take it in public," he said. "People can see in."

Policarpio gestured toward the door at the back of the saloon. "Let's go back there to the *tinacale.* It is quiet."

The brewing room was spacious. It had a door that opened out upon a flowered patio which was also a part of Policarpio's house. In the room itself there were several large wooden vats for the storage of the maguey cactus juice that was fashioned into *pulque.* Slightly apart, there was another stave vat where the *seed-pulque* or mother-brew was fermented. A number of pigskin containers hung from the walls, while above the vats there was a small shelf supporting an altar where a tiny reed-woven figure of Santiago sat on horseback. A votive candle flickered restlessly before the figure.

Father Juniper saw a curious man moving about among the vats. The man was dark and tall and had amazing sloping shoulders and immensely large hands. He moved with a sure panther-like tread. Then, Policarpio presented the man.

"Here is Zapopan," he said. "He's my *tinacalero*. He makes the brew. He also works for you, padre."

Father Juniper looked at the dark man who stared back suspiciously. "You work for me?" he asked.

The man nodded. Then in an explosive shout he said, "I'm Zapopan. I'm the bell ringer. And I clean the church."

"He doesn't hear well," Policarpio explained. "He also thinks that no one else hears well."

"Twice a week," Zapopan shouted, glaring at the priest.

Policarpio stared at Juniper shrewdly. "Do you mind, your sexton being a *tinacalero?*" he asked.

Juniper smiled. "If what he makes is good—" He offered a vague gesture and sniffed carefully, as though judging the quality of the brew by the odors in the room.

A few minutes later Father Juniper and Policarpio were seated on stiff reed chairs, and were sipping the thick, sweet-sour beverage from clay pots. Zapopan had gone out to the bar to look after it. The priest sighed and stirred his cup. After each sip that he took he folded his stubby fingers across his stomach, the better to waylay the flavor of the drink. Nodding and beaming, he went so far as to say, "Good *pulque* is always friendly. This, which I am tasting, is very friendly."

Policarpio gave him a somewhat fixed smile that remained hedged with caution and suspicion. For a little while there was no more talk, and no other sounds than the prolonged smacking of wet lips, the soft gurgles of appreciation and the occasional crunching between the teeth of crisply fried maguey maggots. Policarpio studied the extraordinary roundness of the priest's middle. It was like the dome of Saint Peter's in Rome, but without a cupola. Now, Policarpio felt vaguely perplexed because the priest seemed to give him no excuse for fighting him. He wondered if the new pastor were up to some trickery.

At the same time Father Juniper watched the barkeeper with caution. He suspected that Policarpio was a hard, tough man—possibly a good man, too. He knew that Policarpio spoke for many people in town. He could be a helpful man, for he owned a bar and he heard many things, useful things which probably never got as far as the confessional. For the moment, however, Juniper preferred to remain wary. He had been warned of Policarpio's dangerous anticlericalism. He knew of the troubles in Santiago de Gante and he did not wish to worsen them by taking one side or another. His bishop had told him to gather the facts, then conciliate, if possible.

Following his second cup, Juniper made a tentative probe. "When I was with Don Vasco this morning," he spoke casually, "Vasco didn't tell me why Padre Caldo left the parish?"

"Caray!" Policarpio used his favorite expletive. "He was bombed out!" Then with provocative frankness, he added, "We tried to put a bomb under his window. It was in this very room that we planned it. But Old Vasco made a mis-

take." He looked at the priest challengingly. "This demonstration is a useful thing to remember, padre."

"But why were you against Caldo?"

"He let the general and the gringos make a business of our saint. The saint can't be toyed with, else he'll take his powers away." Policarpio glanced toward the reed replica of the saint standing on the shelf above the vats. "Caldo had no belief in our saint. He would never come here to bless the *pulque.*"

"You are one who has your brew blessed?"

Policarpio nodded. The fact that he was anticlerical had nothing to do with faith. He was well aware that when the moment came for Zapopan to blend the mother-ferment with the raw maguey juice in the vats, a prayer must be offered to Santiago, and there should also be a priest's blessing. For some time now the brew had not matured as it should. Policarpio put the blame for this on Father Caldo, who had not only refused to enter the *tinacale,* but had also forbidden Father Mérida to officiate at the brewing.

"Do they bless the *pulque* in the United States?" Policarpio suddenly asked the priest.

"There is no *pulque.*"

"*Caray!* They are barbarians, then?"

"Not exactly."

Policarpio frowned. "You are for the gringos, eh?" he asked bluntly.

"They are not bad."

"Not bad? They are impossible."

Father Juniper shrugged. "The only trouble with them," he said, "is that most of them are Protestants. This is a mistake which Americans make about religion. It is very careless of them."

Policarpio grunted contemptuously. His suspicions of the

priest flooded back. The man was a clever one, he thought.
He got around things neatly, almost like a Jesuit. Suddenly,
while thinking this, Policarpio hit on a way of testing the
new pastor. He glanced toward his brew vats for a second,
then stared at the priest, impersonally transfixing him with
his eyes.

"Next week," he said, "there will be a new brew. Will
you come for the ceremony and give the blessing?"

"Next week?"

Policarpio nodded and sat back, watching the priest carefully. He felt quite pleased, having set this trap. It would
show whether the new pastor was like Caldo or not.

Father Juniper hesitated. He peered down into his clay
cup as though he expected to find a ready answer lying at
the bottom. Then he glanced up at Policarpio with a speculative, pursed-lip expression.

"Yes, I shall be glad to come," he said. "But on a condition."

Policarpio's face clouded. "What condition?"

"It is this. You said the bombing of the rectory was
planned in this room?"

"Yes. But the rectory wasn't bombed."

"Clearly. Nevertheless, there was a sin of intent. So before I can bless your *tinacale* and the new brew, the sin
should be confessed. There must be a penance. I'll come
here to help, but first you must round up your friends who
plotted the bombing, and bring them to confession. They
will undoubtedly have other sins, too."

Policarpio's jaw sagged and there was a debilitated expression on his face. He had not been to confession, except on
Easters, since Caldo had been in the parish. He had not
even let his wife confess to Father Caldo. It was a matter of
principle. Now, he shot a sickly glance toward the *pulque*

vats, then looked at the priest, saying, "But it was my place, here, that got bombed."

Father Juniper shrugged. "Your *pulque* is good," he murmured. "With a proper blessing it might be better. You will find that the saints are interested in such things."

Policarpio gulped. His glance wavered between the brew vats and the priest's round, confident face. His hands made loose restless stabs in the air.

The next morning a great many people in Santiago de Gante were startled when they observed four men—Policarpio, Old Vasco, Señor Tzintzuntzan and Zapopan—leave the *Parlamento Inglés* in a body. The four men were seen entering the church, where they lined up before the right-hand confessional box.

6

THE MOOR CHASER

A shining shower of green birds flashed through the sunlight around the fountain in the patio of the pink parish house. Father Juniper looked up from his work for a moment and regarded the tiny birds tenderly. There was a fragrance to the morning; the scent of flowers and the woodsmoke smell from the household fires kindled with rosemary twigs. This was Juniper's third day in Santiago de Gante, and he found it pleasant to sit by the fountain and get things done.

He bent over the small sign he was making, and worked again with great industry even though he had to pause at times to scold the parrot which kept biting the hem of his cassock.

"Padre Caldo must have been a strange sort," he said to the bird. "Doña Maria tells me that he was charging two pesos for hearing confessions, and one peso for children. No wonder there was so much dust in the confessional boxes."

He stood up, holding the cardboard sign so that the bird could glare at it with his saucer-like angry eyes. The sign, in neat block letters, read: *Confessions of any length. Free.*

He slipped on his sandals, and gathering up his biretta

53

and long black cloak, he carried the sign to the church vestibule where he posted it on the bulletin board. Filled with a sense of accomplishment, he stepped outside and stared over the plaza, hoping someone there would come into the church and notice his handiwork.

The plaza, however, was almost deserted at this hour. It was still early and the January chill lingered in the air in spite of the sun. At the far side of the square he saw a small procession moving jerkily toward the police station: two policemen and a drunken man who staggered between them. The gendarmes and their captive were followed by Perlimplin, the police captain, whose mustachios drooped sadly. The officer solemnly carried the drunk's straw hat.

Seeing them, it reminded Father Juniper that he had business to discuss with Señor Tzintzuntzan whose house shared a back wall with the police station.

Tzintzuntzan's place was not on the plaza, but was just around the corner. It was a colonial house of some historical importance, though no one knew exactly why. Above its elaborate doorway, carefully carved in the stone lintel, were the Latin words, *Hic Natus Ubique, Notus,* which the guide books usually translate into, "Someone of importance was born here." Although similar legends marked the birthplaces of known national heroes, the scroll over Tzintzuntzan's doorway was a thing that puzzled the entire town of Santiago de Gante. According to Don Leon, the historian and curator of the local museum, there existed no records of anyone of importance ever having been born in the house. Still, a mystery such as this had its value. Whenever a Santiagan felt in the mood to celebrate, and if there were no handy holiday within reach, he made his fiesta in honor of Señor Hic Natus.

It was appropriate that within this house Tzintzuntzan

conducted a business which had to do with fiestas, and one
which made life for the police of Santiago de Gante an heroic
endeavor. The business was fireworks. The police had
grown resigned to having their back wall shaken by frequent
explosions. Tzintzuntzan was used to it, too. Along with
two helpers who could neither read nor write, and who knew
no chemistry, he concocted things of magnesium, of TNT
and black powder into which, for special effects, were mixed
sprinklings of finely ground peyote buds.

Tzintzuntzan hadn't always been resigned to the explosions. In his father's time no such accidents had occurred.
However, being almost a pure blooded Tarascan, and somewhat superstitious, Tzintzuntzan attributed the blasts to a
lack of proper insurance. Ever since the Revolution, when
Santiago had been removed from the church, there had been
trouble. The saint was no longer keeping his eye on the fireworks factory.

Father Juniper found the stocky Tarascan in the back
room of his factory where the latter was busily chopping up
sticks of low-grade dynamite with a machete.

"Good morning, maestro," Juniper greeted him.

The fireworks-maker put down the big cutlass-shaped
knife and smiled shyly at the priest. Although his hands,
his torn blue overalls and the red bandanna knotted at his
throat were grimy, he did not appear embarrassed. It was
this the priest liked about him.

When Tzintzuntzan had appeared in the confessional box
at Policarpio's request, Juniper had been instantly impressed
by the man. The Tarascan had a curious melon-shaped head,
and his thick hair, growing downward like thatch, was of an
electric blackness. He was a very independent man. Even
with the stub of a lighted Vera Cruz cigar clamped between
his bright teeth, as now, and in soiled clothes, he always had

dignity and distinction. These went with him like an invisible garment.

Unlike Policarpio and the others, Tzintzuntzan showed no cautious resentment toward the priest. He took Juniper's arm, guiding him from the workroom to the patio where his assistants were assembling wood and reed skeletal forms which were decorated with paper tubes and sacks filled with explosives. These were the *castillos* or castles and displays that always made up the brilliant climax of a fiesta.

"It is a busy time," Tzintzuntzan commented with an odd turn to his voice, as though it amused him that he, of all people, should be in such a harrowing business. He waved his cigar at an intricate series of pin wheels, adding, "This one here is for Passion Week. But before Passion, there are six smaller fiestas."

"I've come to order one, also," Juniper said. "There will be a small fiesta at the church in a few days."

Tzintzuntzan's grimy forehead wrinkled questioningly. "A church fiesta so soon?" he asked. "How so? There are none marked on my calendar."

"A special one," Juniper smiled. "It will be to honor the return of Santiago to the church."

"*Our* saint?" Tzintzuntzan's teeth almost lost their grip on his cigar. "Have you made the general agree to this, padre?"

Father Juniper smiled confidently. "*Pues,* it isn't a matter of agreeing. The saint does belong in the church. He should be put back now. It is the wish of our bishop."

The fireworks-maker stared at the priest in wonder. His heavy lips began to move slowly as though grasping for words. "And why not?" he exclaimed with sudden emphasis. "Nothing goes right since the wooden saint left the church." He gestured with animation, his burning cigar lashing perilously close to the powder bags. "We have a lot of trouble with explosions ever since Santiago got taken out of the church. The police complain that I am careless. I say back to them, 'Who is careless?'" He stuck his cigar between his teeth again, adding, "Very good, padre. I make you a firework like you never see before."

When Father Juniper stepped out of the Hic Natus doorway, the news that he had promised to get the saint back into his niche seemed to rush ahead of him. Perhaps the festive explosion which shook Tzintzuntzan's house a moment later had something to do with it. In any event the news rumbled and echoed throughout Santiago de Gante's narrow streets. When Juniper arrived at the rectory even Maria knew about it.

Less than an hour later an Indian boy in tattered clothes knocked at the door of the parish house. He brought a message from General Braga, and a loan of three books. Father Juniper sniffed at the message which was enclosed in a scented envelope. The note was penned in a bold script.

Very Distinguished Rev. Fr.:
Precisely, this moment, it has been brought to my attention that you, and our estimable bishop, appear to believe that the wooden figure of Santiago is church property. Upon this, a certain claim is being made for his return. It should be of value if you would read the history of the saint and of our town of Santiago de Gante, noting precisely that the saint pertained to the Monastery of Gante. It is my firm opinion that the saint must remain in my possession.

Your attentive servant,
Gen. Hamilcar Braga.

Juniper turned with curiosity to the books which had come with the note. One of them was that small, fat, green-covered popular mine of misinformation, *Soupçon's Guide to Mexico*. The other two books were very old and vellum-bound, the *Annals of Santiago de Gante, 1549-1909*.

He carried them to his room. Throughout the larger part of the next two days, until Saturday, he read and learned much about the saint.

The *Annals* described Santiago carefully. The saint had been cut from a single piece of dark wood, and he was slightly bowlegged. He had painted blue eyes full of that kind of penetrating depth so commonly seen in horsemen. Time had left his features grained and cracked, and furthermore, one finger was missing from his right hand. It had been cut off by a Moor. Normally, Santiago wore the rich heavy red chasuble that a priest wears at his ordination, but during fiesta-times he was clothed in the garments of a Mexican cowboy, which gave him the freedom of motion needed for chasing Moors.

The scribes who had kept the records of the saint over the centuries were not absolutely clear as to which Santiago he might be. He did not appear to be Saint James, Apostle and son of Zebedee; nor was he the son of Alphaeus; nor was he James, the Lord's brethren. There was some speculation that he might have been a cousin of Saint James of Compostela.

According to the most conservative version in the *Annals*, the recorded history of the Santiago who became the patron of this Mexican town lay well back in antiquity—in the days when Greek, Roman and Saracen blood mixed freely around the rim of the Mediterranean Sea. Along in this period, it is said, the wooden figure of Santiago was captured by Moorish pirates hovering off the coast of Africa. The heathen captain, needing firewood for his braziers, ordered his men to hack the saint into kindling. Santiago resisted the treatment and the angry captain had him flung back into the sea. Moments later a violent storm arose, buffeting the pirate boat without mercy.

During this storm Santiago bobbed in the whitecaps slightly to the larboard of the ship, while around him there seemed to be a luminous halo which might have been taken for a life preserver had such conveniences existed in those days. And, according to some versions of the story, two youngish angels were seen hovering near the scene.

Unnerved by the violence of the storm, the pirates concluded that the wooden figure had something to do with it, so they pulled Santiago back aboard. The sea immediately calmed down. This was the first known miracle attributed to Santiago.

Somewhat later, though most likely on this same voyage, the saint's luck seemed to have run out. The pirate craft was shipwrecked and Santiago was afloat once more. He drifted aimlessly upon the sea until friendly currents carried him through the Straits of Gibraltar, then up along the Atlantic coast of Spain where he was finally washed ashore. The landing took place on a sandy beach midway between the port of La Coruña and a monastery several miles to the north.

The Coruñans and the friars from the monastery suspected that the wooden figure might be miraculous, so they quibbled over the privilege of housing it. They finally agreed to let the saint show his preference. Santiago was mounted upon a dappled horse which was carefully blindfolded, was turned around three times, then given free rein. The good friars and the Coruñans stood back, watching for signs of horsemanship. They were not disappointed. After a mo-

ment of thought, the horse promptly turned and made for
the monastery.

Santiago was properly installed in the chapel there, while
the dappled horse was, from that time on, treated with unusual respect. While the saint seemed to enjoy his residence
in the monastery, he did venture forth on two occasions.
The first time that he left the gray-walled sanctuary was during the ninth century when Christians and Moors were bat-
tling for control of the ravines and valleys of Spain. During
this uneasy era, Spain might have been lost to Christendom,
but for the valor of an unidentified knight who appeared on
the battlefield at Clavijo and saved the day. This unnamed
knight who rode with a markedly wooden and stiff horsemanship, and was accompanied by two very young squires whom
some observers mistook for angels, singlehandedly routed the
heathens. It was on this memorable date that the friars at
the monastery noted that the saint was missing from the
chapel, and that one horse was gone from the stables. After
the battle, Santiago reappeared in his niche, but he was missing one finger.

Santiago's second departure from the Spanish abbey occurred in the mid-sixteenth century when the monks sent an
expedition to Mexico to found another monastery. According to the *Annals,* Santiago accompanied them and kept the
seas quiet.

The friars built their new establishment on the land now
owned by General Braga. As a religious estabishment their
new monastery persisted for about fifty years; then, for reasons unrecorded, all the friars except one returned to Spain.
The single hardy hold-out, a man known as Paco de Gante,
received title to the land and a dispensation from Rome to
beget himself a family. In time a town began to sprout

around the former monastery. Although Paco never distinguished himself greatly, he was eventually given a royal title. One of his sons, the second Conde de Gante (who made a fortune in silver mines located in the distant hills beyond the town), achieved far more note than the father. The second Conde had a habit of celebrating newly begotten sons and daughters in a monumental way. To honor the birth of his first son he built the curious pale green church for the town. The mortar poured into the edifice was made of a mixture of sand, powdered silver and vintage Spanish wines—an obvious attempt, some said, at buying off God, and getting him drunk at the same time.

Having no taste for wooden decorations, the silver-mining Conde had Santiago (who had been left behind by the monks) transferred from his monastery home to a niche in the church. This was how the green church and the town got its name.

As for the beginnings of the fiesta in Santiago's honor, Father Juniper found the *Annals* somewhat vague. The fiesta seemed to date either from the opening of the silver-veined church, or from the affair of the angels, an event which will be gone into later. However, in *Soupçon's Guide*, 1909 edition, Juniper found a precise description of the fiesta itself.

. . . Each year (July 25th) a villager approaches the church doors at an ungodly hour of the morning and sounds an *alborada* upon his trumpet. Following this fanfare, he shouts, "The Moors are coming!" Meanwhile, lurking among the trees in the scented and picturesque plaza, a large body of villagers dressed as villainous Moors set off firecrackers and skyrockets. As soon as the first thunder of the attack subsides, Santiago, mounted upon a painted wooden horse, and garbed in colorful ranchero clothing, charges forth from

the church scattering Moors left and right. While Indian
dancers gyrate in the plaza, the battle between the Christians
and Moors rages throughout the streets to the delight of the
natives. Later in the day there are other spectacles of interest, such as naïvely picturesque parades and a floating of
angels above the square. The traveler is cautioned to beware
of the colorful fiesta foods on display. They are of uncertain
native origin. . . .

On Saturday afternoon Father Juniper closed the books
which the general had sent to him. It was very apparent, he
realized, that Santiago had originally been the property of
the monastery. The general had some rights to him, and
yet—

Juniper decided that he must look at the saint. Putting
aside his cassock again, and dressing in mufti, he gathered
up the general's books and set out for the monastery-resort
which lay at the edge of town.

The *Mesón de los Frailes* or Inn of the Monks, as the restored colonial masterpiece was called, represented General
Braga's idea of how the friars of the old Monastery of Gante
should have housed themselves. It had been rebuilt with a
total disregard for expense, and was so arranged that when
the casual tourist entered its portals he was smothered by a
hotelkeeper's version of colonial Mexico. One could wander
through fretted arches and cloisters, idle in lavish gardens
dotted with Talavera tiled fountains, or swim in a pool where
a festive blanket of exotic orchids floated upon the water.
The floating flower-carpet was changed twice a day.

In that he had been in Santiago de Gante but a few days,
and now wore mufti, Father Juniper was able to reach the
chapel where the saint was kept without being observed.

He slipped into the tiny jewel-like baroque chapel and
peered about. At the far end of the room, shafts of sunlight

angled down from the small colored windows in the cupola lantern, striking an altar of carved pink cantera stone where the saint stood. Juniper approached the altar slowly, then knelt.

The rail-thin saint stared down at him woodenly. Santiago's right hand was raised as though ready to slash at an invisible enemy with the cutlass he held. Visible beneath the hem of his red robe were the pointed toes of a pair of leather *botines,* the Mexican rancher's jodhpurs.

The priest was intrigued by the saint. This is indeed the image of a real saint, he thought. A saint who might do miracles if he were of a mind to do so. No wonder the people of the town love him. Suddenly Juniper frowned as he stared up at the figure. An interesting thought popped into his head, even though he hadn't reached for it. It was a dangerous thought, but it had come almost as if the saint had suggested it.

Juniper wondered: Santiago had often been miraculous. Why couldn't there be more miracles? Couldn't Santiago let people know whether he really wanted to return to his place in the church? It would be just a small matter of doing something, of showing a sign. Perhaps if Santiago didn't wish to do it himself, he could send his two angels, as he had done before.

The priest smiled up at the figure and said, "I am one who has a great faith in you. Perhaps something should be done."

He said a short prayer. Then taking out a pencil and a scrap of paper, he penned a note for General Braga.

My Very Distinguished General:
I wish to thank you for letting me read the *Annals*. They are of great importance. I have learned much from them.

Tomorrow, Sunday, I shall make my sermon about Santiago. It would please me if you would come to hear it.

Your very attentive servant,
Padre Junipero.

He slipped the note within the cover of one of the vellum books, took the books to the office of the inn and left them there for the general. As he returned to the street, he began planning his sermon. He felt a little uneasy, wondering if Santiago would cooperate.

7

SERMON ON THE SAINT

Sunday in Santiago de Gante is always lively because it is market day.

Drawn by the market, and by Mass, the small ranchers and Indian farmers drain from the surrounding countryside into the town. They begin coming in early, streaming down from the distant mountain trails, coming across the nearer muffin hills, along the tracery of roads and trails netting the valley. And they come in fixed order. First, the gray or brown woolly donkey bearing a fat basket of bright produce, then a man dressed in white cottons. The man walks with his knees lifted high in the Indian fashion. Next comes his woman with a child in arms, the child drawn tightly in her *rebozo* so that the shawl, the line of her head and shoulders, has always that Biblical quality, like the Virgin in a church. Strung out along the trail behind her, resembling animated wash, are the children. They come barefooted and dressed in tatters, and they have great brown inquiring eyes and tinkling laughter.

A few minutes before the midday Mass, Father Mérida came to visit with Juniper. Mérida was a friendly, hunch-

backed man who took care of the Candelaria church in the
poorer part of town, and who spent much of his time offering services in tiny isolated chapels around the countryside.
Together, the priests climbed up into the east tower of the
church in order to view the flow of people coming into town.

On the bell platform, not quite at the top of the tower,
they encountered Señor Zapopan. Zapopan and two younger
assistants were pushing the bells, swinging them back and
forth on their huge cradles. The biggest of the bells, *El
Temblor,* a huge rich-voiced giant, was Zapopan's special
care. Upon seeing the priests, the bell ringer greeted them
with a friendly roar. Juniper smiled and marveled, for
Zapopan worked barefooted and catlike among the bells that
shook and thundered in the tower. Zapopan came over and
guided the two panting priests to a small iron-railed platform overlooking the plaza and valley.

After Zapopan had returned to his tasks, Juniper glanced
down at the crowd below, then raised his voice to speak to
Mérida. "Is there always this large a crowd on Sundays?" he
asked.

The hunchback priest shook his head. "Not always," he
shouted. "It is because of what you are doing about the
saint. They are curious. Even most of my parish is coming
to your Mass."

He said it without resentment. Another priest might have
been envious that an outsider such as Juniper should have
been assigned to the most important parish in the town.
Not so, Mérida. He was without envy, and for this he was
liked by the Santiagans.

"Are you sure the general will give up the saint?" Mérida
asked, again raising his voice above the clash of bells.

Father Juniper nodded, but made no answer. He gazed
out over the pinkish-tan of the valley, serene and exalted in

the sunlight. Beyond the rolling hills, the earth rose and became a distant fume, the pleated sierras. Meanwhile, up here in the tower the sound of the bells was like the angry voice of God thundering around the two priests. Out there in the valley it must be different, Juniper thought. The valley air must sweeten the tongues of the bells so they sounded as though it were the Blessed Virgin speaking. That was, all except the tongue of *El Temblor*. He began to think of the giant bell as being the warrior voice of Santiago.

Padre Mérida's shout broke upon Juniper's thoughts. "During the Santiago fiesta," he said, "the two child-angels fly from this platform. They ride out on cables which extend from here, out across the plaza, to the roof of the city hall over there."

Juniper nodded. He knew about the angels. At Santiago's fiesta there were always two of them, a boy and a girl. They were usually not very old, but they were important. During the day they rode beside Santiago on a shiplike float; in the evening, following Benediction and the final breath-taking burst of fireworks, they swung out over the crowded plaza, suspended by pulleys from the cables stretched between the church tower and the city hall.

Although the angels were ordinary children from the town, they were a reminder of another miracle involving the saint. This miracle had occurred in the days of the second Conde de Gante. Shortly after the Conde had built the lime-green church and had installed the wooden Santiago in it, there had been an accident.

The Conde, like most men in those days, had been an avid hunter as well as a churchgoer. One morning he had gone out to hunt ducks and had been delayed in the field a bit longer than usual. Hurrying back to church, he discovered that he had missed Mass. Not being one to overlook the services, even on weekdays, he installed himself in the carved Gante pew, along with his guns, his bag of ducks and dogs, and he ordered the priest to repeat the Mass. According to the *Annals,* the padre was slow in coming and the Conde grew impatient. Suddenly, his gun went off.

No one was sure whether the blast was fired in order to hurry the padre along or if it had been accidental. In any case, the shotgun charge smashed into the saint, filling his wooden face with bird shot and tearing off the end of his nose. The Conde was conscious stricken. To put things right with the saint he took the wooden figure all the way to Guadalajara where it might be repaired by a famous dollmaker.

Although the old craftsman was not in his shop when the Conde arrived, the latter was received by two beautiful children who took charge of the battered Santiago. When the Conde returned to the shop a few days later, he found the shop deserted. There were no children, no dollmaker, but Santiago was ready and beautifully mended. Anxious to reward the dollmaker, the Conde began inquiring after him in the neighborhood. It startled him to learn that the old dollmaker had died the year before and that his shop had been shut down since that day. The neighbors also insisted that he had had no children.

It was obvious that the two lovely children who had retouched Santiago without charge must have been angels. The Conde de Gante was so certain of this that when he died he had himself buried with a silver *real* in each hand. He meant to pay the angels if he ever met them.

Thinking of the angels, Father Juniper looked at Mérida and asked, "Does General Braga also have angels at his fiesta?"

"He has one, sometimes. But it is made of paper. Ours are real."

"Real children, you mean? Not angels?"

Mérida nodded. "Yes, children. But among the people there is a belief that someday, when people are a little holier, the children will be unnecessary. A time will come when there will be real angels, just as there were in the old days."

"Are you one who believes in this?" Juniper asked.

Father Mérida shrugged and smiled vaguely. "Who can doubt the powers of God and the saints," he murmured.

Juniper stared down at the plaza, marveling at the smallness of the people below. They were like ants swarming into church. For two children to fly out from this height, even on strong cables, took a great deal of faith and courage, he thought. They must almost be angels themselves.

The bells had begun to slow down. Zapopan's voice, louder than the bells, called out. "Padres, you go down for Mass, now."

The two priests clambered down the ladder and went to the sacristy where two boys, waiting to serve Mass, were putting on their small cassocks and white cottas. Father Juniper vested himself in the threadbare vestments he had had to borrow from Father Mérida because the previous pastor had taken away all those that the church had possessed.

When Juniper and the acolytes entered the sanctuary, an expectant murmur rippled through the long solemn spaces of the church. The pews and aisles were more crowded than they had been in years. This Sunday, in addition to the faithful communicants, others had appeared: there were those Santiagans who usually came to church only for christenings and funerals; there were some who attended but once a year; and then there were the critics—the old women in black and lace, connoisseurs of ritual, such as the wife of

Señor Villada, the baker, who had come to sample the new pastor's style, how he intoned his Latin, the tip of his biretta, or his manner of raising a chalice.

Juniper devoted himself wholly to the meaning of the ceremony; but after the Gospel, when the moment came to leave the altar for the pulpit, he was touched by an instant of panic. The things he was going to say called for great faith in Santiago.

When he stood in the pulpit, he coughed warningly and motioned toward the niche where the plaster Santiago had stood until yesterday. The statue had been removed by his order. Now, in the sea of faces below he noticed the smiles. To his parishioners it was obvious that the place had been cleared for the real Santiago. Slowly, his confidence began to return. He had a feeling that Santiago de Gante was his town and its people were his people. It was as if he had been here always.

In a quiet voice he repeated the Gospel in Spanish. Then, closing the book and resting his hand upon it, he began his sermon.

"Brethren! It is the opinion of many of you that the Santiago who has been absent from this niche for many years should be brought back. I was of this opinion, also." He paused, shaking his head slightly, then went on, "Now, upon reflection, I have changed my mind. It is wrong for me, for each of you, for anyone to make such demands."

A dozen yards from the pulpit, Policarpio Flores, who had been staring with interest at the halo-like rim of hair about the pastor's head, suddenly jerked to attention.

"Santiago is not an ordinary saint," Father Juniper's voice carried out over his startled flock. "It is not for us to say that he belongs here or there. He is a traveling saint. He has been in many places: pirate boats, Africa, Spain, and for a few years in the old Monastery of Gante, as well as in this very church. Can anyone say, truthfully, that he belongs in one special place?"

The pastor paused. In the side aisles where ordinary people were crowded, people like Old Vasco who had never had a reserved family pew, there was a great deal of frowning. But in one of the front pews, General Braga, who had come prepared to frown, now nodded vigorously. It pleased him that he had not erred in his first estimation of the priest. He smiled triumphantly at the two women who had accompanied him to Mass, and he leaned toward the younger, whispering loudly. "Definitely cooperative, you see. Rumor about the padre ordering fireworks must be nonsense."

Above in the pulpit, Father Juniper wet his round lips and marshaled his words, continuing, "But sometimes our saint seems to like one place better than the others. He shows this by making miracles. When he was with the monks in Spain there was the great miracle at Clavijo. Later, when he was brought to this church there was the miracle of the two child-angels which you all know about. Perhaps he has made smaller miracles, too? Almost everyone in Santiago de Gante who has memories of the days before the Revolution can recall some small miracle which could only have been made by a saint. But, there have been no miracles since Santiago was removed from his place here in the church. Does this mean that Santiago is unhappy where he is now?"

General Braga's full face clouded. Although he maintained good social relations with the Church, he did not make a regular practice of attending services. At fifty-nine, he was a strapping man who wore his uniforms with élan, who pursued the sports of riding, fronton, hunting and bull-fights; and though he did all these things with vehemence, churchgoing was not among them. As a result, he found it hard to follow the thread of a sermon.

From above, Father Juniper's voice pointedly continued: "It would seem, from the fact that there were always little miracles before the saint disappeared, that Santiago's place is here in our church. Yet it is not for us to demand this. My bishop commissioned me to ask our friend, General Hamilcar Braga, to return the saint. I cannot do this. It is wrong."

Juniper paused, his eyes searching the faces below. He saw Policarpio and Tzintzuntzan looking up with angry accusation. He smiled serenely at them and went on: "In order that there should be no hatred in Santiago de Gante, I have thought of something else. Many centuries ago when Santiago landed on the shores of Spain, the friars and the people of Coruña each wanted him. Instead of fighting over the saint, they were reasonable. They let Santiago decide where he wanted to live."

Juniper's glance sought out the general.

"With this in mind, I ask General Braga to let Santiago be put on a horse once again. We shall turn the horse loose in the street, perhaps somewhere near the Hic Natus house which is exactly between the church and the Inn of the Friars."

The priest paused, offering a smile of confidence to his flock. "Naturally, Santiago will know where to go."

8

THE IDOL COLLECTORS

General Braga was stunned. When Mass ended he staggered outside, followed by his two ladies. He was hardly aware of the bold, delighted glances many of the townsmen gave him. He went to one of the iron benches in the plaza and sat heavily while his brows creased in thought. Unhappily, he did not enjoy thinking at this early hour. The weight of a five course breakfast still lay under his Sam Browne belt, and thoughts disturbed his stomach.

The older of the two women who had accompanied him to Mass sat at his side and ruffled herself like a bird. "What are you waiting for?" she asked.

"That priest," Braga grunted.

"Did you send for him?"

When no one answered her, she gave the entire plaza a hawklike glare, and said, "I think he'd make a fine *picador*, don't you?"

"Who would?" asked the younger woman.

"The padre."

"That's ridiculous—a priest, fighting bulls?"

Mrs. Melding, the older woman, ruffled herself again. She

was a woman in her forties, short in stature, and with the unpreened look of a wildfowl. A beaklike cast to her nose and her pinched yellowish lips deepened this impression.

"What's ridiculous?" she demanded. "Wasn't Father Hidalgo very *aficionado* and expert? He had more than just a fan's interest in bulls." She said this, almost as though Father Hidalgo, who had died in 1811 while leading his countrymen in revolt against Spain, were still very active in rectory and bullfighting circles. "This one, Juniper, would make a good one," she went on. "He has the build for a *picador*. Although his arms seem a bit short, he might use a longer lance. Perhaps we can get him to come out to the Ruiz ranch with us. We can try him. Ruiz is having Aguilar there. Some of the best bulls."

She rattled on, enthusiastic. Her conversation, as always, dealt in bulls. To everyone who knew her, this was quite natural. She owned half of the bull ring in Santiago de Gante. In addition, she was comfortably well off, with an income from coupons which permitted her to lead a very active and unfettered life. She favored the sporting crowd. Her small feathery figure was a familiar sight at all the active spectacles: fronton, boxing, fishing at Guyamas or hunting in Chiapas. Of all these pursuits, her favorite was the bullfight. She knew so much about bulls and fighting that even the professionals connected with the *fiesta brava* accepted her, not as a woman, but as a professor of the art of tauromachy.

It was both this, and Mrs. Melding's avid interest in marrying the general that so irritated the younger woman—Miss Goldengrove.

Miss Goldengrove had a stake in the general, too. Unlike Melding, she was attractive. She was always elegantly outfitted, and she usually wore a vacant poetic smile which gave

men a feeling that they could build upon it. She was the
general's current poetess, an author of verses with enigmatic
titles such as, "No Return," and "Tornado What!" Because
of her verse, and the fact that she sometimes posed in the
nude for artists in town (who could get no native Santiagan
to sit with less than four petticoats and a shawl), she was
considered the most daring and brilliant person among the
canapé eaters. Had she not been a poetess, she might easily
have done well in other careers. She had about everything
one needs to become a successful prostitute: she had a brain
like a cash register, she was a teetotaler and she couldn't fall
in love.

Suddenly, Miss Goldengrove forgot her irritation with
Melding. The new pastor was coming toward them.

Father Juniper nodded politely to the two women, then
offered the general his hand. "Good morning, my general,"
he said cheerfully. "I'm pleased you came for the sermon,
and I wish to thank you for the books. They were useful."

General Braga had regained some of his aplomb. He rose,
promptly returned the greeting and introduced the women.

Father Juniper smiled at them with a happy curiosity, and
particularly at Miss Goldengrove whom he had met briefly
once before. He was taken by the vivid contrast of her flat-
brimmed black Cordobése hat, and her gauzelike blue scarf,
so fine it was like a puff of smoke. He was curious regarding
her faith because he had heard she was living with the general.

"You are American, yes?" He asked her. "Are you Catholic, too?"

Miss Goldengrove gave him a smile of terrible purity.
"Catholic? Oh, no. But sometimes I desperately desire to
enter the Church."

"It is very simple. You would not regret it."

"Somehow, I can't quite bring myself to it," she smiled, her eyes crinkling pleasantly. "Still, I do all I can to convert others."

"Tripe!" Mrs. Melding put in.

The general took Father Juniper's arm with vigor. "There is something to be said about your sermon," he muttered. "Let's make a turn about the plaza, eh?"

Juniper inclined his head agreeably. He and the general and Miss Goldengrove strolled slowly around the garden-plaza. Mrs. Melding went off alone. The priest would have preferred to stroll alone, too, for the plaza was alive with color and worth watching. There was a Sunday bustle of people; peons with bright serapes slung over their shoulders, fat women with babies, vendors and children playing. A steady stream of colors and sounds swirled around the plaza and up the Street of Fulano, which went past the *Parlamento Inglés* and came out upon the market.

General Braga noticed that the priest still wore his tattered cassock in public. He began to wonder if he should continue to interpret this as a favorable sign, or if the pastor were slightly mad. "Now tell me, precisely, padre," he said. "You aren't serious about putting the saint on a horse?"

"Don't you think it is a good kind of conciliation of this problem?"

"An absurd idea. Definitely."

Father Juniper smiled ruefully and glanced at the general. Braga's uniform was splendid. It was like something put together out of a number of operas.

"Perhaps you're troubled that Santiago may no longer have horsemanship?" he said to the general.

Miss Goldengrove gave a high, bell-clear laugh. "Aren't you rather putting the saint on the spot, padre?" she asked. "Would he perform another miracle?"

Juniper's glance canted off toward the red-roofed iron bandstand in the center of the plaza where a stubby man dressed in Bavarian leather shorts, an alpine hat with a chamois brush stuck in the brim, was conducting the town band. The man kept shouting in English, "Blay! Blay! Louder!"

The priest turned his glance back upon Miss Goldengrove and the general. "I have faith in the saint," he said.

Braga made an exaggerated grimace. "That's all very good," he replied. "Very fine from the pulpit. But between us, padre, we know the saint is just a wooden image. Miraculous? A fine idea for the people to believe. But between us—"

A faint, rare anger flickered in the priest's dark thumbprint eyes. "And between us?" he asked.

Braga failed to observe the anger. He chuckled expansively, saying, "Precisely. We should arrange something amicably."

"But I've tried this," replied Juniper.

"The sermon? Nonsense. The idea is ridiculous!"

"You do not believe we can find an unbiased horse?"

Braga grimaced. "You're stirring up the people. It's dangerous."

Father Juniper smiled, catching the resentment in the general's voice. He was beginning to suspect the true reason why General Braga resisted returning the saint. The general was not just being a business man. Although Santiago and the private fiesta which the general arranged for at his inn brought tourists and money, there seemed to be more than this behind the man's attitude. Perhaps the ownership of the saint gave Braga a feeling of power? Perhaps it gave him control over the town council?

Juniper looked at the general and said, "I thought up the horse solution in order to spare you."

"Spare me? How, precisely?"

The padre's eyes ran thoughtfully across the crowded plaza. "You've taken a public position about keeping Santiago," he said to the general. "If you were to return the saint to our church now, it might look as though the bishop forced you to do it. Naturally, for a man of your importance it would look bad, this giving in to the clergy." Juniper made a deprecating motion with his plump hand. "So, I thought of this thing of the horse. People always expect generals to gamble on horses, yes?"

Braga laughed with a hint of uncontrol. He had a queer sensation that the priest was winding him about his plump finger. The pastor's strategy was clever. He had mobilized the sentiment of the town. Now the people expected something. The general frowned angrily, knowing that he must think of something quickly in order to turn the tables before it was too late.

Just as the three were completing their second turn of the plaza, Señor Fablehaft, the bandmaster, hurried toward them. He was pulling at his short-cropped hair and gesturing in distress.

"How it zound, general?"

General Braga feigned annoyance, but he welcomed the interruption. "What sound?" he asked.

"You did not recognize?" asked Fablehaft.

The general shook his head. Then, all at once, his features brightened, and he stared thoughtfully at the German. A few years ago, Braga had visited a Black Forest Spa where he had heard Sunday morning concerts of Wagner. Thinking that such entertainments might add charm to Santiago de Gante, he had added Herr Fablehaft to his collection, in

spite of the fact that the latter was neither poetess nor painting. For well over a year, now, he had been renting the bandmaster to the town for Sunday concerts.

"Ve blay Vagner," explained the German. "Ve bractice
all veek, every zingle day. I tell zem to blow. Ven blay the
horn on Vagner, blow, blow, BLOW! Now is Sontag, und
ven comes the horn, vat you sink zey do?" He sank his fat
thumbs into his ears and cursed in German, adding, "You
know vat zey do? Zey toot!"

General Braga watched the bandmaster return to the stand
and blow his whistle to reassemble the musicians who had
scattered about the plaza. At this instant, an idea took complete shape in the general's brain. He could let the church
have the saint, yet keep absolute control of him. It was simply a matter of renting out Santiago, just as he rented out
Herr Fablehaft.

He gave Juniper a friendly grin, saying, "Your sermon
proposition isn't entirely out of the question, padre. To
show you how I feel, let's go through with this business of
the horsemanship. The people seem to expect it."

Father Juniper stopped and caught his breath. "You'll return Santiago?"

"But Hamilcar," Miss Goldengrove objected. "You promised you'd give me the saint when you tired of him. You
can't do this!"

The general tweaked her cheek. "It's nothing," he said.
"I only intend to rent Santiago. Year to year. I don't mean
to lose control of him. He's my property."

"To rent him?" asked Juniper, puzzled.

"To the church."

"How much?"

Braga chuckled jovially. "Thousand pesos."

Father Juniper shuddered. The pinkish color upon his

cheeks blanched. "Each year?" he managed to breathe.

"Precisely. A thousand a year. The saint is quite valuable. Museum piece." Braga waggled his cigar. "Well, padre, what's your word?"

"But . . . but what of this thing of the horsemanship? If Santiago makes a choice?"

"Exactly," Braga grinned. "Good show, and we'll have it to amuse the people. You can do whatever you want to make the horse go to the church. Tempt him with carrots. I'll keep mum. Cooperate. And as far as the fee, the money is concerned, we won't breathe a word about it." Braga nodded vigorously, then added, "I warn you, padre. I know the people of this town. These men like Policarpio Flores and Tzintzuntzan. If they discover you've made a business deal over the saint, they'll drive you out as they drove Caldo out. We'll keep mum. Definitely."

The expression of shock and incredulous outrage that filled the pastor's eyes slowly faded. He looked at the general with a kind of tottering despair. "I'm not sure," he replied. "It is a thing I must think upon."

After the general and Miss Goldengrove had gone, Juniper staggered from the plaza to the stone bench in front of the pink parish house. He had hardly begun musing over the general's suggestions when Old Vasco, looking fiercely piratical with a machete thrust into his belt and a Sunday red bandanna about his throat, approached the bench. The old man removed his big brimmed straw hat.

"Keep it on, keep it on," Father Juniper murmured. "I am just a man, like you."

Vasco grinned admiringly. "For that, I take it off." He set the hat upon the baskets loaded upon his donkey's back, then carefully tied the animal to a post. This latter precaution was a necessity because once, during a moment of political high feeling, the burro had nipped a gringo in the rear. The animal was no longer permitted the freedom of the plaza.

"I hear your sermon this noon," explained the ex-bandit. "I think maybe you can use El Primitivo instead of a horse. Even blindfolded he'll go somewhat in the direction of the church. He is used to visiting next door in the *Parlamento Inglés*. You want him?"

Father Juniper glanced kindly upon the donkey and shook his head. "Thank you, Don Vasco," he murmured. "It will not be necessary."

"You got a horse to do the trick?"

"No."

"It is a good idea, getting Santiago to decide," Vasco observed. "We don't want any deals with the general. Let Santiago ride it out."

The old man glared fiercely at the priest. For an instant, Juniper had been about to tell him of the general's plan. Suddenly he realized that men like Vasco, though expecting something like this from General Braga, would frown upon their priest taking part in it. They would do nothing to Braga, but if the pastor were involved—

"Is the general against this riding?" Vasco asked. He lowered his voice to the pitch of conspiracy. "Maybe you want me to kidnap the saint and put him on El Primitivo?"

Father Juniper smiled uneasily and stared at the reed paniers on El Primitivo's back. To turn the conversation, he asked, "Are you leaving town today?"

"I travel," the old man said.

The priest rose and looked into the baskets on the donkey's back. They were filled with small clay and stone figures packed in straw. Juniper reached for one of the molded figures: a small clay idol that had the feel and the patina of incredible antiquity. The idol seemed to glare at him frogishly. "This one is Tlaloc, the rain god? Isn't it?" he said.

The ex-bandit cleared his throat uneasily. He was troubled that the priest might consider him a heathen because he was carrying the ancient Aztec gods around on a Sunday. "They are not real, padre," he explained. "Don Ignacio makes them. I take them to Teotihuacan."

"To the old pyramids?" Juniper frowned.

"Ayi, there," Vasco replied. "At the big pyramid there are many *pinche* American tourists who buy these."

"This Ignacio, you mention, he is the atheist, yes?"

"He has some beliefs, but not in God."

"He is a friend of Policarpio?"

"Yes, he visits the *Parlamento*.

Father Juniper examined the Aztec idol. "Why doesn't Don Ignacio clean these up? They're soiled. Look at the dirt. You would think he stores them in the ground."

"He does, padre. After he manufactures them, he buries them for a while. The gringos like them this way. They buy them only if they think the idols are from the days of the Aztecs. It is the same when they buy the *santos*."

"They buy figures of the saints?"

"*Si.* Of the saints, and of Jesucristo on the Cross. The gringos are only interested in the very old and cracked *santos*. They use them for doorstops, or they put them over fireplaces."

The priest set the idol back in its straw bed. He began to scowl, remembering that Miss Goldengrove had wanted the figure of Santiago. Suddenly he became worried. Santiago was old; he was crusty and was made of warped wood. Juniper had visions of the saint ending up as a doorstop.

"You'll excuse me," he said to Vasco. "I must telephone the bishop. There is a matter of rent to be discussed."

9

SOMETHING NEW IN SAINTS

The man rapping at the weathered door of the pink parish house was dressed in an impeccable dark suit. He wore a black homburg and a rolled-up umbrella. Altogether, he could have been taken for a diplomat.

When the door opened and Maria peered out at him with suspicion, the man stared back frostily. Maria looked him up and down carefully. With a practiced eye, she read him. He was of the clergy, and of the sort she did not like. Her glance went beyond him, scanning the tiny Fiat coupé parked at the curb. It, too, was painted a diplomatic black.

"Is Padre Junipero in?" asked the man. He frowned steadily at Maria's bald head and face, which had the brown look of smoked leather.

"He's at church."

"I'm Monsignor Gaspar. Our bishop sent me."

"Why do you want the padre?" Maria demanded.

Gaspar frowned. He had come to Santiago de Gante because the bishop was alarmed by certain un-churchman-like behavior on the part of Juniper. Behavior such as this nonsense of trying to concoct a miracle. But it was none of the old woman's business.

"I have business with the padre," he replied.

Maria gave him an unwelcome nod, then shut the door in his face. The monsignor made a note of this impoliteness, for he was a stickler about such things.

The Right Reverend Monsignor Cannon Gaspar was neither a great churchman nor an intensely pious person, but he was without a doubt one of the few men in the Church who had an inside chance of reaching Heaven purely on the basis of protocol. He was a man of great talent which was largely wasted on a diocese that embraced one Mexican state and a bouquet of small towns and villages, including Santiago de Gante. He would have served much better in some cosmopolitan center, either Mexico City or Rome, where there was no scarcity of diplomats.

At his present station, he served the bishop as a kind of superior butler. There were occasions, even in so remote a diocese, when the bishop had to lean upon him for advice: the correct setting of a formal table, perhaps certain matters of ceremonial dress, or the best way to receive a visiting cardinal.

Monsignor Gaspar's specialty was Protocol, but it also included Liturgy and Ceremony. He knew exactly how an Introit ought to be sounded, the proper way to wear a biretta, or the manner in which a Spanish cardinal should sing a High Mass of the Aurora according to the Mozarabic rite. Regarding this latter, however, he was liable to frown for he was most partial to the Roman rite. For ten years he had been engaged in revising Doctor Fortesque's *Ceremonies of the Roman Rite Described*.

In all honesty it must be related that as a young man,

Gaspar had entered the Church with higher ideals, a true faith and a passionate interest in miracles. He had studied in Rome, where for a short while he had specialized in the history of miracles. At that time someone had advised him that the age of miracles was shrinking and it was no field for a bright young man. Reluctantly, he had transferred his studies to Protocol.

Now older and grimly correct, the monsignor sometimes wondered what had happened to his life. He was a dark man, still full of vigor. He had strong cheekbones, a hawk nose and the slender hips of an Arab—all which gave him a hungry, embittered look. He had reason to appear embittered. In addition to his administrative duties at the chancery, he also served as an inspector general charged with popping in on dusty backland villages. It was his task to see that no carelessness crept into the parochial liturgy, and that the right vestments were worn for the proper occasions. Often enough there were things to shock his sensibilities: a village priest wearing a gay Saltillo serape over his vestments during Mass on a chilly morning, or finding a tiny niche carved in the plaster chest of a Saint Joseph, and a harvest god of the Aztecs reposing therein.

As the monsignor went around to the front of Santiago's pale green church, his thin mouth began to pinch in lines of disapproval. A rather magnificent fireworks *castillo* had been set up in the atrium in preparation for a fiesta. Gaspar frowned upon fireworks. In the backcountry people rendered them a kind of religious importance.

Beyond the fireworks display a cart had been drawn up before the church steps. The wagon tongues and the empty harness lay upon the ground, giving the cart an appearance of kneeling. Some workmen in soiled white cottons moved antlike, transporting loads of bricks across vivid patches of sunlight into the black interior of the church. Farther up the steps, the monsignor saw the parish priest. Father Juniper was seated upon a sack of cement. His cassock was bunched up around his thighs, a purple stole hung around his neck, and he was industriously polishing a set of silver coffin handles which belonged to the parish and were lent out for funerals.

"Padre Junipero?" Gaspar addressed him.

The priest looked up, blinking.

"I'm Monsignor Gaspar. From the chancery office. I missed meeting you the day the bishop had you in before sending you down here."

Father Juniper rose quickly. His face brightened. Meanwhile, the monsignor stared sharply at the purple stole.

"Were you shriving?" Gaspar asked in an intense metallic voice.

Juniper nodded. "It has been very busy."

"Confessions on a weekday?" The monsignor seemed startled.

"As on Saturday or on Sunday," replied the padre. "This morning I heard thirty." Juniper blushed. "They think up some strange sins in this town."

"Excellent. You want your people to trust in you. Excellent."

Juniper motioned toward the church entrance. "We can go in," he said. "The shade is useful. The workmen are making repairs but it will not be noisy."

As they entered the vestibule Monsignor Gaspar halted abruptly, glaring toward the Holy Water fount. Father Juniper's green parrot was bathing in it. Juniper smiled apologetically. "I bring him in so he can wet himself," he explained. "You do not mind, do you? Some people feel that

God is against having animals in his house. It is my thought that God gave El Furioso his color and anger. El Furioso is very conscious of God."

The monsignor pursed his lips and made another mental note. Then he went on, inspecting the work being done by the masons, and finally turned to look in upon the sacristy. "What is the condition of the vestments?" he asked.

Juniper opened the vestment chest and showed him the threadbare robes Father Mérida had lent him.

"Gothic," the monsignor observed with distaste. "I didn't realize. Now, padre, I recommend that you get a set of six in colors of the Roman sequence, including pink for Laetare and Gaudete Sundays. I'll take your order and arrange for it. You can pay for them on a monthly basis."

Father Juniper bit his lip with uncertainty. Such new vestments would cost a great deal. He was already in debt to Señor Tzintzuntzan for the fireworks *castillo* which had been set up in the churchyard to welcome the return of the saint to his niche. He was about to object; then he realized that the monsignor must have been sent here to discuss the rental of Santiago from the general. If the monsignor were so free about spending money, he must have some plan for dealing with Braga.

The monsignor wrote: "Vestments, Roman," in a neat black leather notebook he carried. "Now, about the Santiago question?" he said, turning to Father Juniper.

"Has the bishop told you about the troubles in town?" Juniper asked.

"Of course." The monsignor's critical eye roved about the sacristy. "I'm familiar with the problems. General Braga. This Policarpio Flores. The bishop and I had a long discussion with Father Caldo. It was suggested by Caldo that we compromise, perhaps make arrangements with General Braga to build a proper shrine for Santiago at the old monastery."

Juniper's brows pinched. "Didn't Bishop Sierra say anything about my telephone call?" he asked. "General Braga has agreed to return the saint to the church. Tonight or tomorrow we are going to put Santiago on a burro or a horse and let him decide where he wants to go. I am sure he'll ride for the church."

Monsignor Gaspar's mouth stiffened. "Indeed," he said frostily. "That is precisely why I am here. The bishop was horrified by your plan. You can't force a miracle. If you go through with it, it will make a laughingstock of the Church."

"But everyone in town is expecting it. They know Santiago will choose."

"It is barbaric."

Father Juniper frowned. "Is the bishop against miracles?" he asked.

Gaspar pursed his lips rigidly. He did not wish to admit that the bishop might frown upon miracles, and that he himself knew what complications they could cause. In order to turn the conversation to firmer terrain, he said, "We understand there is also a rental fee involved?"

"Yes. General Braga is asking a thousand pesos a year for the saint."

Gaspar's brows arched critically. "The price is preposterous! You can buy a new statue for less than that."

"But this Santiago is the town patron."

"The saint, padre, but not the statue. A statue is but a representation."

"But this one is miraculous. The people believe it."

"Miraculous?"

The monsignor viewed this information with a cautious dubiety. His brows pinched together in a troubled V. He knew well that there could be many a slip between a saint and a relic, and anything might occur. He recalled an instance which had occurred in another village when a dog had broken into a church, making off with the femur of a Spanish saint. By the time the bone had been located, it had been so badly gnawed that no one could have been absolutely sure, except the dog, if it were the same relic. Gaspar himself had been assigned to the case and he had finally decided that the bone in question had come from a mutton. Ever since that day, doubts had troubled him; there was the uneasy fear that he might have consigned a saint to the rubbish heap.

Looking at Father Juniper's expectant face, he retreated to safer ground, saying, "Well, let's have a look at *our* saint."

Bunched in the monsignor's black coupé, the two men drove around the plaza, went past the Hic Natus house and down the twisting Street of the Monks, to the *Mesón de los Frailes*. They turned in through an arched gateway and parked in a courtyard laid out around an exquisite Saracen fountain.

Juniper lead the way. They went through several passageways to the central patio, a huge flowered quadrangle with cloister walks. Here a number of nondescript people whom Father Juniper took to be canapé eaters loitered around low cocktail tables. Suddenly, Juniper saw Miss Goldengrove and a florid man hurrying across the patio to intercept him. Miss Goldengrove's high heels made a merry clatter upon the orange and blue tiles.

"Padre," she cried out. "How delightful."

Father Juniper paused and smiled shyly, amazed as always by the young lady's dress. She was wearing a vivid blue shirt of denim, and knee-length pants of the same material. There was also a blue ribbon tied in her blonde hair.

Juniper introduced the monsignor, then said, "We've come to see the saint. Is the general here?"

"He's at his villa," Miss Goldengrove waved her hand vaguely, as though marking out the location of the modern villa, some distance from the inn, where Braga generally lived. Then, smiling with a tender vacancy of face, she added, "But we'll take you to the saint."

"It is not needed," Father Juniper replied. "I have been to the chapel. I know where it is."

"Oh, we'll join you." She turned to the monsignor, saying, "I want to introduce Señor O'Murphy. O'Murphy is a Catholic. He's an expert on saints. He's writing a biography of Saint Patrick."

Her companion, Mr. O'Murphy, nodded importantly. He was a solid, heavy man with a round cherubic head and pink choirboy cheeks. He was a professional Irish-American who, having once served a Low Mass for a Boston archbishop, had never gotten over being an altar boy.

"I was strolling there with Miss Goldengrove," he said, while pumping the monsignor's hand, "and I saw you come in and I said to myself in that moment, if there's a monsignor walking about, that man yonder will be he."

"You're a Catholic historian?" Gaspar asked.

"I should like to read your book," Juniper added.

"I'm after writing it ten years," replied O'Murphy. "It is in Gaelic I'm doing it."

The three men and Miss Goldengrove strolled through the arched corridors toward the tiny chapel where Santiago was kept. Mr. O'Murphy talked incessantly all the way; little snatches about Saint Patrick, about his voice of gold, the snake population in Ireland, and something about loyal sons of the old sod. O'Murphy was a garrulous man, a lavish spender of words, but they were all small change.

Monsignor Gaspar, whose knowledge of English was put to some strain by the Irish-American, was tempted nevertheless to correct him regarding Saint Patrick. True, there was a Saint Patrick, but his standing probably wasn't too good in Heaven. Gaspar had heard vague tales about a freebooter kind of Irish saint, one who had been too talkative to get along with the other saints. The monsignor sighed patronizingly. Why should he aggravate this Irishman, he thought? After all, O'Murphy was Catholic. With a certain delicacy, Gaspar realized that one must be broad-minded toward co-religionists, even though in distant lands such as China and Ireland, there was often a taint of paganism in their beliefs.

As Father Juniper followed the others into the chapel, he saw an elderly American woman seated on a campstool. The woman had a water-color pad on her lap and she was sketching the wooden saint. Her presence here instantly troubled the priest, and he was doubly anxious that Gaspar should like Santiago.

The lady was dangerous. She was a Sunday painter as well as being the most important real estate operator in Chicago. When she went out to paint, she had a curious habit of always buying the plot of land she painted. Since she had come to live in Santiago de Gante she had become an even more prolific painter. Her paintings were curious things— landscapes that looked like tinted real estate subdivision maps. Even in Santiago she bought everything that she painted. Thus, her sketching of the saint deeply disturbed Juniper.

"It's not much of a saint," Mr. O'Murphy's loud voice broke upon the priest's worried thoughts. " 'T is but an old block o' wood. Now you take Saint Patrick—"

"It's a fine sculpture," Miss Goldengrove argued. "A seventh century Spanish."

From above, from his station upon the pink cantera altar, Santiago looked down woodenly at his visitors. Father Juniper went to the figure and carefully raised a corner of the saint's robe, showing the saint's jodhpurs to the monsignor. "You see," said the priest. "Santiago also has bowed legs. This is from riding." He dropped the hem and turning toward the figure of a dappled pink and gray merry-go-round horse that stood against the sanctuary wall, he added, "And here is San Jocobo."

Monsignor Gaspar's lips drew out thinly. If he had heard clearly, then Father Juniper had called that carousel horse a saint.

"San Jocobo?" he questioned.

"Pues, si," answered the pastor. "San Jocobo is Santiago's horse. The saint rides him during the fiesta. Of course, he is not the horse we were thinking of putting the saint on tonight." Juniper patted the rouged jowl of the gay merry-go-round horse, adding, "He is handsome when he is dusted. *Muy caballo.*" With his sleeve he began dusting the pony.

"Jocobo? There is no such saint," said Gaspar.

"I'm no man to correct you, monsignor," Mr. O'Murphy said with gusto. "But 't is the truth what our padre is saying. In this town, full of its pagan beliefs, it is San Jocobo, patron of the veterinary sciences, to be sure."

Following the visit to the general's inn, Father Juniper and Monsignor Gaspar returned to the parish house for lunch. From time to time throughout the lunch, Gaspar kept glancing up from his plate and murmuring in a distant voice, "Jocobo? San Jocobo?"

This worried Father Juniper, for the monsignor seemed to have forgotten Santiago. The padre tried to be diplomatic, suggesting that San Jocobo really wasn't very important. "The real problem," he said, "is that Santiago should be returned to the church. I don't think the general's price is too unreasonable. The saint is miraculous, remember. And if he does this thing on the horse—"

Monsignor Gaspar frowned and pressed his forefinger to the bridge of his nose. After having seen what had become of the old monastery, he had begun to realize that the inn was no place in which to build a shrine in honor of any saint. "It is a question of the appropriate," he said. "The inn is no site for a shrine."

A happy smile touched Juniper's round lips. "Then you agree that we should honor Santiago in the church," he said eagerly. "That is, of course, if Santiago rides for the church."

Gaspar stiffened. "The bishop utterly objects to your horse riding demonstration. He forbids it. If you attempt it, you'll undoubtedly be removed from the parish."

"Did Bishop Sierra say that?" Juniper asked, startled.

Gaspar didn't answer him.

"But the people of the town want Santiago to ride," Juniper protested. "They love their saint violently."

Monsignor Gaspar pursed his thin lips. "My suggestion is that you forget the wooden image," he said. "Your predecessor, Caldo, had much experience here and he has convinced us that the anticlerical elements in town are using this wooden Santiago as a weapon. You can't take sides in such temporal affairs, padre. Your task is to serve the Church and the people, not factions. Your job is to bring peace to Santiago de Gante. And remember also, General Braga has always been the biggest contributor to the church. I feel you should devote your efforts to making the people of the town see the light."

"What light should they see?" Juniper asked, puzzled.

"That the wooden image is but an image. Let Braga keep it."

"But this Santiago is miraculous!"

Gaspar shrugged. "There are relics, church relics, mind you, in museums everywhere. The Church has no control. This is an irreligious age, padre. I strongly advise you to forget the wooden figure and to get a new statue of Santiago."

"The people feel—"

The monsignor put his hand up, silencing Father Juniper. Again, in a tone that intimated there would be serious trouble if Juniper took sides with the wooden saint faction in town, Gaspar said, "The people will become accustomed to a new statue. Bishop Sierra is very partial to a Danziger."

"A Danziger?" Juniper looked depressed and puzzled.

"Chrome steel statues," replied Gaspar. "They're being manufactured by Danziger & Sons, an ecclesiastical supply house in the United States."

"A steel statue? A steel saint?"

"They're excellent," replied Gaspar. "Weatherproof and handsome. We're placing them in all our churches. I'm sure Danziger & Sons can supply you with a suitable Santiago, and for far less money than you were thinking of paying General Braga."

Father Juniper shook his head desperately. "It wouldn't be the same," he murmured.

Gaspar smiled diplomatically. "You can be certain it will have the bishop's approval. I'll send you a Danziger catalogue."

10

HORSEMANSHIP

After lunch, and before he folded himself into his tiny black car, Monsignor Gaspar glanced across the churchyard and the plaza, noting the fiesta preparations. Several men upon ladders were fastening large vivid paper flowers in the branches of the lime and hemlock trees so that the square began to vibrate with a technicolor bloom. A few awning-covered stands were being put up and displays of festive food began to appear. In one corner of the church atrium Señor Tzintzuntzan could be seen making final adjustments in the complicated structure of the fireworks *castillo*.

Gaspar eyed the activity with disapproval. He turned to Father Juniper, saying, "Better cancel your little celebration, padre. Remember Bishop Sierra's warning. No miracles."

Juniper nodded despondently. Finally, when the monsignor's car had gone, the priest sighed heavily and returned to the rectory. For several minutes he paced around the patio, scarcely noticing Doña Maria and El Furioso, both who seemed to have grown angrier since the monsignor's visit. As he paced back and forth he reflected upon the advice Gaspar had given him. It is a shame, he thought, that there must be no fiesta. Perhaps it was because neither Gaspar nor the bishop really understood Santiago's importance. In recent times, everyone was so busy with the Blessed Virgin, they tended to forget the saints. He wondered if he shouldn't make another appeal directly to the bishop?

With this in mind, he hurried to the small rectory office where the telephone was kept. For a moment he studied the phone, trying to recall how one went about using it. The one time he had made a call, Maria had managed it for him. It was not that he was afraid or unskilled; it was just that telephones in Santiago de Gante were an anarchistic breed, leading a peculiar life of their own. He had heard of one telephone in town which, after the first rain of the season, always rang steadily for three nights and days. Another phone was good only for incoming calls, and then only if the subscriber managed to snatch it up before the second ring.

This apparatus, in the rectory, was one of the few late models in town. One could dial on it.

Father Juniper drew a deep breath, seized the phone firmly, quickly turned it upside down and shook it vigorously. Righting it, he dialed the number 4 and immediately hung up. A second later he shook it again and dialed long distance as rapidly as possible. The bell began to ring as though someone were trying to reach him. He picked up the receiver, and with a sense of satisfaction, heard Señora Trevino's voice. She was the operator at the small telephone exchange on the plaza. He asked for the bishop's residence in the capital of the state.

After quite a long wait Señora Trevino announced that the line to the capital was down. "Someone has stolen one of the poles. They are looking for it. Do you wish to wait, padre?" she asked.

"Will it take long?"

"Who knows?" the operator replied calmly. "It will be as soon as they find the pole."

Father Juniper cradled the phone disappointedly, and as he turned away he saw Policarpio and Señor Tzintzuntzan at the doorway of the office, watching him.

"Good afternoon, padre," said Policarpio. "Are you busy?"

"No. Not really. A telephone pole is lost."

"I saw the black one, the monsignor, leave," Policarpio said. "It would be useful to know what he was doing in Santiago de Gante."

"He came about the saint."

"Was it friendly business?" Policarpio asked suspiciously.

Father Juniper shook his head, saying, "He came to tell us that we cannot have the fiesta tonight. The bishop has forbidden the demonstration of horsemanship." He glanced at Tzintzuntzan, adding apologetically, "You will have to take away the fireworks. There will be no need for them."

"*Ah, Caray!*" Policarpio exploded. "You can't do this. The whole town is waiting."

Juniper made a helpless flourish with his plump hand.

"The bishop is a good man," Tzintzuntzan put in shyly. "But he doesn't know our saint, I think. Our Santiago has the ability to make up his mind. He did it before, didn't he?"

"In any case," Juniper shook his head sadly, "the bishop has forbidden it."

Policarpio snorted contemptuously. "Bishops are notorious forbidders of everything," he said. "It might be wise for you to remember Father Hidalgo."

Father Juniper frowned uneasily. He thought of Father Hidalgo who had led a handful of lace-cuffed revolutionaries and the people of Mexico in their struggle for independence. He did not feel much like Padre Hidalgo who had bravely counted his beads and his ragged army while defying his bishop who dangled the sword of excommunication over his head.

"I do not have the courage of the warrior priest," he said. "And maybe this that we argue over is not quite as important. I don't think I should disobey Bishop Sierra."

Policarpio flashed a dark look at the priest, then shrugged, saying, "I think this bishop needs to be shown something. He seems to have forgotten that a priest who is not for our saint does not last long in Santiago de Gante. This is not personal, you understand. It is just a fact."

The barkeeper motioned to his Tarascan companion and turned to leave. Señor Tzintzuntzan hesitated, then following the old custom, he took the priest's hand and kissed it. As he did this, it entered Father Juniper's mind that Tzintzuntzan had undoubtedly kissed Caldo's hand, also, before fabricating the bomb they had planned to use against Caldo.

Father Juniper called after Policarpio. "You are not going to do anything foolish?" he asked worriedly.

"We take the matter from your hands," Policarpio answered cryptically. "Our saint has a right to brush up on his horsemanship."

That evening, as he lingered over a simple supper from which he took no pleasure, he was suddenly startled by the deep wrangling sounds of the bells in the church tower. A rocket soared above the plaza, tracing a wavering pencil line of orange against the darkening sky. Then he heard the great booming of *El Temblor,* the big-voiced bell that was rung only on very special feasts such as Christmas, Easter and Santiago Day.

"Doña Maria," he called. "Go see what they do."

He himself hurried to the rectory door and peered out

across the plaza. With a sinking feeling, he saw the crowd
which had gathered outside. Someone had ignited the fireworks display and a sputtering, snarling snake of burning
powder raced up one of the poles supporting the *castillo*.
The entire structure burst into white, blue and green flaring
pin wheels, glowing globs and huge clumsily rotating figures. From somewhere across the plaza, in the direction of
the Hic Natus house where the crowd was the thickest, he
could hear voices shouting, "Santiago . . . Santiago!"

Maria's bald head, glistening in the flare lights, for she
had gone out without her *rebozo,* reappeared. Her eyes were
shining with excitement. "Don Vasco has kidnaped Santiago," she cried breathlessly. "At this very moment he is
in front of the Hic Natus house. They are preparing to put
the saint on El Primitivo so he can ride."

Were the *Annals of Santiago* still being compiled by the
town's chroniclers, Don Vasco's feat of kidnaping the wooden
saint from under General Braga's nose would indeed have
been included in the records, for it was no simple accomplishment. The deed had called for an old-time highwayman's ingenuity, because at the hour set for the kidnaping,
the Inn of the Friars was filled with people dining and drinking. To make it doubly difficult, Monsignor Gaspar, while
on his way out of town, had dropped in on the general, telling him that the bishop had forbidden the demonstration—
a bit of news which both relieved and pleased the general.

Just before sunset Old Vasco and his mouse gray donkey
appeared at the Inn of the Friars, delivering a load of mesquite firewood for the kitchen. Thus getting in, more or
less unobserved, he made his way to the chapel where he
removed the wooden saint's red garments and dressed him
in a rancher's clothing—the tight suede *charro* pants, the

blouse and sleeveless jacket. For added effect he let the saint wear his big cart-wheel sombrero and slipped a brace of horse pistols into the saint's belt.

Mounting El Primitivo, Old Vasco supported the wooden saint in front of him. As the burro trotted out into the street and up toward the Hic Natus house, Vasco, in his old-man's voice, began singing a wild and raucous *ranchero* song, just to make sure that no one would notice them. Anyone who saw him and the saint scarcely looked twice. It was exactly as if he were taking a friend home, a friend who had had a bit too much to drink and who wobbled upon the donkey with a wooden stiffness that comes from alcohol.

Naturally, El Primitivo deserved a great deal of credit, too. The gray donkey was one of those rare animals of complicated intelligence. In addition to being able to play dead, as well as to take commands in Catalan, in Spanish and in the difficult pre-Columbian Tarascan tongue, El Primitivo was a burro who could sense occasions of importance. On this critical evening he played his part to the hilt. After reaching the Hic Natus house where a large crowd had gathered, El Primitivo stood very still while a new saddle was put to his back and Santiago was strapped on in preparation for riding alone.

Even Old Vasco, knowing his burro better than anyone else, marveled at how amiable El Primitivo had become. When Policarpio had blindfolded the burro and had turned him around three times, Vasco gave the animal a warning whack, shouting at him, "*Ya!* Now don't be stubborn. Let the saint guide you. He has horsemanship."

Father Juniper reached the area of the Hic Natus house just as the burro and the saint were left to their own devices. The priest watched with mixed emotions. He experienced a feeling of dread over what his bishop would say when he heard of this, and at the same time he worried about the wooden saint. Although this Santiago upon the burro carried himself with cavalier airs, looking quite dashing and handsome, yet a little lonely in the manner of a bachelor—was he not just the image of a saint? Could miracles be expected? Juniper glanced at the flare-lighted faces around him. There seemed to be no doubts in the faces of his parishioners. Their fervor impressed, and shook, him.

He crossed himself quickly, and silently said a prayer to the real Santiago in Heaven.

El Primitivo stood for a moment, as though waiting for instructions from the wooden figure weighing him down. Then he wheeled and trotted toward the plaza. A great shout went up and firecrackers began to burst deliriously in the midst of the crowd jammed on each side of the street. Upon reaching the plaza, he veered to the left and headed toward the *Parlamento Inglés*. Old Vasco, Policarpio and several other personal acquaintances began shouting at him, but he paid them no attention.

Arriving before the doorway of the leaning saloon, El Primitivo hesitated. His large fuzzy ears semaphored and for a moment he seemed to struggle with temptation, like someone who had taken the pledge in a low moment and now had afterthoughts about it.

Suddenly, with a kind of straightening of his animal shoulders, El Primitivo turned and trotted swiftly toward the church. He went up the steps as if something were after him and entered the vestibule. Behind him, the cheering of the crowd was deafening.

Actually, no one will ever know what impelled El Primitivo to turn from the saloon so abruptly and head for the church. Most Santiagans believe the saint applied a firm hand to the reins. Some dubious persons claim the fireworks

frightened him. Others say it was just a whim on the part
of the donkey. To the people who knew El Primitivo, it
was a miracle even if the saint had no hand in it, because
Vasco's burro had never ever been known to pass up the
Parlamento Inglés without getting at least one bowlful of
pulque.

The friends of Santiago, however, had no time for such
debates because at the same moment that El Primitivo was
entering the church, the police, led by Captain Perlimplin,
tumbled from the police station and raced across the plaza
to recapture the saint. General Braga had heard about the
kidnaping of Santiago.

There was a short battle in the churchyard; then the police withdrew empty-handed. None of them were really
anxious to take the saint, and yet because it was their duty,
a siege was begun.

By mid-afternoon the following day, Santiago was still in
the pale green church. Throughout the bright morning and
afternoon a steady stream of men, women and children filed
through the cool church interior to greet their saint. Afterwards, the men usually drifted toward the *Parlamento Inglés*
to shake hands with Don Vasco, who had become a popular
hero. At the same time, an atmosphere of tension also vi-
brated through the crooked streets of Santiago de Gante.

Since the first clash with the police the evening before, a
small band of vigorous looking men had taken to loitering
on the church steps. Some of them passed the time sharp-
ening the machetes they carried. One of them sat in the
sunlight cleaning an elderly gun with the neat and fussy rub-
bings of his bandanna, almost as a man in a bathroom might
clean a set of false teeth. Meanwhile, upon the far side of
the plaza, the police watched the church with a frustrated
caution, while other people near and around the plaza

glanced curiously toward the doorway of the pink parish house.

"They are waiting," explained Father Juniper, to Doña Maria who had just come in. "They wish to know what I have decided. They feel it is up to me to say whether our Santiago should stay, or be returned to the general."

"But Santiago has decided," Maria replied flatly.

"Pues, si. But that is something else."

"Do you have a decision, padre?"

Father Juniper made a large motion with his hand. "I have one," he murmured. "And I am going to take a walk. Perhaps while I am out I may come upon General Braga's house."

"It is not hard to find," Maria said. "It is the most erect house."

THE DEAL

In Santiago de Gante a house is not considered old until it has reached its two-hundredth year. At about this age it is expected to sag against its neighbor, and for this reason most of the houses in town cluster together so they can lean and stagger and crumble without danger of completely collapsing. Only in one section, the newer part of town, do the houses stand upright. These livelier and aloof homes, surrounded and set apart by spacious gardens, occupy an area called the *Colonia Americana,* the habitat of the canapé eaters. Of all the houses in the colony, General Braga's was the most erect and easily recognizable.

His villa was set back upon a small hill behind the Inn of the Monks. Unlike the hill, which retained its age-old simplicity, the house atop it was a jungle of geometry—glaring mauve and blue cubes, rectangles, huge sheets of plate glass and frowning overhangs. It took a young man to live in such a place. Although the general was no longer young, he did his best to keep in condition. Within the high walls of his estate he had assembled an athletic-club collection of swimming pools, tennis courts, a great screened-in fronton

court, a pigeon-shooting range, stables, and as a kind of frivolous pivot for all this to swirl around, he had a fire-engine-
red kiosk bar set in the center of extensive lawns.

When Father Juniper made his way alone to the general's
villa, a servant showed him to the fronton court where General Braga and Miss Goldengrove were at play. As the priest
approached, the game stopped.

"*Hola, padre,*" the general shouted, bounding toward the
priest. He wore white duck trousers, and though he was
naked from the waist up, it was still evident that he was a
military man, for he had the insignias of a field general tattooed upon his shoulders. "I was expecting you, padre,"
Braga said with a faint acidity.

"I thought you would expect me," Juniper replied uneasily.

The general wrapped a towel around his neck. A long
curving wicker basket that resembled a gourd split in half
was strapped to his right hand. He offered the tip of this
cesta to the priest.

Juniper shook the end of the wicker solemnly. At the same
time he gave Miss Goldengrove an embarrassed scrutiny. He
was uncomfortably aware of her tanned shoulders and golden
smooth thighs, and of the tiny gold crucifix suspended from
her neck by a black ribbon. It seemed as if, of all things
about her, the crucifix stood out boldly, while her shorts,
the wisp of kerchief cupping her small breasts and the ribbon
tying up her blonde hair were but afterthoughts.

The priest turned to the general, saying, "I've come to
discuss the saint."

Braga scowled darkly. "Indeed you should," he said. "Definitely. Things have gotten out of hand. My saint being
stolen! Townspeople defying the police! A fine mess."

Father Juniper smiled contritely. "I truly had nothing to

do with it," he murmured. "I am sorry that I even suggested the horsemanship of the saint. I had hoped it would be a way of solving a problem. Instead, it has caused more trouble."

The priest's words tempered the general's feeling that this man might be dangerous. Perhaps the padre was unaware of his ability to arouse the people? Braga shrugged his tattooed shoulders. "You'll send back my saint, then?" he said. He put his muscular arm around the priest's shoulder, urging him toward the geometric house. "We'll have a drink on it," he added. "Make the good will flow. Cooperate, eh?"

Father Juniper nodded and supposed he could utilize something mild. The day had not been an easy one for him. He had come to a decision about the saint, but it was a decision full of risks and uncertainties. All morning long he had wandered about his patio, thinking about the saint and the people of the town. Then, at noon, Mother Monica, the mother superior in charge of the nuns who taught at the parochial school, came to see him.

The cheerful nun had strolled with him in the patio and her biscuit-brown face had been bright with plans. It was her duty each year to select the two children who would be trained to fly as angels over the plaza during Santiago's fiesta. This year, because the wooden saint had chosen to return to the church and take part in the fiesta, she now proposed something daring.

"I have picked two of Don Ignacio's children," she had explained.

"Don Ignacio, the atheist?" Juniper had raised his brows. "But not for angels?"

The good nun had nodded firmly, saying, "God has never struck down Ignacio for his atheism. Do you know why, padre? It is because he is saving him so that Santiago can convert him. Now, with the miraculous image back in our church, and if these children become fiesta angels, Santiago will surely take note of Ignacio."

When the nun had gone, Juniper thought about it deeply. It seemed to him that if someone like Mother Monica had such faith in the powers of Santiago, it was not a faith one should destroy by putting up false steel saints. Thinking upon it, he began to believe in his heart that the event of Santiago's horsemanship last night had meaning. The saint had shown where he wanted to reside. Thus, Juniper had come to his decision, in spite of Monsignor Gaspar and the bishop's warnings. Santiago must be left in the church, and some arrangement must be made with the general.

It is really not disobedience, he reasoned. The bishop sent me here to bring peace. If Santiago can bring peace into Ignacio's troubled atheistic soul, then can't he bring peace to the town? It is simply a matter of having him in a place where he has shown that he wants to be.

When Juniper, Miss Goldengrove and the general entered the house, the latter disappeared, leaving the padre with the girl, who promptly curled her smooth limbs upon a couch and stared entranced at the priest's dusty cassock.

"They're saying in town that our wooden saint really rode a horse last night," she commented.

"It was a burro," replied Father Juniper.

"And he guided the horse, I mean the burro?" She laughed lightly. "Do you believe that, father?"

Juniper smiled. "The burro was not accustomed to going to church," he said.

The girl gave a poetic sigh, murmuring, "I do love a good theological discussion, padre. Like this of the burro. Or do you like poetry? Liturgical poetry? Why don't you drop in here, an evening this week, just to see me?"

Juniper stared uneasily upon her semi-nudity. He did not mind seeing naked statues—they didn't move, sigh or breathe. Now, he found himself intrigued by the tiny cross at the girl's throat. She wore it with a curious grace which, in spite of her lack of costume, conveyed the impression that she was not, theologically speaking, naked or unvirginal.

"You're not a Catholic," he said with a note of puzzlement, "yet you talk as though you ought to be."

The girl smiled earnestly. "I can't bring myself to it," she said. "But I push others into it. My writing—" She assumed her purest expression. "You know, I'm a church bell."

"A church bell?"

"Of course, padre. I call others into church, yet I remain above and outside." She made a charming little sound, like the tinkling of a bell. "You see," she said. "I ring."

Juniper smiled uncertainly.

"You haven't seen Mrs. Melding, have you?" the girl asked with a sudden note of venom in her voice.

"The lady who owns the bull ring?"

Goldengrove nodded. "Be careful of her," she warned. "Melding is not a nice woman. She has such stupid ideas, so dogmatic about the bullfight. What do you think of it, padre? Isn't the bullfight a cliché? Just like the Mass? It's a ritual. Mass on Sunday morning, the fight in the afternoon. A sacrifice of blood—both. Symbols."

Father Juniper made a helpless motion with his hand. Miss Goldengrove writhed upon the couch. "What do you think of war and poverty, father?" she asked abruptly.

"They are things to worry deeply about," he replied carefully. "Solutions are not simple."

"How wrong, padre!" The girl frowned prettily. "Never

concern yourself with solutions. The most important aspects
of war, of poverty, are not their solutions, but their use.
Don't suggest solutions, please. Did I ever tell you, whatever
diverts your attention, whatever makes you look toward the
future, toward consolation, is evil?"

Father Juniper scowled politely. "Then you think Heaven
is evil?" he asked.

Miss Goldengrove's voice filled the room with its flight of
laughter. "The politics of redemption; that is what you're
in, father. It's false. It's an opiate."

Juniper began to feel disturbed and angry. He was sure
now that his decision about Santiago was good. With ideas
like these of the young lady rampant in town, there was need
for a good saint to keep his eye on things. Perhaps there was
need for another miracle; if Santiago would consider converting some of the gringos . . .

When General Braga, wearing a colorful Cossack uniform,
strode abruptly into the room, the pastor felt immensely relieved. The general slashed at a potted rose tree with his
cavalry saber, and Father Juniper stared in awe at the man's
long flared coat, the flashing red boots and high karakul hat.

"So," said the general. *"Niet. Niet."*

Father Juniper stood up immediately, feeling that this was
expected of him. Braga made another circuit of the room.
With his saber he cut at a vase filled with flowers, shortening
them considerably. At the same time, Miss Goldengrove rose,
and stretching her lithe limbs, she offered her hand to Juniper.

"You'll excuse me," she explained. "I must dress. We're
going to a costume party with Mr. Spire." Her laughter
tinkled again. "We're so fond of masquerades. You *must*
attend one."

Father Juniper shook her hand and nodded vaguely. Al-

ready, in less than a week he had received several invitations
to the canapé eaters' masquerades. All of them had come
from complete strangers, and invariably, each invitation suggested the party theme; that he come as a song, or that he
come as a thought.

When the girl had gone, Braga studied the priest searchingly. Although he would not admit it, he feared the latter's
ability to arouse the people. In some manner, he must win
over the man, or rid the town of him. The first approach was
best, he thought. But within limits. He brought Juniper
a glass of wine. "To Santiago de Gante, and to our good relationship," he said.

"To Santiago," Father Juniper murmured.

"To our saint, precisely," said the general.

He raised his glass, drained the contents with a gulp, then
flung the glass into the fireplace. Father Juniper put down
his glass. The general picked it up and flung it after his own.
"And now, padre," he said, "Have you ordered those bandits
to send back the saint?"

"I haven't asked them."

The general looked startled. "You what?"

"Last night," Juniper said softly, "Santiago decided that
he wants to reside in the church. My bishop objected to it,
but it has happened. What can I do?" He smiled helplessly,
adding, "And you agreed, too, that if Santiago made a
choice—"

"Exactly," Braga replied stiffly. "But there was a rental
price. The monsignor . . . the bishop . . . they're intelligent
men. Did they agree to it?"

Father Juniper bowed his round head. "I discussed it with
the monsignor," he said evasively.

"Precisely. And he must have said no." Braga sliced at
a mote of flying dust with his saber. "Good! Now, I've been

thinking . . . if you care to act as chaplain during my little fiesta at the inn."

"No, señor."

The general's face clouded. "There'll be a plump fee. Definitely."

"I'm sorry. I can't take part in such things. It is my duty to serve the Church and the people. Your fiesta is only for tourists."

"Nonsense," replied Braga, his voice becoming angry.

"It is best to be independent in temporal affairs," Juniper replied softly.

The general regarded him warily. "Then, precisely, you plan to keep the saint?" he demanded.

"That is why I came here."

"My terms haven't changed."

Father Juniper sighed. "Santiago himself decided it."

Braga grunted and thrust his saber forcefully into its scabbard. He realized that if he relinquished the wooden saint it might put an end to the fiesta at the inn, but it would enhance the town fiesta and, undoubtedly, draw more tourists. He did not deeply mind releasing Santiago as long as he had control over the priest. "The terms are ridiculously high," he said. "A thousand pesos."

"It is high, but—"

"Has the monsignor agreed?"

Juniper ignored the question. He smiled, saying, "Santiago will surely help."

General Braga stared fixedly at the two empty buttonholes on the priest's cassock. Although he was annoyed and angry because he felt the priest had maneuvered him into this position in spite of the monsignor and the bishop, and all the temptations he himself had offered, he controlled his feelings. "You're a clever man," he said. "You've gotten the town to expect the saint's return to the church. You've engineered it, hardly lifting a finger. You've brought about an explosive situation. However, since I am a peaceful man, there's nothing to do but let you have the saint. At least for a year. Do you have the thousand pesos?"

Father Juniper shook his head. "I'll get it. That I can promise."

The general looked unimpressed.

"I shall need a little time," said Juniper. "Perhaps until the date of the fiesta of Santiago."

Braga weighed this shrewdly. "Will you sign a contract?" he asked.

Juniper nodded. "If you will give me until one day after the fiesta."

Abruptly, General Braga's attitude changed. He was suddenly very satisfied. He called for his secretary, a young man with liverish lips and greenish skin. Braga cleared a desk which was cluttered with clocks and knickknacks simply by sweeping everything off into a dog basket kept under the desk obviously for this purpose. He then poured two new glasses of wine for himself and Father Juniper. At the same time, he dictated a contract to the secretary.

". . . agreed the statue of Santiago will remain in the parish church for one year, on a rental basis. If, however, the fee of one thousand pesos is not paid by July 26, General Hamilcar Braga retains the right to remove said wooden statue from the church without further notice."

The general finished dictating. He snatched the papers from his secretary and offered them to Father Juniper to sign. The priest read them carefully. Then, as he looked up at the general, his Mexican instinct for bargaining surged up.

"It is a great quantity of money," he said.

"Precisely."

"Perhaps it ought to be seven hundred pesos? The figure is made of wood, and it has cracks."

"A thousand."

"Will you include San Jocobo?"

"The carousel horse?" Braga smiled. "You drive a hard bargain, padre. Make it eleven hundred."

Father Juniper shook his head and stood firm.

"What do you offer?" asked Braga.

"Nine hundred."

The general shrugged. "I'll let it go at a thousand, and with the horse."

"*Bien.* A thousand."

Father Juniper put his signature to the copies of the contract.

After Father Juniper had gone, General Braga reread his copy. It put him in an expansive mood, for this was exactly what he wanted. He had the weapon, now, for getting rid of the priest. It pleased him that he had been clever enough not to have told Juniper that, yesterday afternoon, he had conferred at length with Monsignor Gaspar, also.

12

THE BIRDS

When Juniper returned from the general's villa, a table had already been set for him in the cloister-patio of the parish house. Here he sat before a clean cloth, eating a little, watching the sunset light glaze the patio, and listening to the play of the water in the fountain. Maria brought delight after delight from the kitchen.

It was Juniper's habit to marvel that she could find plates, or even knew which foods she was putting upon them when she vanished into the kitchen. When Maria cooked, and when she was not cooking, her kitchen was filled with a dense cloud of rich brown smoke. It poured steadily from the doorway, the only apparent opening in the cavernous room. The happier she was, the more smoke.

Maria was happy these days. Whenever she waddled out of the pall of smoke, her eyes watering slightly, but no more than was necessary for a woman of her age, she would stare at Father Juniper and at El Furioso with a bashful pleasure which she was too timid to reveal except through her cooking. This was the exact truth. Since Juniper's appearance in Santiago de Gante, Maria had become an inspired woman.

Although she had been the housekeeper and cook over many years, she had seldom gotten on with the previous pastors. Her feuds were famous. She had carried on a guerrilla warfare from behind the kitchen smoke screen, sniping at clerical palates by forgetting to salt the stews, or lacing the ranch eggs with too much *serrano,* a small explosive green pepper related to the fulminating cap. Once, she had even served a fried rubber sole taken from a discarded sandal. Father Caldo had been the victim, and from that time on he had taken to dining out with General Braga or with the canapé eaters.

Maria's reasons for such warfare were sound. In some instances pastors had been too curious about her kitchen, insisting upon snooping about, as though searching for unassorted sins. Father Caldo had drawn her fire because he wanted her to wear a uniform and a curious white chef's hat that he had ordered from Paris.

With Juniper, there was none of this nonsense. The plump priest ate with gusto, and he never inquired whether she had been to confession. And now, on this early evening, as he smacked his lips over each spoonful of black tarrish *zapote* pudding, Maria sensed that something important had come from his visit at the general's house, something that might bring her even more happiness.

The priest seemed less worried, and he ate with happy relish. When he had finished the pudding he smiled at Maria, saying, "What do you think, Doña Maria, if I tell you some news? It is definitely arranged that Santiago will remain in the church."

"Santiago alone?" Maria asked.

"Santiago and San Jocobo, too."

At this very moment—just at sunset—and as the words slipped from Juniper's lips, a thing happened which Maria and many townspeople were to call a miracle. A flight of birds winged over the pink parish house and whirled toward the plaza.

Maria looked up. "The starlings," she cried. "They've come back!"

For some centuries, ever since the dedication of the lime green church and the laying out of the garden-plaza facing it, starlings had been a familiar sight in Santiago de Gante. Each evening at dusk, with the punctualness of night watchmen, great flights of these largish blackbirds skimmed over the rooftops into town. For some twenty minutes they chattered and twittered gaily among the branches of the laurel trees in the plaza; then as darkness came, they went to sleep in the branches. Each dawn they were gone; no one could say where they spent their days.

Few people paid much attention to the starlings until the coming of the canapé eaters. One day a careless starling dropped a bit of something on a few tourists who were sitting in the plaza. A complaint was lodged with the town council.

This had occurred at a time when the town fathers were becoming very conscious of the value of gringo tourists. The councilmen had already refused to repair the old bridge spanning the gorge because it was being painted and photographed so much. They had already initiated a project to make the streets of Santiago even more crooked and colonial so as to attract more tourists. For a starling to threaten all this was grounds for action. An exterminator was called down from Mexico City. This man succeeded in trapping several birds while they slept. A few others were poisoned. The remaining starlings promptly left town, and for ten years they absolutely refused to return.

When other less sensitive Americans appeared distressed

because this picturesque phenomenon had vanished from the life of the town, the city council discovered its mistake. The starlings were one of the reasons why canapé eaters were settling among the Santiagans. Naturally, the council tried to get the birds back. They baited the plaza with titbits of food; they imported bugs; they bought chick starlings, but even these disappeared as soon as they could fly. The best that could be done was to convince a few shabby sparrows, an occasional hawk and some parrots to inhabit the laurels.

But not the starlings. Their feelings had been hurt.

Now, on this evening when the first dense flight of birds swirled over the town, circling above the plaza, dipping downward into the trees, a shout went up in the square. The news swiftly spread through the town, and within a few minutes, a great part of the population came to the plaza, watching.

Because she had seen the starlings at exactly the same instant that Father Juniper had announced that the saint would remain in the church, Maria was positive the priest had brought the birds back. The next morning she was up early, spreading this information about.

"It has something to do with Santiago," she told Policarpio's wife. "Naturally, it must be some kind of miracle. Perhaps there will be more."

Policarpio's wife took this information to her husband, who was already pleased because of the stand the priest had taken. He took the information back to his *pulque* brewery and mentioned it to Zapopan. Zapopan carried it into the street where he happened to meet Don Ignacio, the maker of idols. He shouted it at Ignacio. The latter took it home, but having no use for it, and feeling that his children should disregard it, he gave the information to Old Vasco.

In that he had become a strong admirer of the new pastor, Don Vasco passed the news about the birds and their relationship to the priest on to Don Juan de la Basura. Vasco embroidered it somewhat, explaining that his donkey, El Primitivo, had actually overheard the birds conversing with the priest. "The starlings carry messages between our priest and the saint," said Vasco. Deeply impressed by this, Don Juan de la Basura, the town refuse collector, and a man of some historical importance, took this information along on his route. Soon the stories about Juniper penetrated almost every house.

Some of the tales that popped up were rather difficult to verify. For example, the story sworn to by the wife of Popotla who claimed that she had seen the fringe of tarnished silvery hair which grew around the priest's crown floating slightly above his head like a halo. But some notable changes were very evident. For instance, now that the starlings were back on their old beat, not all of them left town each morning. Instead, twelve of them, like faithful disciples, went with the padre whenever he strolled out of the parish house.

As far as the people of Santiago de Gante were concerned there were also other firm signs that Father Juniper had connections with the saint. One day, shortly after the return of the birds, Juniper had carried a small silver bucket of Holy Water into the brew room where Policarpio and Zapopan fabricated their *pulque*. In a simple ceremony, the priest blessed the new brew and begged Santiago to look after it carefully. A little later, after the fermentation had set in, it was noticed that the brew had a remarkable flavor. It was truly an elixir. Men began coming from great distances to drink in the *Parlamento Inglés,* and the place was always busy. People brought their guitars; they sang songs; they admired the fighting bull over the bar, whose sickness began to disappear. The men occasionally pulled out their guns and fought, but for a change, no one got seriously hurt.

On the other side of town, in the *Colonia Americana,* General Braga and some of his friends were troubled by the growing popularity of the priest. Sensing the mood of the people, and realizing that the Santiago fiesta at the church would be a bang-up affair this year, Braga quietly canceled plans for his private fiesta at the Inn. Instead, as *presidente* of the town council, he leased out shooting rights for the big fiesta to a television company.

But the general didn't stop with this. He had no intention of losing his hold over the priest, or his control of the wooden saint. He set out to make certain that Juniper would never raise the thousand pesos rental money for the saint. "We'll see this man come crawling to us," he told one of the councilmen.

Thus, on the Sunday following Santiago's memorable burro ride, General Braga and the pro-gringo merchants began a subtle boycott. Although they attended Mass as usual, they stopped contributing to the collection. This happened Sunday after Sunday, until by Easter there was scarcely enough in the parish treasury to pay for the food Maria and the padre ate.

THE PARLIAMENTARIANS

Although most of the friends of Santiago, even Policarpio, had begun to accept the new pastor as being their man, Juniper remained uneasy and worried. He knew that Policarpio and his friends were curious as to how he had convinced General Braga that the wooden saint should remain in the church. Up to now he had avoided explanations because he was afraid they might not like the deal he had made with the general, or would frown on the condition of the church treasury. This made for a dilemma. He needed help, yet he was fearful of asking for it.

It was Policarpio who first noticed that the priest was not at ease with him. Misunderstanding the pastor's shyness, Policarpio thought it was because he did not like to visit with his friends in a crowded saloon. The barkeeper made certain changes in his place. Over the doorway leading to the brew room, he had a sign painted. It read: *The Vicarage*. This was done so as not to embarrass Juniper and the Church. Here, the padre could come and sip *pulque,* and, according to Policarpio's reasoning, if anyone saw him they would think they had caught a glimpse of a Protestant, most likely an Anglican clergyman.

In spite of his fears, Juniper himself liked the vicarage room. During the hours of the siesta, a small group of friends could gather there to drink, and to play complicated games of dominoes in which the partners worked out elaborate and surreptitious systems of signals. They belched, pursed their lips, farted, hoisted their eyebrows or scratched various regions of the body, as was needed. When anywhere else, particularly where their womenfolk might watch and make slurring remarks about a man's game, the signals were more complicated. In The Vicarage, the play was friendlier and more satisfying. At the hour of drowsiness, when the hour bell in the green church tower tolled four, and when the sun softly bronzed the small patio beyond the brew room, friendship and philosophy flowered.

In the back room one could always find men like Old Vasco, Tzintzuntzan, Policarpio or Zapopan. Sometimes Señor Popotla, who worked at the bank, took part in a game. He was a good man for dominoes. He liked confidences and concealment; these were second nature to him. His eyelids were normally drooped, his gaze darting out between them, following the game narrowly. If Popotla were not there, then the baker, Señor Villada, or Don Leon, the historian, or Señor Penjamo who was the town's night watchman, usually filled in. Villada and Panjamo always came together, for they were close friends. Although the baker was not a skilled player, he was a very good Catholic. He was the chief of the Cristeros, a subversive party which held weekly secret meetings, the hour and place of which, and all attending, was known to everyone in town. His friend, Penjamo, was useful to him in many ways, but not as a domino partner. By virtue of his profession, Señor Penjamo knew pretty well exactly who

in Santiago de Gante had insomnia, or if someone by chance
was not sleeping that night in his own bed. Being a charitable man, he passed these titbits on to Villada, who embroidered the scandals somewhat and whispered them to his
wife. The Señora Villada was most grateful because she was
in the habit of going to confession daily, and without these
additions to her repertoire, there were times when she would
have had little to say.

One afternoon, several days after Easter Sunday, while
Juniper took part in a game of dominoes, and had just carefully parried a query about how he had gotten the saint back,
there developed an argument about the duties of the saint.

"Santiago is the protector of *pulque*. This is a thing I can
swear to," Policarpio said as he held up a domino, then
slapped it down upon the table.

"He is God's bodyguard," said Vasco. "God is important
enough to need a *pistolero*. Still it is the kind of a job that
gives our saint much leisure."

"No," Señor Villada objected. "His main duty is to convert the heathens. Now that he is back in the church we'll
surely see Don Ignacio converted. It is high time."

The other players looked at their pastor, awaiting his
opinion. Father Juniper sighed thoughtfully. "Everyone in
Heaven has a job," he said. "God thinks up jobs for them."
He glanced about sadly, toying absently with his dominoes.
It troubled him that everyone so depended upon Santiago.

"Your play, padre," Policarpio nudged him.

Juniper aroused himself from his reverie, put down the
domino and smiled gently. Then, as Old Vasco made his
play with a fury worthy of big stakes, Juniper fumbled in
his cassock and took out a printed catalogue which Señor
Madriaga, the postman, had brought this morning.

It was a fat booklet from the liturgical supply house of Danziger & Sons in Detroit. He leafed through it, staring worriedly at the colored illustrations of vestments, of chalices, and the section devoted to sculptured saints. The saints were catalogued like farm equipment. There were three kinds: the plaster ones, which looked insipidly cherubic, some that resembled business executives, and lastly, the chrome steel saints.

The catalogue reminded him with force of the contract he had made with General Braga. He also thought of the expensive new vestments which had arrived on Easter Saturday. He winced, remembering how thin the collection had been the following day. Along with the pennies given by the poor of the parish, there had been a silver peso in the collection. A note had been wrapped around the coin; a note saying, "When you need help, call me. Your Servant, Braga."

Policarpio leaned over, looking at the catalogue. "What is it, padre?" he asked.

"Some supply things," replied the priest.

Policarpio's attention was caught by the picture of a steel saint. There was a blue check-mark beside it. Beneath the illustration, was a brief description.

> SAINT JAMES (Santiago) Model #342
> Dimensions: 82 x 24 x 12
> Wgt: 300 lbs. Incl., pedestal
> Chrome finish, halo incl.
> List price, FOB, Detroit, $60.00

Although Policarpio read no English, he recognized the saint's name. He looked at Juniper with sudden suspicion. "It would be useful to know," he said, "if you're thinking of turning in our Santiago for something like that?"

Juniper shook his head morosely. Don Vasco, Villada and

Popotla peered at the illustrated saint. "He's an ugly one," remarked Villada. "He probably lacks the miraculous qualities of our saint."

"He's only worth sixty dollars," agreed Policarpio. "How much is that?"

"It is less than eight hundred pesos," said the priest.

The barkeeper's eyes widened. He gave a sardonic smile. "That much? Whoever would pay that much for any kind of a saint is a fool."

During the discussion Señor Popotla slipped a double-six domino which he didn't want into his left sleeve. Having managed this successfully, he craned his neck toward the doorway that opened out upon Policarpio's patio, then whistled loudly to attract attention.

"Ayi, there is something that really needs thinking upon," he said, pointing at a single slim cloud extending finger-like across a visible wedge of blue sky. "If you were God, would you ever bother to think up an object like that skinny cloud?"

Father Juniper shot Popotla a quick grateful glance for having turned the conversation away from the high cost of saints. Meanwhile, the other domino players studied the cloud and shook their heads. Not one among them would have thought of putting a cloud in the sky.

"For shade, I would first think of making a tree," Villada said.

"Or a well, for the thirst," added Old Vasco. The ex-bandit frowned as he spoke, but the frown was because he had seen Popotla slip the domino up his sleeve. Vasco wondered if it were one he might make use of. Then, because Popotla was looking at him and he didn't want the man to know that he was aware of the missing piece, he commented casually, "A cloud is really something to think up."

"*Caray!*" Policarpio agreed forcefully. "For most of us, a cloud is hardly useful. We don't think of making such things unless we happen to be birds or aviators. They might have some use for a cloud."

"*Chingada!*" Old Vasco abruptly swore as he studied his hand. He looked apologetically at the priest.

"Does God think up every cloud?" Villada suddenly asked Father Juniper, as though he were testing him on his theology. "Or, does He just think up the first one, like Adam and Eve?"

Juniper's attention had again drifted both from the game and the discussion. Villada had to nudge him and repeat the question. The priest jerked to attention, then shook his head as though he were coming out of a bad dream.

"The clouds?" he murmured. "Ah . . . they're not God's work, exactly."

"Not God's work?" Villada rolled his eyes around in a shocked, overpious way. He came from a family which had great respect for God and the saints. His maternal grandmother was a woman of some note in Santiago de Gante because she had once purchased three hundred crucifixes to hang throughout her house. She had had them shipped to Rome, with orders that His Holiness should bless them, one by one.

"I believe the Blessed Virgin has something to do with clouds," Juniper explained. "She looks out for these small details of the universe. She cares for the color, the size, and where a cloud ought to be put. God may only bother with the big problems in creation."

"I know of something that only God could have thought of, and it isn't big," said Popotla.

"What's that?" Vasco demanded as he glared up Popotla's sleeve.

"An onion!"

"An onion?" Juniper frowned.

"Imagine anyone inventing a thing as complicated as an onion out of nothing," said Popotla. "That's a job for someone who has much time for thinking."

Suddenly Old Vasco pointed accusingly at the domino which had slid down Popotla's sleeve and had become visible. "You dog!" he shouted, pounding the table so the *pulque* jars and dominoes danced. "Dog of a ——" He flung back his chair and lunged for his machete.

Acting as though he had been startled by the mention of a dog, Popotla ducked under the table. In this manner he cleverly transferred the troublesome domino to Señor Penjamo's lap. Meanwhile, Policarpio had pushed back his chair and was struggling with Old Vasco for possession of the weapon. For a few minutes a heated argument blazed around the table. Popotla came up from beneath the table, unbuttoned his sleeves, shook his arms and spat disgustedly. "Who is hiding dominoes?" he demanded. Villada pounded the table. Señor Penjamo felt thoughtfully in his lap, came upon the domino and passed it on to Old Vasco's place.

Finally there was a lull. Villada noticed that the padre was gone. "It's strange for him to go away like this without a word of *adiós*," he said.

"Perhaps he is ill?" said Señor Penjamo.

Policarpio shook his head. "Something bothers him," he said thoughtfully. "I've noticed it for several weeks. And on Friday last, during the Good Friday procession when he carried the heavy wooden cross on his shoulders, he reminded me a little of Jesucristo. The priest has a burden."

"It could be that woman, Señora Melding," Popotla suggested. "I have seen her talking with him in the plaza. She's always anxious to get in bed with people."

The others looked at Popotla and frowned. It wasn't that they could not envision a priest sleeping with someone, but not one of them thought of Mrs. Melding as a woman. For a man to try sleeping with her would be like bedding down with a turkey.

Policarpio rose. "I'm going to see about the priest," he said.

Juniper was kneeling before the figure of God the Father. He had been praying for guidance and trying to make out whether the ferocious expression on the face of the statue was more marked than when he had first come to the parish. He wondered if God were angry with him? How else could the things which had happened recently continue in the same way? It was as if God were punishing him for failing to abide by Monsignor Gaspar's suggestions concerning Santiago.

A cough sounded behind him. He turned and saw Policarpio standing there alone.

"I came because you seem to be in trouble," the barkeeper said.

Juniper nodded. "There is some trouble."

"What, padre?"

The priest hesitated, wondering if it were wise to confide in Policarpio. However, since he felt so alone, so like a stream caught in a gorge, eddying and running in whirlpools, he finally gave in and poured forth his troubles.

When he had finished, he smiled sadly and added, "It is very difficult here in Santiago de Gante."

Policarpio shrugged and said nothing. The barkeeper walked over to the place where the wooden Santiago stood on a stone pedestal surrounded by flowers. He stared at the saint long and thoughtfully. It struck him as odd, how the saint seemed to add something to the church; a sense of completeness, perhaps. Then he remembered what he had said about the value of saints. But this one? Who could measure its value?

He turned and looked at the priest again. Up to this moment his anticlericalism had prevented him from really seeing Juniper. Somehow, now, the priest stirred him as no man had done in a long time. To his surprise, he felt a deep emotion, the kind he was accustomed to disdain. All along he had avoided thinking through the reason why his *pulque* had become so good. It was clear now. Seeing Juniper—troubled, childlike in his distress, and bumbling into foolish deals for the sake of the saint, and being followed through the streets by those ridiculous starlings—well, the vague notion began to stir in Policarpio's mind that Juniper was no ordinary priest. No matter how farfetched it might seem, in some way, he must be the representative of the saint.

"It is bad," Policarpio said at last. "You should have spoken to me before making the deal. Braga is a fox. It is useful to think that he got you to make the contract so that he has proof in writing that you disobeyed the bishop. You're in a mess, now. What you need is a good business man to help you fight Braga."

"A business man?"

"Clearly, yes. A manager. I'm going to manage you. One must know Braga to fight him. I know him. It is plain that the general is trying to trap you and to get you out of the parish. Now, we'll have to raise the thousand pesos for this year; then we'll have time to think of something else for next year."

Policarpio paused and a frown clouded his features. It was as if he were slightly puzzled, finding himself involved in such a venture after all these years of anticlericalism. Watching him, even Juniper sensed what went on in the barkeeper's mind. It was a thing he was familiar with: the struggle between worldliness and faith. And though he wondered how much Policarpio might be able to help, he remained hopeful.

"We'll raise the money, but quietly," Policarpio said abruptly.

Juniper gave a sigh of relief. "Do you have a thousand pesos?" he asked.

"Me? No."

"It is more than most Santiagans make in a year," said the priest. "And the Sunday collections—" He shook his head in distress.

"We'll get it from Ignacio," said Policarpio.

The padre looked startled. "From the idol-maker? He won't give anything. His atheism prevents it."

"Not that way," replied Policarpio. "The way you do it is to collect the reward."

"Is there a reward on his head? A thousand pesos?"

"Exactly a thousand."

14

THE IDOL-MAKER

The Church hangs on to its straying sons with the tenacity of an installment-plan company's credit department. It lets go only when the son becomes an outstanding atheist or a bishop of the Episcopal faith, and even then there are reservations.

Although Don Ignacio, the idol-maker, was Santiago de Gante's most notorious atheist and outspoken anarchist, there were reservations. In spite of his violent attitudes, he was looked upon as a respectable citizen—a thing probably not easily understood in any other community. Santiagans did not really mind his anarchism since they had a touch of it themselves. Furthermore, except for the subject of God, Don Ignacio went along with the townsmen on almost all other important topics: he liked fiestas, he had been against Father Caldo and he respected the legend of the Mare Lady. But most important, his atheism in no way prevented him from believing in the Virgin of Guadalupe, in Santiago, and in most of the other important saints.

Numerous pastors in Santiago de Gante had worked on Ignacio, attempting to better the man's relations with God.

Even Father Caldo had tried and had failed. According to some people, Caldo had made the mistake of presenting God as a stern old dictator. Ignacio was against dictators of every sort. When priests were not at work on Ignacio, the towns-people tried their hand at converting him. They brushed closer to success because the God they offered to Ignacio wasn't as grim as the priests made Him out to be. God might be somewhat eccentric, according to the Santiagans, but He was essentially good-natured.

The thing that kept people interested in Ignacio's conversion was the reward, a prize of a thousand pesos, offered to whoever could get the idol-maker to believe in God. The money had been put up by the wealthy Don Emilio Prado who had died during Caldo's tenure in the parish. This bounty, deposited with the town council, had originally been offered for another purpose. That it had ended up, as so many things do in Mexico, being used for something other than it was originally intended, was not the fault of Don Emilio.

What had happened was, some years before, Ignacio had organized the workers in the Fuente cotton weaving plant which Don Emilio had owned. There had been a strike, and one day a harmless and anonymous small bomb had frightened Don Emilio into signing with the union. To even things, Don Emilio had offered a reward to anyone who would come forward with evidence that it was Ignacio who had planted the bomb. Of course, no one came forward, and everyone thought it was a shame that this money was going to waste.

When Don Emilio died, and the money was still on the town council's hands, someone had an idea. Why not put the money to work in such a way that it would keep Ignacio too occupied to organize any more unions? Why not offer the reward for his conversion and thus keep him busy arguing? So the story was let out that Don Emilio, in his will, had specified the conversion reward. Naturally all the merchants, who feared Don Ignacio's talent for organization more than his atheism, breathed a sigh of relief and hoped it would take a long time to convert the idol-maker.

Familiar with some of this history, and having been coached by Policarpio, Father Juniper set out one afternoon to collect the reward.

The pastor was full of confidence. He was aware that Ignacio had great respect for both Santiago and the Virgin. Obviously, it should not take much to push him a little further. He actually mentioned this to the twelve starlings who flew about him as he crossed the plaza and strolled down the Street of the Monks.

It was a fine day and he felt that good would come of it. As he went down the street he could see the distant valley where the fields were burned to a yellow and brown crispness, and where the farmers were preparing the soil for the May planting before the coming rains. Out in the distance, the only touches of green were the maguey and cacti plants which stood in groups, like people engaged in dry, whispered conversation. Closer in, the sun struck less harshly. It glazed the cobbled roadway, fell and molded about the ancient houses of the town, coloring them with a film of unreality. This climatic condition, most noticeable in spring and fall, was one which delighted the tourists and canapé eaters. Though all of Santiago de Gante was touched by such alchemy, the Street of the Monks, particularly in the vicinity of the Inn of the Friars, wore it spectacularly.

Five years ago this area, with the exception of the old monastery and Don Ignacio's house, had been vacant fields and clay pits. But one day, a remarkable change had taken place. An American movie company had invaded Santiago de Gante to make a film about bullfighting. Because they had found nothing in Mexico that really appeared sufficiently Mexican, the film people had brought their own stage sets. They had rented the property from the general, and had constructed a typically picturesque Mexican street scene. When they had finished their work, General Braga had bought the sets, had hired workmen to throw up some rooms behind the false fronts. In this manner a new street and housing development had been born.

The houses were quickly snatched up by the Americans. The finest house was the one occupied by Señor O'Murphy. It resembled the Alhambra in Granada, though sometimes it was mistaken for a bordel by Mexican traveling men. Next to it there was a California ranch house, a copy of the site where Ramona had lived. In the midst of these purple, pink and orange façades, stood Ignacio's house, a place that was colored a dry red, as though someone had bled all over it.

Juniper rapped on the door. A squat, solid man without much neck opened the door.

Though Father Juniper had never spoken to Don Ignacio, he had seen him about town. Ignacio had a family made up of eleven children, and no wife. On Sundays he dressed in a good black suit and took the children to the plaza to listen to the band concert. The children, even so many, were not difficult to manage. They clustered around him like tiny boats moored to a pier.

"I'm Junipero," the priest explained.

Ignacio's glance seemed to take in the pastor's Roman collar, his dusty cassock and black cape, in one gulp. "I'm glad to see you," said the idol-maker as he drew the priest through the doorway. "I have been expecting you."

"Expecting me? You have?"

Ignacio did not explain that Policarpio had already warned him of the priest's coming. It was thought best that the padre should not know. Now, Ignacio merely shrugged, saying, "Why not? You come to convert me, eh? All the priests eventually come."

Juniper nodded cautiously and studied the man. He was impressed by Ignacio's flowery brown handle-bar mustache which clung vinelike to cheeks that were like a dark and pitted map of a tired volcanic region. He was impressed, particularly, by the gregarious friendly twinkle in the man's eyes.

"I thought I should visit with you," Juniper said. "Two of your children have been selected as angels for the fiesta."

"Sure. Raimundo and Eulalia," Ignacio laughed warmly. He slapped his thigh and a cloud of clay dust billowed around him. "But you didn't come for that, padre. You came to argue God, yes? Maybe you have better luck than the others?"

Juniper's feeling of confidence took another upward leap. The conversion of Ignacio was going to be easy, he thought. When a man is ready to argue about God, the battle is half won. It is the silent ones who are difficult.

Don Ignacio led his guest through two gloomy rooms and out into a patio where several sheds stood around the enclosure. In the patio's center there was a shallow pond filled with dull green clay cut into oblongs and drying in the sun like a pan of bilious fudge. Farther back, stood a deeper pit, the clay well. A windlass, a bucket for drawing up the moist mastic, and two brick kilns were also visible. In the midst of all this, countless children scurried about; the kind of small active animals who climb in and out of hot kilns, fall into wells, fight up and down piles of pink cantera rocks, scream, kick and bawl, yet without ever damaging themselves.

Ignacio shooed them aside and showed Father Juniper into his workroom. The priest stared curiously at the potter's wheel, the workbenches piled with stone-cutter's tools, as well as half-completed figures of Tarascan and Aztec gods. A fine film of dust covered everything. Ignacio lifted a huge tub of clay from a bench and invited the priest to sit down.

"Are there eleven?" Juniper asked, motioning toward the patio where the children could be heard screaming.

"Sure, eleven," Ignacio nodded with pride.

Father Juniper had heard that there were some people in Santiago de Gante who, after seeing Don Ignacio's brood, were wont to think kindly of Herod. Ignacio paid no attention to such people. He was a man who liked children; he liked them so much that his family had kept growing even after his wife's death. "Six come from my wife and me, the rest just got collected," he explained to the priest. "Before my wife died she was always taking up orphans. I do the same. There are a lot of orphans on the streets; somebody has got to feed them."

"They must be a great expense?" Juniper said, though he was pleased by what he had heard.

"Kids help me a lot," replied Ignacio. "The two oldest girls cook and make tortillas. The little kids go up on the hill and collect cactus leaves for us to eat. The boys, they help me here."

Ignacio's twinkling glance moved about the shop. It was evident that he took great pride in his business. The small stone and clay figurines of the ancient gods sold well to the tourists, and indeed, they should. Some of Ignacio's work looked so authentic that certain pieces had found their way into the glass cases of at least three important museums of archeology.

Don Ignacio seemed so burdened with responsibilities, Juniper marveled that he even had time to think. Atheism took a great deal of thought, a lot more than faith. How did Ignacio manage it?

Thinking again of the children, Father Juniper began his attack. "How is it you permit the nuns to educate your children?" he asked.

"Why not?" Ignacio shrugged. "The nuns are good women and they do no harm. Anyway, when the kids get to be fifteen or twenty years old, and have their use of reason, they'll become atheists, maybe even anarchists. For three generations in my family, there have been anarchists. I bet you don't have three generations of priests in yours? My grandfather, he was anarchist since the time of Benito Juarez. My father, he hated governments so much, he even refused to talk to the postman." Ignacio looked at the priest carefully, thinking to provoke him. "I'm for revolutions," he added. "Do you think God is?"

Father Juniper gave a wry smile. It was reassuring to hear Ignacio say this. It was at least an admission that there was a God.

"If God came out in support of revolutions, would you believe in him?" he asked the idol-maker.

Ignacio sat up, interested. "But there is no God! How can he come out for anything?" Ignacio said this, then waited like a checker player for the priest to react.

Juniper smiled with a disarming patience. "Just because you don't see God each day," he replied, "it proves nothing. Do you know Señora Treviño who works with the telephone company?"

"The hunchedbacked one? I know her."

"God is a little bit like her," said the priest. "Señora Treviño sits up in that little office above the bank among all those wires. Nobody sees her, yet she arranges it so that everything moves in the right way. She makes messages go where they should go."

Juniper set this out like a saucer of milk. Ignacio sniffed the argument carefully; then he chuckled and pulled at his mustache.

"Sure, maybe God sits up there in his own telephone office," said Ignacio. "But once in a while I see Señora Treviño. I talk to her. When I telephone Mexico City about selling some idols, she gets somebody on the line for me, even wrong numbers. But from God, what do you get? You call all day. He's not on the line."

"Prayers are not always answered directly," the priest replied nervously. "That is a fact everyone knows."

"*Sí, claro.*" Ignacio grinned, sensing that he had the priest in a corner. "How do you know which is the right prayer? Is that why there are so many different prayers in the book?"

Father Juniper tried to smile, but it came off badly. He felt as though his brain were being gently bruised by the idol-maker. To keep his confidence from frittering away, he took a desperate grip on himself and leaned forward, saying, "God exists! You must believe me!"

For an instant Ignacio seemed startled by the pastor's earnestness. He rubbed his jaw with a clay-roughened hand. "You are working hard for that reward, padre," he said. "I like to see a man work hard. Maybe I help you."

Hope suddenly surged through Juniper.

"Why do you need so much money?" Ignacio asked.

Father Juniper hesitated, then humbly he explained how he had signed a contract with General Braga, and what had happened lately to the church revenues. Ignacio listened thoughtfully, without showing that he already knew all this.

"Good, I'll help you," he announced when the priest had finished.

Father Juniper smiled happily. He began to feel that God might be helping him through Ignacio. "Then you're ready to believe in God?" he asked. "But it must not be just for the sake of helping me. You must truly believe."

Ignacio smiled, liking the priest for this. He shook his head and waggled his mustache. "No," he said. "I am not one to believe in God under any conditions. But I am glad to help you in anyway short of being converted."

Father Juniper frowned. "Then, do you have a thousand pesos?" he asked.

Ignacio shook his head. "Naturally I don't have it myself," he replied. "We'll have to organize it. We'll work up a committee. Is tonight good, eh?"

When Ignacio offered his hand, Father Juniper hesitated. He felt uncertain about accepting such support without first converting the man. Then, it entered his mind that God might want him to accept the idol-maker's help because it might be a step in the direction of his eventual conversion.

"Tonight," Ignacio repeated, as he let the priest out of the door.

Juniper shook hands with him and smiled. Something about the idol-maker's tone, his air of decisiveness, reminded him of a few priests he had met in the United States, men who had a great knack for organizing money.

Finally, when he stood alone in the sunlight upon the street and saw the twelve black starlings waiting for him on a telephone wire, a new wave of uncertainty swept over him. He thought of the things he had done which might annoy his bishop. Were they sins? He had visions of the philosophic brothers at the Wisconsin monastery compiling a new list of transgressions: sins of disobedience, of rejecting the monsignor's orders, and now, of receiving aid and comfort from an atheist. Where was it going to end, he wondered?

15

THE BUSINESS MEN

Don Ignacio's committee differed very little from the group of domino players who usually gathered in the back room of the *Parlamento Inglés*. The only real change was that the meeting was held in the patio of the pink rectory. There were the same familiar faces: Policarpio, Villada, Old Vasco, Popotla and Father Juniper. Both Zapopan and Señor Penjamo were absent; the former was tending Policarpio's bar and the latter was guarding the streets of Santiago de Gante. Tzintzuntzan, also, couldn't be found.

Under Policarpio and Ignacio's guidance, the meeting took on a businesslike atmosphere.

"There is a matter of a thousand pesos to be raised," said Policarpio. He gave the pastor a quick glance, and an old note of sardonic anticlericalism crept into his voice. "It is useful to remember that the money is for the parish. One would expect the *señor cura* to raise it."

Father Juniper smiled without resentment. He was deeply relieved that these men had been willing to share his burden. "I wish to do something," he said. "It is my responsibility. I have toyed with the idea of making cheese."

140

"You'd need a factory," Ignacio objected.

"No. This cheese requires only some old shoes and milk. We might get the shoes from Don Juan de la Basura."

"How long does it take to make?" asked Villada.

"Not long. But it takes time to package and sell it." The priest looked at his stubby fingernails thoughtfully. "Three months, perhaps."

Old Vasco shook his head furiously. "That's too long. The fiesta for Santiago comes sooner. It would be better if someone lent me a pistol, and—"

Policarpio interrupted the old man. "Ignacio and I have already discussed things," he announced. "We think the padre can make money out of the gringos. These Americans have money and they are a curious lot: they are always anxious to spend, but they need guidance. It is a known fact, for example, that the greatest ambition of most of the canapé eaters is to be invited into the homes of Señor Gancho, the grocer, and of Señor Patrullas, the hardware salesman. The gringos are of the impression that these shopkeepers are descendants of the nobility. No one has bothered to tell them that the only real nobleman in Santiago de Gante is Don Juan de la Basura."

"Policarpio is right," said Ignacio. He waggled his finger like a schoolteacher. "Up to now, the padre has been running the church for the Santiagans who never have much money. Do you think General Braga runs his inn for the likes of us? No. He has his eye on the gringos who have the money."

"But they're Protestants," said Villada.

Ignacio looked at the pastor, giving him a smile so suddenly and elastically broad that the priest could not help but become wary. "You convert the Americans," Ignacio said. "I'll bet you, you'll get plenty of money."

Juniper rubbed his face dubiously. "How many Americans are there?"

"Seventy," said Villada. "Not counting the tourists who never stay long."

"Eighty gringos," Policarpio corrected him.

"No. There are seventy," insisted the baker. "The other ten are Catholics."

Father Juniper thought this over critically. "The baptizing will take a great deal of water," he mused. "Fortunately, we come into the rainy season."

Popotla glanced at the priest with a staggered awe. "*Caramba!* Do you think you can do it?" he asked.

The priest thought again, then shook his head. "I might do it," he replied. "But it wouldn't be right. There is a question of morality."

Policarpio nodded. "The simplest thing is just to get the gringos into church. Once they come to church they'll give to the collection, and we might also interest them in the fiesta for Santiago. They might even raise a fund to pay for the rental of the saint. It is useful for the padre to remember that he must compete with the general for the tourist money."

Father Juniper frowned. "I don't like it," he objected. "Santiago and the church are not in business."

"You've no choice," Ignacio reminded the priest. "You made the deal with the general."

"But there must be some other way?"

Policarpio and Ignacio shook their heads. "The people don't have money," said Policarpio. "Only the gringos."

"*Pues . . .*" the priest murmured with some distress. "Well, as long as it is just for Santiago."

"How do you get Americans into a church?" Villada asked.

"You were in their couutry, padre," Policarpio said, looking at the priest.

Juniper's brows pinched thoughtfully. He scratched his head, tipping the halo fringe of silvery hair. "Well, it isn't the same as here," he said. "We should have an usher in church, like in a theater. The Americans like that. And there should be music. Maybe there should also be clubs and sodalities."

"Clubs?" Villada asked, somewhat shocked.

"Yes. There could be one for a game called bingo," Juniper explained. "Also, there should be men's clubs like the one which they call the Knights of Columbus."

Policarpio smiled sarcastically. "They wear armor, eh?"

Juniper shook his head. "Spiritual armor, which is not the kind you are thinking about."

"Good," Policarpio nodded, amused. "We'll leave the armor out. It would be difficult for there is but one suit of it at the museum. Nevertheless, we'll do what we can. It is clear that we must cater to the gringos."

During the following week Father Juniper controlled his qualms concerning the new project, and he set out to win over the canapé eaters. He studied the tourists who stopped at the small hotel on the plaza and at the Inn of the Friars. The canapé eaters and tourists were not quite like the Americans he had known in the United States. These traveled in bands of five or twenty, rather than in a manner less expeditionary. They also had a habit of bestowing a kind of civic importance on reptiles and insects, which the latter, themselves, did not assume. As a result of this study, Juniper and Zapopan fumigated the church.

Father Juniper's next task was to call on the handful of Catholic canapé eaters: Señor O'Murphy and his red-haired wife who painted crosses; the Dugans who were retired brokers; and Mr. Cavanaugh, the liquor man. Most of these people had been successful in business, but unlike other retired gringos who were satisfied with country clubs, hot dogs, television and Sunday picnics, these had been infected by an odd romantic virus which impelled them to live in distant places. As an apology for such behavior, they took up painting, or writing, or drinking.

The canapé eaters whom Juniper visited were startled by the new pastor. Back home in Boston they had been accustomed to having priests put the touch on them. When Father Juniper visited, it was not at all like that. In Juniper they met another kind of priest. When he failed to sit down, and did not begin with the usual edging forward on his chair, at the same time making a businesslike clearing of the throat, followed by the quick salesman-like pitch, the Catholic canapé eaters took an instant liking to him. They decided that the Mexican bishopric had sent this plump, untidy, otherworldly little man as a good-will exhibit.

Father Juniper asked for no money. He stood around in an apologetic way, gently explaining that he should have visited sooner. He wanted his church in Santiago de Gante to serve the Americans, both the Catholics and those who were not.

"The noon Mass on Sundays is especially for you," he explained. "There will be a sermon in English as well as in Spanish. There will be other improvements, and some clubs."

"We'll be there in force, scraping and bowing," Mr. O'Murphy assured the pastor.

Although Mr. O'Murphy and his friends actually meant what they said, on the following Sunday, the increased attendance that Father Juniper had expected and prayed for failed to materialize. That Saturday night, General Braga gave an especially brilliant party. As a result, only half the Catholic gringos appeared at Mass; and Señor O'Murphy was able to get out only one other canapé eater who, having once been a member of the opera claque, and not knowing the etiquette, applauded loudly after the English sermon. Thus, both the sermon and the one other American touch—Señor Popotla acting as an usher and taking up the collection—were wasted on the Santiagans.

After the Mass, Father Juniper went to the sacristy where he said the Thanksgiving. He hurried through the Latin words, stumbling upon some of them because his thoughts were half involved with wondering how the collection had come out. *"Trium puerarum cantemus himnus, quem cantabant."* He paused. He could never remember if it should be *puerorum* or *puerarum*. He made a small act of contrition because his thoughts had been on money during the prayer.

There was a rap on the door. "Popotla?" Juniper called out expectantly. "Come in."

Instead of Popotla, his visitors were nuns: Mother Monica from the parochial school, and another nun who pushed two ragged children before her. Juniper smiled. He liked the twinkling-eyed, plump, brown-faced mother superior. In spite of her middle years and her heavy white Dominican habit, she gave the impression of being spry and athletic. She took the children from the other nun, banged their heads together gently to quiet them, then presented the boy and the girl to the priest.

"These are Don Ignacio's children," she explained. Her voice went on, pleasantly pebbly, saying, "The girl is Eulalia; the boy, Raimundo. They are the angels for this year." She handed him a sheet of paper with typing on it. "It has always been the custom that the padre of the church teaches them the speech which they will deliver as they fly over the plaza. It is here."

Juniper patted the children on their heads; then he glanced toward the other nun who had withdrawn to the farthest corner and was nervously saying her rosary. He was on the verge of offering her a blessing, but Mother Monica shook her head warningly.

"Please don't," she whispered. "It may frighten Sor Juana."

"She is frightened of a blessing?" Juniper glanced cautiously at the younger nun. Her features, framed by the white wimple, were sweet and plain. Her face was rosy-cheeked. Then he noticed how she trembled.

"When she sees a man," explained the mother superior, "she takes on a fright. It unnerves her even to look upon statues of men saints. It's a problem, padre."

"But this is a rare thing?"

"The fright was caused by a streetcar."

"How could a streetcar frighten anyone? Was she under it?"

The mother superior blushed delicately. The thing that had happened to Sor Juana on a streetcar was known to her and a few other nuns, but it was not a subject she could discuss with a priest. She glanced toward San Jocobo, the dappled carousel horse who stood in one corner of the sacristy, watching everything that went on with his gay, fixed stare and merry-go-round smile. "I would suggest," said Mother Monica, taking her glance from the horse and nodding toward the children, "that you baptize them first. Then you can prepare them for the fiesta. They should learn to say the speech loudly. There will be much noise and it will be a great distance down."

As the two nuns departed, Juniper smiled reassuringly at Mother Monica, saying, "At least, in Santiago de Gante, the good sister will not be troubled. There are no streetcars."

He turned his attention to the children, but he had scarcely finished washing them in advance of coaching them in the Latin prayer, when there was another interruption —Policarpio rushing in with the disturbing news that Señor Popotla was dead.

Juniper sent the children home. He turned to Policarpio, shaking his head in shock. "Popotla? Our Popotla?" he murmured. "But only a short while ago I heard him making the collection in church. I've been waiting here for him."

Policarpio laid the collection basket on the vestment trunk. "Here's the collection, but Popotla is dead!"

"But how can this be?"

The tragedy of Popotla was an entirely logical event. It stemmed from the man's lively interest in banking and finance.

Although Señor Popotla's connections with banking were looked upon with some amusement by the parliamentarians, Popotla took himself seriously. He was employed by the town's only bank, *El Banco Internacional de Santiago de Gante*. Of the bank's three employees, he worked the longest hours because he was the *mozo* or janitor. Despite this limited role and the long hours, he always had faith that he would rise in the banking fraternity, and but for his accident, he might have done so. He could read; he loved to figure out deals; and he studied the investment market closely. Because of this knowledge he had insisted upon serving on Ignacio's committee as the financial adviser as well as undertaking to be the usher and collection taker in the church. He had a talent for knowing to a centavo exactly how much everyone in the parish had. He knew how long to hold the collection plate under a person's nose to get the most out of him.

Today, however, he had been thrown off slightly. He had estimated rather shrewdly how much more should be in the collection due to the several Catholic gringos at Mass, but because of some unaccountable accident, someone had dropped an extra twenty peso bill in the basket. When Popotla spied it, his eyes had grown wide. It opened entirely new vistas.

"This is exactly what the committee has been waiting for," he murmured to himself. "A bit of capital to invest properly."

Familiar with the intricacies of finance, he knew how money could be doubled in a day, quadrupled the next, and so on. Ignoring the other money in the collection basket— the centavos, the *tostons,* the *lana* and the buttons—he slipped the twenty peso bill into his pocket, then hurriedly sought out Policarpio and begged him to count the collection while he went off on business.

To get his bearings, Popotla paused for a moment at the *cantina* beyond Policarpio's place. After breaking the twenty peso note there, since it would be difficult to invest so large a sum in one lump, he proceeded to deposit smaller amounts here and there, mostly in the less reputable saloons and *pulquerias* around town. In less than a half hour, or shortly after Mass had ended, he had become quite inspired.

At one point, he looked through his pockets and discovered that there were but twenty-five centavos remaining. "Just the right amount," he mumbled unevenly. "I'll go buy'n egg."

His voice petered out happily and he staggered up toward the Old Bridge, intent upon going into the countryside where an egg could be purchased by a sharp investor for twenty-five centavos. He saw himself selling the egg to some gringo for fifty centavos.

"With such capital, and my profit," he murmured happily, "there's no telling . . ." He began thinking in terms of four hundred eggs. Before he got around to totaling up the profits he came to the house of Señor Ibarra who owned the bank where he worked. He halted, swayed unevenly, carefully thumbed his nose at the banker's ornate colonial house. Now visualizing well beyond the four hundred eggs, he hiccuped festively and pissed elaborately upon the Ibarra gate.

The Old Bridge was not much farther uphill. He wobbled up toward the edge of the arroyo and wove out upon the suspension bridge. When midway across the ancient span he stopped to admire the gorge below. "If there's a gringo down there painting the bridge," he muttered, "I'll sell him an egg."

Forgetting the Santiago de Gante rule that a male must never look down into the gorge while crossing the bridge, he gazed down. For a moment the thin ribbon of silvery water, the rounded boulders and the palo blancos with their white flowers that looked like crushed cambric, soared and swayed in his vision. Suddenly he thought he saw something stirring among the rocks.

"La Yegua!" he gasped.

This was a rare sight—the Mare Lady abroad in daylight. Then he heard the curious whinnying. He leaned too far over. The hemp railing gave and he felt himself tumbling headlong down into the gorge.

In the church sacristy, Policarpio shook his head. "It's a queer thing, padre," he observed. "Popotla asked me to count the collection money and bring it here. That's not like Popotla."

"You say, he was found under the rope bridge?"

"*Si.* An American found him. This Señora Melding was down there in the arroyo."

"It's sad. A great tragedy. He has a wife and children."

"They are not all his."

"Nevertheless, they are children."

Policarpio shrugged. "It's curious that he let himself fall from the bridge. Perhaps he was disappointed in the collection today?"

"You counted the collection? How much is there?"

"Seventy-one pesos and some buttons."

Father Juniper shook his head. "It isn't good, is it?"

"It isn't as good as we had expected," Policarpio agreed. "But it's a beginning."

Juniper shook his head sadly. "It's a bit more than last Sunday, but not much. And we've lost a man."

16

WAKE

When Father Juniper arrived at Popotla's house, in the block behind the market, he was by no means the first to be on hand for the vigil of the dead.

Old Vasco, Señor Zapopan and Don Anselmo, the town mason and woodworker, had set up shop in the street and were constructing a coffin for Popotla. The cobbles about them were covered with bright yellow wood shavings. Their friend, Don Coconino, sat on the doorstep and with one hand tapped out a hypnotic beat on a small drum while he played an altogether different tune on a three-note flute. Normally he did not play both instruments, but on this occasion his friend, Don Temerio, the town flutist, was in jail.

Juniper nodded to the men in the street, then entered the house. Popotla's place was not an elaborate one. Like the homes of the poor, it was so typical it could have been moved to a different location in Mexico each night and not have looked out of place anywhere. There was only one room, likewise typically furnished. It had a small Santiago shrine which the saint shared with the Virgin of Guadalupe; there was also a *metate* of gray stone for grinding corn, a huge clay waterpot, two stubby wooden chairs with cane bottoms and gaily painted legs, some straw sleeping mats, and on one wall, a large calendar with the face of a handsome Tehuana girl who held a bunch of impossible cherries between her flashing teeth. Beyond the room there was a dusty patio filled with flowerpots, a well and a thatch-roofed cook shed.

Popotla's place was already jammed with friends and mourners. The women had gathered in the yard and kept the Widow Popotla company. Some patted tortillas and prepared food for the wake, while others, from time to time, helped her grieve. Their menfolk did not mourn in this manner. The duty of the men was to keep Popotla's soul amused until it was time for it to move on. They sat around drinking, telling such jokes as Popotla used to enjoy, and singing his favorite songs. They sat in the living room with the dead man.

Popotla was laid out upon a cross of lime made upon the earth floor of the room. This lime was important for it would definitely shorten his stay in purgatory, though none of his friends were sure how this would come to pass. Popotla's head was propped up upon two chalky red bricks. Except for his face, the rest of him was blanketed with freshly cut flowers. In addition to the candles thrust in Coca-Cola bottles, he was surrounded by other little comforts. There was a small wooden box packed with fingernail cuttings and clippings from his hair and mustache. If these happened to be left behind during his journey into the next world, his soul would have to return for them, because it was known that everything must be delivered, intact, to Jesucristo. There was also a neat bundle of work clothes and a piece of fresh green cactus lying at his side. The cactus was included because on his journey across the plains to purgatory, one never knew when he might encounter a wild black bull. On such occasions a traveling soul throws the

cactus to the animal and slips safely by while the beast is
sniffing at the bribe.

Father Juniper anointed his dead friend and said the
prayers for the departed. He stared down upon Popotla
with tenderness, and he marveled over how well Popotla
looked, considering the fact that the man had fallen into
the gorge. Much of this was due to Ignacio who had remod-
eled Popotla's face with wax so that the dead man looked a
little more like Tlaloc, the rain god, than Popotla had ever
looked.

The priest sought out the widow. This wife of Popotla
was *morenaza,* very dark skinned and handsome. Although
thin and young, she was deeply saddened by her husband's
death. She had not had too much experience with men and
she loved Popotla passionately, even though he had never
beaten her as was the custom among more thoughtful husbands.

It startled the priest when he saw General Braga in the
patio with the women. For a second, Father Juniper frowned,
suspecting that the general was being hasty in paying court
to the handsome widow. In actuality, he shouldn't have worried about this. At the moment, Señora Popotla had eyes for
no other man. She was quite sure that, even though her
husband was dead, he lingered in spirit and might still be
jealous. Once before, when Popotla had vanished from the
house for several days, a curious thing had happened. An
owl had begun roosting in the cook shack, watching her with
unblinking suspicion. She had gone to Doña Inez, an old
woman who lived near the gorge and who specialized in such
problems. Doña Inez had given her several herbs to burn in
the cook shack. Almost immediately after this had been
done, the owl flew away. An hour later Popotla reappeared.
When he had been informed about the owl, he had admitted

that Doña Inez's sister, who was something of a witch, had turned him into an owl. Now, scarcely an hour after the wake had begun, the Widow Popotla had found another owl in the cook shack.

"Hola, padre," General Braga exclaimed, sighting the priest.

"You come to these things?" the priest asked.

The general smiled expansively. "Definitely," he replied. "We Mexicans must stick together." He turned to the young widow and added, "I've been told that Popotla had little money?"

The widow nodded.

"Precisely," Braga said. He dug into his pocket and brought forth a handful of money that he carried like soiled and crushed handkerchiefs. He gave the widow a fifty peso note, then glanced at the priest challengingly.

Juniper fished under his dusty cassock, but the most that his pockets disgorged were a rosary, several small coins and a crumpled invitation to a gringo masquerade party which commanded him to come dressed as a dinosaur.

"Well, there will be a Mass, without charge," he said to the Widow Popotla. "And I'll see to it that the funeral is paid for. Perhaps there will be a little extra money to keep you going until there is another husband."

The general now drew him aside. He smiled at the padre with a fondness and caution one reserves for a worthy adversary. "This business of the sermons in English, definitely inadvisable," said Braga as he solemnly shook his head. "You make a mistake, padre. The Church in Mexico is Mexican. Remember that."

"It is for everyone. We are catholic."

"What's the purpose of such things, precisely?"

Juniper shrugged and said nothing.

"If you think you'll make money from the gringos you're mistaken. Definitely." Braga shook his finger in warning. "When you want help, padre, you come to me."

"*Pues,* no." Juniper murmured stubbornly.

Afterward, when the general had gone and Father Juniper went back into the house, he began to worry. He wondered if he should bow to the general. After all, he had already lost a man, and it did not look as if the Americans would fill the church coffers. General Braga could just go on giving parties each Saturday night until no one at all would attend Mass on Sundays. "It is not going to be easy to find money, both for Santiago and for Popotla's widow," he murmured to himself. Such disastrous thoughts continued to trouble him, even after some jars of *pulque* had been brought over from the *Parlamento Inglés*.

He watched the wake for a while longer. It became clear to him that no one was really thinking about the widow and her children. More and more people came in to mourn. There was a great deal of music, shooting off of fireworks and drinking. Toward evening the dancing began, and there were also two fights: a short encounter between Zapopan and Señor Madriaga, the postman; and a battle between two orange-colored dogs who rolled and snarled through the room, finally upsetting the corpse. By the time Father Juniper took his leave of the wake, Popotla, though not exactly forgotten, was no longer the center of attention.

As he returned to the pink rectory, a plan began to shape in the padre's mind. It was simply that he would borrow a little money from the slim parish fund and lend it to the Widow Popotla. It would have to be a bit more than the general had given. He also decided not to tell Doña Maria. She usually looked after the rectory money, and he was afraid she might frown upon his lending out so large a sum.

Going to his room, he wrote out an IOU for one hundred pesos, a sum large enough to cover Popotla's funeral expenses and to leave something over for the widow. Folding the note into his pocket, he wandered casually about the patio, looking for Maria. He paused at the doorway of the smoke-filled kitchen.

"Doña Maria?" he called.

There was no response. He slipped into the pitch dark, acrid smelling kitchen. The smoke was blinding as he stumbled about, feeling his way along the walls, encountering curious indefinable objects. He came to a fissure in the wall which was not quite large enough for him to go through, then he returned to the door. He took a deep breath of fresh air, then made another circuit of the kitchen, this time, shaking each pot and jar that he could lay his hands on. Somewhere within the kitchen, there was hidden the clay pot in which Maria guarded the parish treasury.

Unable to bear the smoke any longer, he staggered out to the patio and stood there gasping and coughing.

"Are you ill, padre?"

It was Maria's high, cracked voice coming from the kitchen entrance behind him. He wheeled and saw her emerging from the smoke.

"Were you in there?" he asked uneasily.

Maria nodded her bald head vigorously.

"How is that possible?" Juniper asked. "I didn't hear you."

Maria lowered her eyes in embarrassment.

"Have you heard of the tragedy?" Juniper went on. "Señor Popotla is dead."

The old woman nodded. "I have been waiting to go over there," she said.

"It would be good if you took along some food, particularly for Popotla's children."

"There is nothing but your supper."

"Then take that, yes."

Maria smiled shyly. She could remember the times when the former pastor, Caldo, had never offered more than a few dry crusts to the poor.

Juniper appeared to hesitate; then, clearing his throat, he said, "While you are gone, I've been thinking I should go over the parish funds. There are a number of expenses . . . Some planning is necessary . . ."

"The treasury?" Maria looked at him blankly, adopting a curious stance and a witless grin. *"Pues,* it is the same, padre."

"Naturally it is the same. But I wish to go over it."

"Tonight?"

"Now."

There was an odd recuperative silence. Juniper had an uneasy feeling that Maria was questioning his motives regarding the money. This, of course, was quite understandable, for when Caldo had left the parish, he had owed Maria six months salary.

"There is the value of one hundred and sixty pesos in it," Maria explained. "This includes the collection from this morning. Do you want me to take out a little wool for you?"

"No. I simply wish to do some bookkeeping," Juniper insisted.

"Then you want the jar?"

With a glance of odd hesitancy, Maria turned and plunged into the smoke-filled kitchen. For a moment or so there came a great crashing of cutlery and dishes, the forceful gushing of water and some curious strangled cries. Then Maria appeared, bearing the blackened clay pot.

Juniper took it in his arms, hurried across the patio to the rectory office where he locked himself in. Fishing the hundred peso IOU from his pocket, he laid it upon the desk. Then he turned the jar over, spilling out the coins and paper money it held. He began counting, but did not get very far before he commenced to frown. There was much less in the pot than there ought to be. He counted again, slowly. It was still short. Then, staring into the pot, he spied a slip of paper caught just within the rim. It was an IOU for fifty pesos, and it had been signed by Doña Maria.

Juniper stood for a moment, blinking at the slip and pressing his stubby forefinger thoughtfully to the bridge of his nose. "Should I question her?" he murmured aloud. Finally he decided against it. Undoubtedly, Maria had some personal reason for borrowing money, and to question her might be embarrassing.

With a sigh, he counted out the hundred pesos he wanted to give to the Popotla family. He carefully redeposited the ten pesos that remained over, and added to this the pair of IOU's.

Thus it came about that the Widow Popotla, on her night of tragedy, was made richer by one hundred and fifty pesos, in addition to what General Braga had given her. And at the same time, the treasury of the pink parish house was reduced to almost nothing.

It was only some days later that Father Juniper learned the purpose of Maria's borrowing. He said nothing about it, but during the following Sundays when the collections were small and there was almost nothing to add to the treasury, he would look at her IOU nestling there in the clay jar, close to his, and he would experience a feeling of warmth for the old bald headed woman who had had pity for Popotla's widow.

17

THE KNIGHTS OF SANTIAGO

Nothing seemed to be going quite right. For lack of listeners Father Juniper finally gave up the English sermons. Only the Catholic canapé eaters came to Mass, and these, somewhat spasmodically. Then one day, Zapopan reported other disturbing news.

Each day the powerful, cat-footed Zapopan was accustomed to exercising the corps of bells that hung high in the pale green tower of the church. He rang the smaller bells daily, while on Sundays all the bells except *El Temblor* were given a strenuous workout. Since the giant bell was tolled on special occasions only, Zapopan usually let it rest upside down. This way, a slight push was all that was needed to send it rocking. However, because its mouth faced upward when it was left at rest, dirt sometimes filled its throat, and Zapopan was called upon to dust it out from time to time.

One day, when he was about to clean out *El Temblor,* he discovered that some starlings were busily building a nest in the throat of the bell. He hurried down to tell Father Juniper.

"If they build a nest," said the priest, upon hearing this,

159

"there will be eggs. Naturally, we cannot disturb them."

Zapopan shook his head, and in his accustomed way, shouted, "It's an omen, padre."

"An omen?"

"Maybe there won't be a Santiago fiesta," the bell ringer replied loudly. "Maybe the starlings know it."

"But why?"

Zapopan pointed up toward the tower. *"El Temblor* always rings in the fiesta. If there are eggs, or baby birds, how can there be a ringing?"

"Perhaps they'll be large enough to fly by then," Juniper said hopefully.

"Pues, sí. They might be, and they might not be, but who knows? Maybe Santiago is angry and plans not to have the fiesta because we are so slow getting up the rent money. Yesterday, I saw General Braga in church, looking at the saint."

Juniper nodded solemnly. A few minutes later he stood with Policarpio on the steps of the *Parlamento Inglés.* The two men, priest and bartender, stared up at the church tower where the bells were hung. Juniper glanced at Policarpio, saying, "Perhaps Zapopan is just being superstitious. But lately, I have had a strange feeling that Santiago is disappointed in us. I have been thinking maybe this club we talked about should be started."

Policarpio didn't reply at first. Instead, his gaze moved from the church tower, swept toward the distant mountains and the sky. He seemed to be feeling the weather, sensing the changes in it.

It was already mid-May and the first of the rains had come to the region around Santiago de Gante. The folded hills and slanting fields, tilled and tucked with seeds, had begun to lose their scorched crispness and to take on the tender colors of yellow and green. Each day, now, the clouds gathered, spotting the tile blue sky with puffs of white, piling up in gleaming monumental towers, darkening toward afternoon and finally breaking over the valley like an enormous demoniac concert. For an hour or so rain drove and jumped upon the ground, and rushed in torrents down the sloping cobbled streets of the town. By nightfall the sky cleared and the evenings were again sweet and bright. The stars seemed so close they hissed and crackled across the sky.

"Yes," Policarpio observed at last. "It is time to do something. This is canapé weather."

"Canapé weather?" Juniper asked, puzzled.

Policarpio nodded, explaining, "All of us like rain. But of all the people in Santiago de Gante, the greatest rain lovers are the canapé eaters. They like the wet season because the power plant breaks down regularly, and it forces them to use oil lamps or candles for light. It is a useful thing to remember that nothing appeals more to the gringos than the romance of eating canapés and drinking cocktails by candlelight. Now is the time for you to get a club going—and by candlelight."

It was on one such evening that a handful of canapé eaters, prompted by Juniper, held the first gathering of their new organization, the Knights of Santiago. At eight-thirty, Father Juniper set out for Señor O'Murphy's house to join them.

The instant the priest stepped from the rectory doorway, twelve black starlings whirled out of the laurels in the plaza to greet him.

"You really need not come," Juniper addressed them, although he was not at all sure if the birds understood him. "I shall be late, I think."

The birds twittered noisily, but they insisted on accompanying him. Father Juniper frowned at them, wondering which one among them had been building the nest in *El Temblor*'s throat. As though to reassure them that he was busily working for Santiago, he said, "It will be an important meeting. Something good should come of it."

He sniffed deeply of the night air, sensing that it was one of those evenings that conspire for happiness and success. The electric power was off again, and the night was clean and fresh. A moon soared brilliantly, showing upon its face an interesting green splotch like verdigris upon a chalice. Its reflected light fell across the plaza, making it look like the ghost of noon. In one corner of the plaza, Juniper paused to exchange greetings with two heavily armed policemen and their prisoner, Don Temerio. The police and their captive had set a victrola on one of the iron benches and they were celebrating a private fiesta of their own.

The priest continued on down the Street of the Monks to the *Colonia Americana* where O'Murphy lived. When he reached the door, he waved good-by to the starlings.

The O'Murphy home was one of the larger gringo show-places in Santiago de Gante. It had most of the conveniences that foreigners had demanded in the houses they occupied: there were fireplaces, bathrooms with plumbing, a patio with a banana tree, a tiny kitchen equipped with a refrigerator and a sideboard for making canapés. In addition, there were countless rum bottles supporting candles that glowed cheerfully.

"And let me be showing you about," said Mr. O'Murphy when the padre came in. He took Juniper's arm, leading him through the various rooms, introducing him to his guests. "It is a small group, as you suggested. We're all Romans, except for Miss Goldengrove and Señor Spire. He's High Church, to be sure. Ah, here, meet the Corrigans."

Father Juniper shook hands with a man who had a smooth diplomatic face that reminded him of Monsignor Gaspar. The man was accompanied by a woman whose figure was like an inverted Coca-Cola bottle. The man, Mr. Corrigan, offered him a glass. " 'T is Bushmills," he said in a tone that implied this was an important code word.

"To be sure, father, you don't mind that we invited the ladies. Perhaps, later they'll form a sodality," said Mr. O'Murphy.

Father Juniper smiled. He sipped from the glass. The taste was not one that intrigued him. It had too much of the flavor of chlorinated potatoes.

" 'T is like a breath of the old sod, eh, father?" Mr. Corrigan enthused.

Father Juniper held his breath, swallowed again and smiled sheepishly.

"Ah, and begging your pardon," O'Murphy broke in. "Here is Mr. Spire and the general." O'Murphy dragged at the pastor's arm.

The priest frowned as he was led to a group clustering around General Braga. Along with the general and Miss Goldengrove, there was an Englishman, Mr. Spire, and a Mr. Quin, a man with a faint but impervious New England hauteur. General Braga smiled broadly upon seeing Juniper. The priest smiled back, but it rubbed him wrong that the general should be here.

"Spire is doing a cookbook, he is," explained O'Murphy.

Mr. Spire nodded wisely. He wore thick-lensed spectacles which cast a jelly-like film over his eyes. His enlarged pupils seemed to float vacantly behind them.

Since Mr. Spire's glance missed him entirely, Father Juniper turned toward the general with a look of query. "Are you just visiting?" he asked.

General Braga grinned broadly. "I'm a knight," he said.

"A Knight of Santiago?"

"Precisely. I have an interest in our saint."

For an instant Juniper's features clouded and he scratched his halo-like tonsure. It was obvious that General Braga was here to spy upon him and to disrupt his plans.

"You don't mind, eh, padre?" the general asked with an edge of irony.

Juniper moistened his lips. He stared at the general and the others. At the same time, the Bushmills began to stir about in the pit of his stomach. It gave him confidence and he began thinking that it really didn't matter if the general were present. The canapé eaters here were Catholics. In a pinch, they would back him in any struggle with Braga.

To show his confidence, he turned away from the general and spoke to Mr. Spire. "You are writing a cookbook?" he asked casually. "Is it a book of English cooking?"

The Englishman's gaze floated vacantly toward him. "An Aztec cookbook," he replied. "The ceremonial dishes."

"Spire isn't a Catholic," Miss Goldengrove broke in happily. "But he's drawn . . . The Sacrifice of the Mass, you know."

"What makes you do an Aztec book?" asked Father Juniper of the Englishman.

Mr. Spire loosened up somewhat. He smiled distantly at the priest. "The book is based on a crashing recipe," he said. "A little thing called, *tloco pozole.*"

"What is that?" asked the priest, puzzled.

"It's a ceremonial recipe, a stew prepared for the Aztec god, Xipe." Spire explained as his gaze wandered about the room, jellifying.

Juniper shook his head in wonder, and Mr. Spire sighed without explaining this emotion.

The gathering of material for his cookbook had become a trying task for the wealthy Englishman. Originally it had begun when he had found the recipe for *tloco pozole* slipped between the pages of a cookbook that had been lent to him by Georges, the chef-in-chief at the Perigord-Ritz in London. The dish had captured Mr. Spire's imagination, for it was brilliantly simple, yet it appealed to the gourmet in him. It had called for nothing more complicated than the thigh of a prisoner of war, a quart of hominy, a few pinches of marjoram, chili and just enough salt to taste.

Intrigued by the logic of the ancient Aztecs who seemed to have devised wars for the purpose of capturing prisoners intact—and just enough to make up various interesting ceremonial stews—Mr. Spire had come to Mexico to look into the matter.

"What time is it?" O'Murphy asked.

Mr. Spire withdrew his floating gaze from the heavy thighs of a gringo lady who moved through the room bearing trays of canapés. He took out an English timepiece and pressed a button on its rim. The watch, ingeniously fitted with tiny Westminster chimes, struck ten times. Father Juniper looked at his own potato-like watch and realized that the Englishman must have listened to burros on a gray day. He was an hour fast.

O'Murphy clapped his hands. "It's time we get on with the meeting," he shouted.

Mr. Cleary, an active little man with a peaked head and trembling ardor in his wrists and fingers, began moving chairs about. When everyone was seated, O'Murphy smiled enthusiastically and waved a cocktail as he addressed the gathering. "Are you wanting me to chair the meeting, or do we elect a knight-chancellor to do it?"

"A knight-errant," someone cried.

O'Murphy made some infinitesimal movements with his glass which Father Juniper mistook for a blessing. "Father," O'Murphy said. "With the heavy burdens of the parish upon you, t'would be too much, asking you to be the chair. We'll find someone suitable, to be sure. I nominate General Braga."

"Second," cried Cleary.

The pastor caught his breath. He rose to protest, but it was too late. All the male knights voted quickly because it included a toast. The general was rushed to the chairman's table where he raised his hands, calling for silence.

"Is there a program?" Braga asked. "We must have a program. Definitely." He glanced at Father Juniper. "Any ideas, padre?"

Juniper hesitated. He was conscious of the general's eyes thoughtfully transfixing him. They seemed to challenge him to reveal his plans and hopes for the Knights of Santiago. He thought of his discussions with Policarpio and Ignacio: together they had worked out a strategy, a bold plan to invade the American camp quite openly and organize gringo support behind Santiago.

"Speech!" Mr. Corrigan called. "Say something, padre."

Father Juniper stood up again and let his thumbprint eyes rove about carefully. Yes, he thought, perhaps the very boldness of his plan might confound the general. He coughed politely, and began, " 'Though I speak with the tongues of men and of angels, and have not charity, I am become as sounding brass, or a tinkling cymbal. . . .' " He paused, and seeing from the expressions upon the faces of the knights that they knew the rest, he smiled. Then he began talking about the saint and his fiesta.

"This year," he said, "General Braga has kindly let Santiago return to his accustomed place in the church so the fiesta will be more important than at any time before. This means a great deal for the people of Santiago de Gante. We would like to outdo ourselves in honoring the saint, but it is a thing that takes much money." Juniper hesitated, fumbling for the right words, then added, "There is the upkeep on Santiago, the fireworks, the floats, the vestments." He paused again and smiled uneasily. "It has been my thought that the natural duty of the Knights of Santiago should be to make certain that our saint is properly honored. If the knights would raise money for the parish treasury, for its part in the fiesta . . ."

He hesitated again and squared his shoulders. Looking away from the general, and toward O'Murphy and the others, he went on, " '. . . and now abideth faith, hope and charity, these three; but the greatest of these is charity.' "

Mr. O'Murphy leaped to his feet and shook Father Juniper's hand enthusiastically. "And me, after drinking for years, to forget charity. 'T is a shame." Waving to the other knights, he shouted, "And wasn't I telling you; and he's a fine speaker. He moves the heart."

"Charity. A charity ball. We'll throw a charity ball and raise funds for the fiesta," someone suggested.

"Second," cried Mr. Cleary.

"Right," O'Murphy responded. "A charity masquerade ball. To be sure, it's a way of getting the entire town behind our patron."

"Definitely, a ball," said General Braga.

"The theme?" someone asked.

For several minutes there was much discussion of this vital aspect of masquerade balls. In order to attract the widest attendance, it was finally decided that the invitations would go out, saying, "Come as Anything"!

"When is it to be?" asked one of the women, Mrs. Corrigan.

"It should take place the night before the fiesta of Santiago," O'Murphy decided.

"A prize for the best costume?"

Mr. Spire raised his hand. "I'll offer the prize. How much?"

Although Juniper was aware of how enthusiastic the canapé eaters could be about masquerades, he was startled by the swiftness with which they planned this one. Even the quibbling which developed between Spire and General Braga as to who should offer the prize for the best costume was quickly settled. The general and the English gourmet each put up five hundred pesos, making it a grand prize of a thousand.

Father Juniper smiled happily. The Knights of Santiago were now knit in a project. It seemed to him that even the general had been caught up in the enthusiasm for the event.

"Father, we'll raise a fortune," said O'Murphy.

"It's good," replied the priest. "However, the fiesta is more than two months away. There will be need for some money to finance the ball, and for other expenses."

"Right, to be sure. So we'll pass the hat. No. We'll take pledges." O'Murphy turned to the general. "As the chairman, General Braga, will you entertain pledges?"

General Braga rapped upon the table. "Pledges. Definitely," he said. "But first, does someone move that we toast our good friend, the padre?"

"Second," shouted Mr. Cleary.

The Knights of Santiago, and their ladies, rose in a body, lifting their glasses in a toast to Father Juniper. This gesture cemented the atmosphere of knighthood and good will. The priest looked about at the zealous faces of his new friends,

and he was sure he could expect wonderful deeds from them.
He even entertained a charitable warmth toward the general.

"Pledges, it is, now," said O'Murphy.

General Braga rapped the table sharply again. "Pledges,
precisely," he boomed. "But first, let us also toast our
bishop." Cocktail glasses were filled all around. "To Bishop
Sierra," said the general.

Juniper smiled generously. However, when the toast was
completed, Señor O'Murphy, suspecting that his father's sod
had been slighted by the general, proposed a toast to the
Bishop of Dublin. The salute was welcomed. Then, to satisfy
the others, a toasting excursion through the various Irish
bishoprics, including Boston, was found necessary.

Following twenty or so toasts, the Knights of Santiago were
patriotically afire. Their speeches careened high above the
spires of common sense. Fearing that they had forgotten the
plight of the parish treasury, Father Juniper rose to remind
them.

"Ah, the fiesta, to be sure," O'Murphy remembered. "The
saint. A toast to Santiago."

Someone else thought of another saint worth toasting, and
from here onward, it was but a short step to a brawl.

General Braga, being experienced in these affairs, drove
Father Juniper back to the rectory. As he let the pastor out
in the dark plaza, he chuckled with amusement and stared
blandly at the priest. "Definitely, padre," he said. "The
Knights of Santiago will be of no aid to you. Always, before
business, they come to the toasts."

"You started them on this," Juniper replied angrily.

"Precisely. You invaded gringo territory, which is mine.
If you continue to try raising money for the saint's rental,
I may have to inform the bishop about the deal you made
with me."

"But I'm going to get the money."

"I'll lend it to you."

"No. That wouldn't be right."

"Pues, then it is no quarters, padre." The general chuckled ironically and stepped on the gas.

Because he was so depressed by the general's remarks and by the chaotic first meeting of the knights, Juniper did not particularly notice the combination corkscrew and bottle opener that came out of his pocket when he fished for his door key. He thought nothing more of it until, after switching the light on in his cell-like room, he noticed that the object was gold-plated and there was a ruby-colored stone set in it.

18

THE TREASURE

Something strange had been taking place. Father Juniper was not altogether certain what to make of it. While waiting for Policarpio to come to the rectory, he sat on the edge of his hard bed and stared musingly at the small reed basket filled to bursting with an odd assortment of jewelry and trinkets. The gleam of gold and silver and flashing stones appeared oddly out of place in this room which was furnished with nothing more than a hard bed, a worm-eaten wardrobe, a single naked electric bulb of low wattage and a crucifix upon the wall.

Juniper picked up a jeweled Renaissance dagger from the basket and examined it critically. It was indeed a wonder of sorts how this object and the others in the basket had come to him. His thoughts went back over the weeks since the first meeting of the Knights of Santiago.

The history of the treasure in the reed basket dated from that night. At first, he had not been fully aware of what was occurring for he had been too distressed by General Braga's sabotage of the meeting and, later on, by the conduct of the knights themselves. The knights were good men, and they always began their meetings with great enthusiasm: order of business, motions, discussions of the masked ball, suggestions for pledges, the parish fund and the reading of minutes. Then they came to the toasts. It was obvious that there would be a masquerade ball, but it was equally clear that no one would sell tickets nor raise funds for the parish treasury. It seemed that no one really had to organize the ball. Among the canapé eaters, such cocktail parties and masquerades sort of started up by themselves, perhaps by a kind of osmosis.

After attending the second meeting held by the Knights of Santiago, Father Juniper had been surprised to find a silver cigarette lighter in his pocket upon reaching home. Then, following other meetings, more such baubles filled his pockets. He began to suspect that Mr. O'Murphy or one of his friends had dropped the objects into his pockets by mistake, and for this reason he had failed to return them immediately.

He explained his hesitancy to his parrot, El Furioso, in this way:

"They are all heavy drinkers, you know. One just can't go back and say, 'You've been careless with a jeweled bottle opener.' The gringo is noted for his ability to hold strong liquors. If I return these things right away it would embarrass them. It would be like saying they are drunkards and can't keep track of things. So, I'll wait for the proper moment."

The opportune moment never seemed to come. While the padre bided his time, more and more trinkets began popping into his pockets whenever he visited with the canapé eaters. There were gold cigarette lighters, letter openers, crystal and silver ash trays, and on one occasion, a tiny chrome garlic press. Gradually these unasked for gifts filled his reed wastebasket.

The strangest thing about it was, that for all the world,

he could never remember exactly when the Americans had pressed the treasures upon him. He began to suspect himself of stealing. One evening, to test himself, he carefully sewed up all his pockets before going out to visit with the gringos. When he returned to the rectory at midnight he found a suspicious bulge. Although all the pockets of his coat were still tightly stitched together, there was a rent in the lining of his coat. He trembled as he explored and pulled out a silver pillbox. He stared at it somberly, looking at the tear in the coat-lining which he had never noticed before; then he made a sign of the cross and knelt down to murmur a troubled *Ave*.

This was a turning point. Although he continued meeting with the Knights of Santiago, even extending his circuit of visits to include the non-Catholic canapé eaters, he no longer spoke to them regarding the fiesta fund and Santiago. He just went from house to house, sitting quietly, beaming a little, waiting to see if something stirred in his pockets.

Now, while he sat in his room, he heard footsteps crossing the patio. He laid aside the jeweled dagger and went to the door. It was Policarpio.

"You sent for me, padre?" the barkeeper asked.

Juniper drew him into the room and shut the door. He pointed to the basket, and while Policarpio stared at it open-mouthed, he explained how he came to have the things.

"You didn't steal the stuff?" Policarpio asked, still startled.

Juniper shook his head with dignity. "I told you," he repeated. "There must be something miraculous about it. Perhaps Santiago has had something to do with it. But I am puzzled. What does the saint want me to do with such treasures? Were they given to me so as to pay for the rental of the saint?"

"Did you have the old bandit, Vasco, along with you when you got these?"

"No. Certainly not."

Policarpio pursed his lips, picked up a few of the pieces, weighed them in his hand, then glanced at the pastor with an expression of shrewd amusement. "Why don't you return them?" he asked.

"Return them?" Juniper's stubby hands played through the air as though unraveling a spidery argument. "I planned to," he replied, "but if I go about trying to return these things, people might misunderstand. If they gave them to me, they'll be angry because I don't value them. If they do not remember having presented them, they may think a priest stole them."

"It would be a useful thing to know whether they were stolen!" said Policarpio.

Juniper shook his head. "It would be a sin to steal," he said simply.

Policarpio's dark eyes twinkled with sardonic amusement. "Ah, *caray!*" he exclaimed. "It is plain, then. The gringos gave you the stuff?"

"I don't know, exactly. But the things have been presented. Perhaps to help pay for the saint. This is my only interpretation."

The barkeeper picked up the ruby-set corkscrew and the tiny garlic press and studied them wonderingly. It secretly amused him that such objects should catch the eye of a priest or a saint. He dropped the two pieces and frowned at the pastor. "These things have value," he said. "I think, more value than you imagine."

"I know. That's why I asked you to come over. I don't know what the saint has in mind, in case he has arranged all

this. Do you think we should sell these things? Perhaps on
Sunday, in the market?"

"It would be dangerous."

"Dangerous?"

"Yes. Quite dangerous." Policarpio shrugged. Although
he suspected the gringos had given the trinkets to the priest,
he was prepared to humor the priest by agreeing that, perhaps, Santiago had engineered the transfer. Undoubtedly the
gringos were slipping the things to the padre so as not to
embarrass him, or Juniper himself was trying to hide the fact
that he was accepting gifts from gringos. Policarpio smiled.
And then, of course, there was the other possibility . . . Juniper had seemed a little desperate lately.

"To sell the things in the market might be dangerous,"
Policarpio went on. "Sometimes the gringos forget they give
things away. They go about shouting that they've been
robbed. The gringo is always complaining of being robbed
in Mexico. It is as if there were no robberies in their own
country."

"What do you think of a lottery or a raffle?"

Policarpio shook his head once more. "Listen, padre.
These toys look too much like gringo stuff. If you sell raffle
tickets, and if the canapé eaters happen to win some of the
things, they'll say they were stolen."

"But they weren't stolen. It is something of a miracle how
these things got into my pockets."

Policarpio gave a preposterous snort. *"Caray!* How do we
know if the gringos believe in miracles? I have a better
thought. Let's get Don Ignacio to turn these things into
antiques. He's good at that. And it is useful to remember,
the canapé eaters are interested in collecting antiques. This
is an American habit."

The suggestion appealed to the priest. He smiled happily,

asking, "How much do you think we'll get? Will it be much?"

Policarpio lifted the reed basket to judge its weight and value. Setting it down again, he nodded and said, "I would guess that we don't have to worry any longer about the money for the saint. Maybe, if a few more trinkets were added—"

He glanced up at the pastor. Juniper's gaze was withdrawn. The padre was deep in thought: he was trying to remember if there were still some Americans he had not visited.

19

THE INVESTIGATION

While Father Juniper and Policarpio went to Ignacio's house to discuss the business of antiquing the gringo treasure, Police Captain Perlimplin was taking up another facet of the same matter with General Braga.

For Perlimplin, it was not an easy conversation. He had patiently followed the active *presidente* of the town council about the shaven lawns of the latter's estate, for at this moment the general, shirtless and garbed in blue shorts, was pursuing a battered croquet ball. While the military insignia tattooed on his shoulders fried in the sun, the general knelt on the lawn, rump stiffly up as he sighted carefully over the top of the wooden ball as though surveying a dangerous terrain from behind a bunker. Suddenly he jumped up and wacked the ball toward a wire wicket. "Definitely," he said. "This is a serious situation. The crime wave must stop. Arrest someone!"

"It is a difficult thing," replied the captain.

"Difficult? Why, precisely?"

Captain Perlimplin cast a bleak and distressed glance at the general. Although he was almost as large as General

177

Braga, he was far less athletic. The pace set by the latter as he pursued the foolish red-ringed wooden ball was rapidly exhausting the policeman. Perlimplin mopped his brow with a blue bandanna, and began again.

"It isn't an ordinary crime wave," he explained. "It has been troubling me for weeks. Each day there is a new complaint from the Americans. Always from the gringos."

"Good. Round up someone. The maids, the gardeners, the woodcutters."

"I have done that, but it does not help."

The general threw his head back and stared down his nose at the police captain as though he were sighting down the barrel of a rifle.

The walrus-mustached police chief appeared amazingly sad. Of course, he always looked sad, and this made him an ideal police captain for a town that attracted tourists. When he had to arrest people, he accomplished it with politeness, and with an unchanging expression of deep melancholy. In actuality, he was not one who enjoyed arresting citizens. With the exception of Don Temerio, the flutist, who was a special problem, he usually only made arrests toward the end of each month when the police force budget was apt to run low.

"These crimes are a reflection upon police efficiency," said General Braga. His voice carried a note of warning.

Captain Perlimplin winced and glanced about uneasily. His attention settled momentarily upon a buzzard wheeling high in the bleached sky. Meanwhile, the general scowled, sensing that the police captain was hiding something. "Well?" Braga demanded.

Perlimplin gave an embarrassed squirm. "There is a suspect," he admitted.

"Who? Old Vasco? Good. Arrest him."

"It isn't Vasco."

"Well? Precisely, who?"

"It's the priest."

General Braga stiffened abruptly. "Our *cura?* Junipero?"

Perlimplin nodded. "The padre has been the only person who has visited all the gringos who now complain of being robbed. But it means nothing."

"Hah!" the general muttered vigorously.

He wheeled abruptly, striding across the lawn in deep thought. Although he did not show it, he was deeply elated. He was worried, not only by how popular the pastor had become in the town, but also among the canapé eaters. Now he turned toward Perlimplin, saying, "You'll investigate the priest. But thoroughly."

The captain hesitated. Even though he realized that the general's suggestion was in order, it filled him with qualms. He was not a religious man, but ever since the return of the starlings to Santiago de Gante, he had begun to regret certain anticlerical attitudes that he had assumed in the past because they had been the thing for a civil official to display. Of late, he had even begun feeding the starlings in the plaza.

"How should I investigate?" he asked.

"Search the church, the priest's house."

"That will be difficult."

General Braga waved his hand airily. "No trouble," he said. "Search the priest's place for antigovernment tracts. This is expected of a civil official. It will arouse no suspicion. Now, let's have a drink on it."

Perlimplin nodded uneasily. The general grinned broadly, put an arm around his captain's shoulder and led him toward the kiosk bar on the lawn. As they walked together, the general paused to pick up a bow and arrow lying in the grass.

With an air of enormous well-being, Braga launched the arrow at a pale gray cloud hovering in the sky; then he sighed because the feathered shaft didn't puncture it.

A half-hour later Perlimplin knocked at the door of the pink parish house. When he discovered that neither the pastor nor Maria were there at the moment, he slipped inside cautiously and began going through the various rooms surrounding the patio.

The task filled him with a certain uneasiness. It was almost as if he were daring to search in a church. From time to time he grew taut, overcome with a sensation of secret watchers, of eyes peering accusingly at him from behind flowerpots. Finally, he came upon Juniper's simple room and his eyes fell upon the basket filled with the gringo treasure. He crouched over the reed basket nervously.

An abrupt scream came from behind him.

"Pecador! Pecador! Sinner!"

He spun upon the sound, his nerves vibrating with fright. For an instant he saw no one, but then his glance dropped, coming upon the vivid green Huaxtecan parrot. The bird glared at him with yellow demoniac eyes and Perlimplin stared back in horror.

"Sinner!" the bird screeched accusingly.

El Furioso, usually too angry to speak, had suddenly found his voice. It was the only time he was ever known to have spoken.

The screeching of the bird capsized Perlimplin's senses. Abruptly grabbing up the basket of treasure, the police captain fled from the rectory and did not stop running until he reached the safety of the police station. It was only after he caught his breath while hiding in one of the back cells that he realized he was clutching the basket. It was the last thing in the world he wanted around.

Had he found the basket of glittering trinkets anywhere else, Perlimplin would have known what to do. But now it was too much for him. He was aware of what the townspeople thought of the pastor, and what certain small blackbirds, and possibly even Santiago, seemed to think of him. This was church business, and he was afraid of it. He wished desperately that Santiago would take a hand in the affair, perhaps send his angels, or come himself to remove the evidence. When nothing like this seemed likely to occur, the worried captain did the next best thing; he set out to shift the responsibility to someone else. An hour later, he called upon General Braga again.

The general was simmering in a steam cabinet in his private bathhouse. He didn't trouble to leave his cabinet for Perlimplin, but insisted, instead, that the police captain strip and steam himself in the adjoining box.

"Well?" asked the general when he saw Perlimplin's sad face, protruding from the top of the box, steaming adequately. "You made your search, yes?"

The police captain nodded unhappily.

"You found evidence?" asked Braga.

The captain licked at his walrus mustache. He stared uneasily at the general's domed head. "There were things in the padre's room," he murmured.

"The loot?"

Perlimplin inclined his head again.

"Good," Braga exclaimed with relish. "Definitely a clear-cut case, eh? The priest needs money badly. Steals from the Americans. Evidently he must have a crime ring. He may have confederates, Policarpio Flores, Old Vasco. Where's the loot?"

"It's at the station."

"Guarded?"

Perlimplin nodded. The loot was locked in a cell, but its presence in the police station left him uneasy. In his opinion this kind of an affair was church business, not a thing for the police to handle. If he had his way, the entire matter would be turned over to the bishop. Glancing in distress toward the general, he said, "Perhaps there has been some mistake."

"Mistake?" Braga scowled darkly.

"Maybe the evidence is circumstantial," Perlimplin hedged. "Before we arrest him, I should like to ask the bishop. It doesn't seem right, arresting a priest, especially this one."

General Braga pursed his lips and thought this over. "The bishop," he muttered. Although he had come to respect the new pastor as an adversary, he felt that the time was at hand for some sort of action. He realized, however, that he must proceed with caution. In Santiago de Gante, the seizure of a priest could be dangerous. Nodding, he swiveled his head toward the police captain, saying, "You may have a point. Definitely. We won't arrest him. At least not before the fiesta. We need him during the celebrations. Lead the processions. For the moment, we'll give him a bit more rope, then tie the knot."

"The knot?" Perlimplin looked puzzled.

"Absolutely."

The general gave an enormous heave and burst out of the steam cabinet. He began pacing back and forth, naked as a poached egg. Finally, after he had arranged some thoughts, he picked up the telephone from the table near the massage bench and put through a long distance call to the bishop's office.

"A knot," he muttered vigorously as he stood there holding the phone. His connection came through. "Monsignor Gaspar?" he shouted into the phone.

Meanwhile, Captain Perlimplin watched him and wondered vaguely if he, too, could have his captain's insignia tattooed on like the general's.

20

JUNIPER'S SACRIFICE

Neither Maria nor anyone seemed to know where the basket filled with treasure had gone. For several days she and Father Juniper turned the rectory upside down, searching frantically.

"It is nowhere about," the priest finally admitted to Policarpio.

"You didn't have a change of mind and give it back?" Policarpio asked.

Juniper shook his head. "I would like to believe that Santiago changed his mind, and removed the treasure as mysteriously as he gave it, but I am not so sure," he said.

Policarpio's gaze curved about the patio of the rectory thoughtfully. It paused on the green parrot, went on to the fountain, then rested again on the priest. "The police haven't been here, have they?" he asked.

"I don't think so."

"It would be interesting to know," replied the bartender. "Zapopan tells me he saw that walrus of a police captain snooping about in the church."

This information startled the priest and he frowned worriedly.

"If Perlimplin has found the treasure," Policarpio continued, "then you are in serious trouble. I had better get Old Vasco and Zapopan to keep an eye on him. With the Santiago fiesta so close, we don't want trouble, eh?"

"The fiesta is close, isn't it?" Juniper agreed uneasily.

Policarpio nodded. During the last few days he had become keenly conscious of the signs of the approaching days of fiesta. This, of course, was not difficult to sense. Were there no soaring moon, no calendars nor other means of accounting for the days of the month, people in Santiago de Gante would still know when they had reached the twenty-second of July. On the twenty-second, as regularly as clockwork, a man named Don Jesus always changed the tires on his dilapidated red autobus.

Don Jesus, a plump curly-headed Santiagan who resembled a renaissance cherub on an opera house ceiling, was the owner and operator of the town's only bus—a colonial-looking contraption which he had named *El Delirio,* or The Delirium. Once each day his bus made the ten-mile round trip to the town of Fuente de Ovejuna, the nearest railway terminal to Santiago de Gante. The trip was a thing of uncertain duration, not so much because of breakdowns, but because of Don Jesus' attitude toward tires. Throughout the year *El Delirio* managed to roll on tissue-thin rubber because it was Don Jesus' custom whenever he spied glass or dangerous rubble upon the road, to halt the bus, then take out a broom which he kept handy, and carefully sweep the highway.

But each year on the twenty-second, exactly three days before the festival of Santiago, Don Jesus put aside his broom and performed a ceremony. He changed the paper-thin tires for the heavy-duty ones which he kept in reserve for the huge loads his bus would haul into town during fiesta week. The jacking up of *El Delirio* was a signal touching off a great flow of activity in town and in the surrounding region.

For several days before the fiesta the roads and donkey trails leading into Santiago de Gante were jammed. The railway trains to Fuente de Ovejuna were packed to the roofs since the railroad never dreamed of adding on more cars. *El Delirio,* and other buses pressed into service at this time, barreled back and forth over the pot-holed roads.

Usually, the change of tires, also served as a reminder for Captain Perlimplin to let Don Temerio out of jail no matter whether the flutist's current sentence was completed or not. On such occasions Temerio's friend, Don Coconino, was always waiting at the jail door; when the two were reunited, they went about the streets, tirelessly playing their primitive flute and drum, thus announcing the impending fiesta, just in case someone had failed to notice the jacking up of the bus.

Meanwhile, during these days before the fiesta, the basket-weavers, toy-makers, the farmers and ranchers crowded into town. Tradesmen put up awning-stalls in the market and along the curbs of the plaza. There was often a heavy rain about this time, and after it, the sun seemed to shine with a happy brittleness, the air smelling cleaner and sweeter, like the air at a seaside resort on a spring day. People everywhere reacted to the change. Little rashes of celebrations broke out here and there: anticipatory rockets sailed into the night sky; Indian dancers tried a step or two; and in the *barrios,* over-anxious celebrants held modest fiestas for Señor Hic Natus.

The nearness of the fiesta for Santiago had an opposite effect on Juniper and Policarpio. The loss of the treasure as well as every explosion of a firecracker reminded them that they were no nearer to securing the rental money for General Braga than they had been months before.

It was also clear that the masquerade ball planned by the Knights of Santiago would add no money to the parish treasury. Although the charity event would take place the evening before the fiesta, no one had sold tickets. Instead, General Braga had offered his villa for the usual pre-ball cocktail party, and he was letting the knights stage the ball itself at the Inn of the Friars.

On the evening before this event, Juniper met with Ignacio, Policarpio and several friends in The Vicarage behind Policarpio's saloon. They made a last desperate attempt to solve the problem.

"There is but one thing for me to do," Father Juniper explained. "I have been thinking I should attend the masquerade in a costume and win the thousand pesos in prize money." He looked around at Old Vasco, at Ignacio and at the bell ringer, Zapopan. "But I can think of no suitable costume."

Zapopan grunted tiredly. He had spent the whole of the previous night and much of the day spying on Captain Perlimplin. The police captain seemed to have developed insomnia and gave him no rest.

"How much money do we have?" Policarpio asked as he noisily mixed up the dominoes.

"There is a hundred in the parish treasury, now. It isn't much."

"Not enough at all," said Ignacio.

Old Vasco, frowning and mumbling angrily at the domino that seemed to have no useful place in his array, looked up, saying, "Now, if someone were to offer me a pistol and a mask—"

"What would be a good costume?" Father Juniper mused.

Policarpio grimaced at the priest. It had taken him some time to be convinced that the pastor really didn't know where the basketful of treasure had gone. Now, having heard from Zapopan about the police captain's insomnia, he was deeply worried.

"It wouldn't do for you to go to the masquerade," he said to Juniper. "Perlimplin may be watching you. And by chance, if you went to the party, Santiago might slip another of those trinkets in your pocket. There could be trouble."

"But if I won the prize?"

"If you won the prize, it would be a disaster."

"A disaster?"

The bartender nodded wisely. "It is a useful thing to remember," he said, "that there are people in town who still distrust the gringos. They'll think that the Americans gave you the prize money. If you accept it, they'll say that you are being bought out. Remember Caldo's bathtub. It would be better if one of us were to win the prize. I have been thinking Old Vasco should go as a Don Quixote."

"Me? Don Quixote? But I'm a Basque." Old Vasco glared about uncertainly.

"They'll recognize him," Zapopan yawned.

"Not if he's in a suit of armor," said Policarpio. "There is an old Spanish one in the museum. Don Leon will lend it to us."

Old Vasco thumped the table with his gnarled fist. "Good. I'll win the prize. I'll carry my machete and make certain of this."

"No machete," Policarpio waggled his finger in warning. "And the prize money is for the parish treasury, you understand?"

"For the padre," Vasco agreed fiercely.

By this time, Juniper and the others had noted that Ignacio

had been shaking his head dourly. "It is no good," Ignacio objected. "Even a Don Quixote in gold armor can't win. I know all about these masquerades. No one but the general ever wins. He buys the best costumes. This time he'll be dressed as a bull."

"A bull?" Zapopan asked.

Juniper shrugged, unimpressed. "A bull isn't much," he observed.

"Not an ordinary bull," replied Ignacio. "He'll be one with a pedigree. The general has sent to Pastije where they raise the best fighting bulls. It is said that he bought one of their best *toros de lidia*. The animal has been killed and its head and hide was sent to a man in Mexico City who stuffs animals. The general will get inside the front part of this bull and Señora Melding is to be in back. The Goldengrove one will also accompany them. She will be dressed as a bull-fighter."

A heavy silence settled around the domino table. The men stared at one another and it was evident from their expressions that all felt General Braga and his team were invincible. For a little while there was a gloomy sipping of *pulque*. An occasional thoughtful belch or a nervous tapping of a domino upon the table were the only sounds.

Suddenly Policarpio's features brightened. He flashed his sardonic smile, saying, "What is to prevent the general from getting sick? Now, if he doesn't appear at the masquerade—!"

"He's like a bull," Ignacio snorted. "He never gets sick."

"*Caray!* It might be arranged for tomorrow night."

"Like breaking his leg?" Zapopan suggested loudly. He flexed his massive sinewy hands.

Policarpio shook his head. "It is a useful thing, at times, to have a kind of powder which can put a man to sleep quickly," he said. "I never use such powders, but I keep them against the day when I might be moved to open a bar in Mexico City. The powders are used there. You drop a little bit into a man's drink and . . . pooft . . . he's knocked out. Now if someone were to go to the cocktail party late tomorrow afternoon, and if the powder fell into General Braga's glass—"

There was a sage nodding of heads around the table. "Who is the one to do it?" Zapopan thundered in a wide-awake voice now.

"Old Vasco," Policarpio suggested. "He'll be in costume."

The ex-bandit shook his head vigorously. "How can I?" he demanded. "Are there pockets in a suit of armor."

"Ah, I see," Policarpio agreed. "You have reason. The one who carries the powders should be someone with pockets. It must be someone who can attend the cocktail party and the masquerade without arousing suspicion."

He had no sooner said this, than the others turned to look at Father Juniper. No one spoke now. They simply stared— there was Old Vasco's saturnine leer, Zapopan's open gaze, Ignacio's challenging glance and Policarpio's smile of friendly, sardonic amusement.

Juniper began to fidget and blush. "Me?" he asked helplessly.

Policarpio shrugged. "Who else, padre? You must only take care that you let nothing get slipped into your pockets."

Juniper's brows knit as he stared at his *pulque* jar. "Your powder?" he asked. "Does it make a man unconscious?"

"For a short while."

"Well, then I can't do it," replied the priest. "When a man is made unconscious, he is deprived of his reason. For me to deprive another man of his use of reason would be a sin." He paused, examining the faces of his friends. Then in desperation, he added, "It is a sin of stealing. Reason is God's property; he lends it to us just for our lifetime. To take reason away from a man, even for a moment, is no less than stealing something which belongs to God."

Having laid out his argument, he glanced about anxiously. Gradually his face clouded and he experienced a sinking feeling. Each of his compatriots continued staring at him exactly as they had done before. Their silence and their solemn attitudes spoke more clearly than words. Juniper raised his eyebrows in semicircles of query. Still no one spoke.

Finally the pastor made a wistful, helpless motion with his hand. There are times when a man has no choice, when even a saint might be called upon to make the sacrifice of sinning for the greater good. Juniper shrugged his shoulders and said, *"Pues, yo lo hago*—I'll do it."

THE BATTLE OF THE BIRDS

At 5:30 P.M., on the eve of the fiesta of Santiago, the streets of the town took on a gay operatic appearance. In car and on foot, the canapé eaters and the wealthier Mexicans, dressed in vivid costumes, made their way to General Braga's villa for the premasquerade cocktail party. A handful of centuries were confusingly blended as the viceroys and their ladies, the Spanish monks in medieval cowls, the dukes and bandits and Lüger-packing *rancheros* converged upon the Street of the Monks.

Meanwhile, in the patio of the pink parish house there was some trouble over a suit of armor which had been run up for a fashionable knight of the fifteenth century. Policarpio, Zapopan, Ignacio and Father Juniper had gotten Don Vasco into the borrowed suit, but now none of them knew how to close it up. The metal shoulder pieces, the elbow joints and the shin guards kept falling off of the old bandit's spare frame and crashing to the flagstones.

"Someone go get Don Jesus," Zapopan shouted. "He has a welding outfit."

"Don Jesus is in Fuente de Ovejuna with his bus," said Policarpio.

"Perhaps if we had some rivets," Juniper suggested. He gave Don Vasco's chest a ringing clank with a hammer.

At this moment Maria appeared. She was leading Don Juan de la Basura across the patio. The town's refuse collector carried a can opener, a soldering iron and some odd scraps of tin. "I brought Don Juan," Maria explained. "He has a way with metals."

"Evening, señores," the garbageman greeted the others with great formality, and at the same time brushed an invisible speck of dust from his tattered sleeve.

Although Don Juan de la Basura had a loose front tooth, larger than the others, and one couldn't take one's eyes from it, still, he was a person of great regal bearing. He carried himself with tremendous pride, difficult as this was, considering his attire. He wore the white flyless cotton pants and pink shirt of the peon, but these were so relentlessly patched up that little of the original garments remained except as a discolored crust around the patches. His sandals, woven of coarse leather thongs, and utilizing discarded automobile tire treads for soles, were as dirt encrusted as his feet. He also wore a short, frayed woolen serape, flung over his shoulders in the manner of a poncho. His head was crowned by a shapeless straw hat that had begun to unravel.

In spite of his dress, typical of the poor in the region, Don Juan was memorable. His matted hair and Biblical beard made him look thoroughly unreliable, and yet there was an air of importance about him. He was the only living, direct-line descendant of the Conde de Gante, the founder of the town.

Don Juan took out his complicated American can opener while he scrutinized Old Vasco and the suit of armor. He pursed his lips, scratched himself in various places, walked completely around the armor, then broke wind with an air of competency. "This should not take long," he said.

"How long?" asked Juniper.

Don Juan de la Basura shrugged. "A half-hour, maybe an hour, perhaps only a fraction of an hour, or a fraction of two hours, but most likely—who knows?"

Policarpio took Father Juniper aside. "You'd better go ahead to the cocktail party, padre," he advised. "You can prepare the general. We'll send Old Vasco along as soon as he's assembled. Do you have the powders?"

Juniper patted the pocket beneath his cassock. "I do it with heaviness in my heart," he murmured.

When he left the parish house and crossed the plaza, a contingent of starlings (those who seemed to have been elected for night duty) flew down from the laurels and twittered around him. By now, he had come to know many of them by name. Whether they understood, or not, each day he lectured them about vacating *El Temblor*. Several eggs in the big bell had hatched, and the chick starlings up there were being stubborn about abandoning the nest in the bell and learning to fly. Tonight, however, he warned them that he might be out late and there was no need for them to follow. The birds insisted, nevertheless. It was not often they got a chance to visit in the general's garden.

General Braga's estate had been turned into a fairyland. The trees, the winding paths, the clean-shaven lawns were all festooned with colored Japanese paper lanterns that warmed and quickened gaily against the darkening sky. The villa, on its slight rise, stood with all its doors and windows open and blazing with lights like an overthick crepe suzette.

As Father Juniper crossed the grounds a cardinal archbishop wearing a flame red cassock, a little red skull cap and a matching red mask, hurried forward to greet him. "Ah, it is a grand thing to see you here, father," exclaimed the cardinal. Juniper recognized Mr. O'Murphy's infectious conviviality.

O'Murphy thrust a drink into the padre's hand and ringed his arm around the priest's shoulder so as to guide him across the lawn. Wandering thus, they skirted various groups of canapé eaters and an unhappy contingent of tourists who eyed the drinks, the canapés and the drinking water with unrelieved suspicion. A large group of people were clustered about an illuminated lawn fountain which rained a concoction of pink rum punch. Tinted cakes of ice and sportive fruit rinds floated within the fountain, while deeper in the rum concoction, goldfish dawdled numbly. Father Juniper nodded pleasantly when he saw Mr. Spire, who was dressed as a gaudy Aztec chef.

For a moment the priest lost Mr. O'Murphy, so he wandered on alone. When he came to the terrace of the house a *mariachi* orchestra began playing the opening bars of *La Macarena,* the two-step overture that formally launches every bullfight. Suddenly, a youthful masked bullfighter twirled through the doorway, spinning a brilliant cerise and gold cape as though it were a broad tongue of fire. It was Miss Goldengrove, and she came to a halt before Juniper.

"Why padre," she cried out. "How utterly novel! You've come costumed as yourself!"

She whirled off again in a haze of gold that dazzled the priest. Bewildered by all the sights, Juniper stood still and watched the masqueraders: the Arabs and Zouaves, those dressed as conquistadors, as Tarascans and as Aztec chieftains. What he could see of the costumes pleased him. As yet, no one seemed half as impressive as Old Vasco would be in his suit of burnished armor. It relieved him for he felt there would be no need to use Policarpio's knockout powders.

All at once a trumpet within the house sounded the *Macarena* once more. Then the musicians took up their instruments and there was a crash of music as the orchestra burst into the bullfightingest part of *Carmen*.

"The general is coming!" someone shouted.

People hurried up to the terrace to watch. They saw Miss Goldengrove pirouette out through the doorway again. Hot on her heels, snorting and pawing the floor and terrace flagstones, came a magnificent bull. It was utterly startling.

Father Juniper's heart sank. He found it difficult to believe that General Braga and Mrs. Melding inhabited the skin of the animal, for in the beast's every movement there was the absolute appearance of a *toro de bandera,* the very best of fighting bulls. He stared in awe at the animal's glossy black pelt, the small frank head, the strength of horns curving forward, and the short thick neck with its monumental hump of muscle. It was only after Miss Goldengrove had brought the bull to a halt at her heels that the difference became apparent. A servant brought a tray of tall iced drinks. He handed one of the glasses up under the stomach of the bull. A woman's hand grasped it. Then the servant fitted a long silver straw up through the bull's nostril so the animal could sip from the iced glass held beneath its nose.

While people crowded in to congratulate the general and Mrs. Melding for their costume, Father Juniper had trouble digesting his thoughts. It was clear that Old Vasco in his armor, or even the real Quixote, wouldn't have the slightest chance of winning the costume prize in competition with the general's bull. The pastor sighed unhappily and pressed the vial of knockout powders that lay in his pocket.

The general noticed Juniper and moved in his direction. "You begin to find our company lively, eh, padre?" the bull asked.

Juniper smiled. "Your costume is magnificent."

"Thank you," replied the general. "Will you have a refreshment?"

Juniper nodded. Remembering his mission, he realized that here was his opportunity. He must certainly have a drink with Braga.

Additional drinks were brought. The monumental bull dipped his silver straw into the frosted glass. Father Juniper raised his own glass and sipped thoughtfully, deciding that for the moment it was not exactly time to use the powders. The general should be permitted the pleasure of a few cool drinks for it was undoubtedly hot within the leather skin.

"How do things go with you, padre?" Mrs. Melding's hawklike voice came from the rear of the bull.

"Good," replied Juniper, marveling. "You arc truly Señora Melding back there?"

"Another drink?" the general suggested.

Father Juniper nodded agreeably. He needed something to wash his conscience down. The bull gave a frivolous toss of his horns. It saddened the priest to think that it would soon be his duty to deprive the general and Mrs. Melding of so much fun.

The white-jacketed servant brought another round of refreshments, and then another. Within the bull's hide, General Braga was chuckling to himself. Only this morning, he had spoken again with Monsignor Gaspar at the bishop's office. Gaspar knew all about the basket of gringo loot. The monsignor had announced that he was coming to Santiago de Gante to investigate, and would arrive in the evening. It would be interesting, the general decided, if in addition to all other things, the monsignor were to find the parish priest drunk.

The general commanded more drinks for the priest, for Mrs. Melding and for himself. Although neither the general nor Juniper realized it at the instant, this marked the beginning of a spectacular drinking bout. General Braga had great capacity, and a motive for getting the *cura* drunk. At the same time, egged on by his mission, and seeking an opportunity for administering the powders, Juniper matched him, glass for glass.

As the number of drinks increased, Father Juniper grew more and more desperate. Each time he thought the moment had come, somehow General Braga would empty his glass before the powder could be fished forth. By the eighth round even the guests had begun to sense something unusual in the air. They crowded around the priest and the bull, watching eagerly. Some of them began taking sides, and betting. Their interest made Juniper's task doubly difficult. By the twelfth drink the priest forgot which of his pockets held the hidden powders.

The *mozo* brought the fourteenth round of drinks. Juniper gulped his down and suddenly showed signs of sagging. He began sipping from the same glass as the general. All at once, he stiffened, he stood bolt upright, and with a cheerful wave of his plump hand, such as travelers give when they depart on a transatlantic voyage, he smiled radiantly and wandered out across the lawn and through the gate into the darkness beyond.

Having forgotten the initial reason for the drinking bout,

the bull drained off another glass, hooked his right horn
playfully at Miss Goldengrove's slender flank; then, giving
a triumphant bellow, he cantered toward the gate after the
priest.

This was a signal for the cocktail party to break up. The
guests began to move toward the Inn of the Friars for the
next stage of celebrations, the masquerade ball.

When Father Juniper strayed beyond the gateway of the
general's estate, he promptly got lost.

He didn't much mind, for he was in a jolly mood. He
was amused by the starlings who joined him, and he completely forgot the cocktail party, or why he had gone there.
He wandered about through the crooked streets of Santiago
de Gante, progressing uphill as far as the Old Bridge; then,
almost as if the town had tipped precariously, he came staggering hurriedly down in the opposite direction.

At one point he encountered Señor Penjamo, the town's
night watchman who went through the streets from sunset
to sunrise, blowing a mailman's whistle forlornly. Juniper
tried to trade hats with Penjamo.

Then, staggering on alone, he burst forth in song, little
uneven shards of sound that echoed up the dark streets.
When he became too raucous the starlings circled about him
anxiously, whirring their wings to muffle the sound of his
voice. For more than an hour after leaving the cocktail
party he wandered haphazardly, singing and talking with
himself and the birds. Finally he sat down on a curb to take
an accounting of things, and this was a mistake. Something
within his stomach turned over abruptly. He gave a tremendous belch and began hiccuping with the steadiness of
a metronome. The birds, sitting on each side along the curb,
gazed at him sadly.

He broke into another song, *The Swallows:*

> "Volveras, golondrinas de ojos negros
>   Que te vas cruzando el mar
>   Volveras, porque sabes que te quiero
>   Y no te puedo olvidar . . . ."

The birds began twittering to one another. Now they were convinced of the pastor's condition. He took them to be swallows.

Juniper rose unsteadily and began weaving down the street, but in a direction away from the parish house. By now the people of Santiago de Gante were aware that their pastor was lost in the narrow streets and couldn't find his way home. In that most of them had come to respect this man who was so unlike Father Caldo, they naturally suspected that there must be some very good reason for his behavior. No one wanted to embarrass him by intimating that he was drunk and needed assistance; so, like the citizens of Coventry who had deliberately refused to gaze upon the nakedness of Lady Godiva, the Santiagans closed their shutters and abandoned the streets to their pastor.

The delicacy of the citizens was not enough, however, to help Juniper. There remained the fact that on this eve of the fiesta, there were a great many strangers and visitors around the market and plaza. They might get a wrong impression. And there was the presence of a monsignor who had driven into town. So it remained for the starlings to see Juniper home.

At first the birds tried humoring him. When this had no effect, they began pulling at his sleeves, picking at the hem of his cassock, pulling at the halo fringe of hair on his head as they tried to guide him homeward. When the pastor and the blackbirds had drifted somewhere near the market, there

occurred a furious battle in the moonlight. Juniper began
flailing at the birds. His biretta flew off. Several starlings
picked it up in their beaks and tried to set it back upon his
head. The birds whirled around him, pulling, jerking, confusing him with the beat and whir of their small black wings.
In the end the birds were victorious. They guided him to
the rectory doorway.

Once within the doorway, Juniper knew his way. He
stumbled through the patio, took vague note of the group
of people who were busily setting an armored knight upon
a donkey. He nodded to them with a tolerant dignity, murmuring, *"Señores y caballeros—"* Then he staggered into his
room.

Policarpio, Zapopan, Ignacio and Old Vasco exchanged
glances. None of them dared call out to their pastor, for
they saw his condition.

"I would suspect the general has been done away with,"
Policarpio commented.

"Naturally, man," Ignacio replied, glancing toward the
bedroom. "You see his condition." The idol-maker turned
toward Old Vasco. He gave the donkey a whack that almost
sent the ex-bandit reeling from his mount. "Be on your
way, now," he said. "Don't fail us."

Meanwhile, in his bedroom, Juniper stumbled around uncertainly. Although his head was pounding enormously,
with the aid of the wall and a chair he managed to reach the
safety of his bed. He tried to sit and undo a shoe. He had
scarcely begun, when suddenly, with a heavy sigh, he col-
lapsed upon the bed.

When Policarpio entered the room a few minutes later,
the pastor was fast asleep. Policarpio carefully touched the
pastor's pockets to make certain there were no incriminating
trinkets in them. Then he gently laid a blanket over his

friend and gazed down at him. "He's out like a light," the bartender murmured to himself. He nodded his head, thinking, there was no doubt that God would absolve the *cura* from any defects on earth. "But when you get to Heaven, padre," Policarpio whispered, "most likely, they'll make you stand in a corner with your face to the wall."

THE BRAVE NUNS

When General Braga and Mrs. Melding trotted into the town, they were in every sense of the word the gayest fighting bull ever to run wild through the streets of Santiago de Gante. They cavorted, galloped and snorted around corners. But when they had gone several blocks from the villa, the front half of the bull noticed that the rear portion had developed a mind of its own.

"You're dragging," the head complained to the rear. "Definitely, we ought to get back to the inn."

"I'm not dragging," retorted Mrs. Melding. "Let's go to the bull ring."

"At this hour, woman?" The bull cocked his head and looked at the moon ripening in the sky.

"We've time," insisted Melding. "Come on, you old scrunch! I've always wanted to know what it feels like to be a bull in the ring."

General Braga was feeling just gay enough to agree; so together, they charged down the street, went past the Hic Natus house, entered the plaza and turned left. Just as they trotted into the Street of Fulano, the head of the bull halted and the beast eyed the crumbling old convent building where the nuns lived and taught school. Of all places in Santiago de Gante, this was the only one which the general had never been permitted to visit.

"Let's knock here," he said. "See what's inside."

The bull rapped on the ancient carved door with his right horn. A moment later the door was opened by none other than the timid Sor Juana. The shy nun's eyes widened at the sight of the beast. She gave an abrupt piercing scream and fled, leaving the door open. Her wail startled the other nuns who were at prayer in the convent chapel. They hurried into the patio.

Delighted by the excitement, the bull rushed through the doorway, and for a few minutes ranged about in the convent, charging furiously, bellowing with a taurine pleasure that thoroughly frightened the nuns. Most of the sisters screamed and scurried for their cells. One or two were a bit slow. When these were cornered by the bull, they let out high-pitched wails, for the bull had learned to pinch in the Parisian manner.

Only Mother Monica and the convent's cook had their wits about them. At various times in the past, Mother Monica had gone to the bullfights, just to be up on things. Although the bull's rear hardly seemed as spry as the front, she didn't think about it at the moment. Instead, she ran into the chapel, seized an altar cloth and reappeared in the cloister corridor, holding the cloth like a bullfighter's cape. She stood there with her small left foot pointed forward. She flicked the cloth slightly, citing the animal in the classical manner. Then she challenged the bull, crying, "*Toro! Huh! Huh! Toro!*"

Both General Braga and Melding marveled at this touch of professionalism. Neither of them could resist it, and they charged. The good nun was ready: she executed a creditable series of passes, thus gradually playing the bull down the corridor until the animal roared past her and through the doorway into her cell. The cook, waiting behind the door, slammed it shut and barred it.

The other nuns came out from the safety of their cells. "What is it?" one of them asked.

"A bull. A fine one," the sister cook explained. "It's here in mother superior's cell."

Mother Monica looked about, and seeing that the animal had caused almost no damage, smiled, saying, "This must be the work of God. Never before have we been sent so fine an animal. Tomorrow, we'll call in Señor Amador, the butcher."

The nun-cook, taking a professional interest in such largesse, stood on tiptoes to peek through the tiny grill window in the door. Suddenly she gasped and backed away. "It speaks!" she cried.

Mother Monica, remembering uneasily that this bull had seemed somewhat different than most bulls she had known, also peered through the grill. Then her face blanched and she gave a startled cry. "It speaks in the devil's tongue!"

Within the cell, the general and Mrs. Melding, discovering their state of imprisonment, had begun arguing in English. Melding was for throwing off the stuffy bull's hide and revealing who they were. The general, having sobered somewhat, was embarrassed and thought it best not to unveil themselves.

On the other side of the door, the corridor filled with twitterings of alarm as each nun was scandalized in her own way. Some wanted to peek through the window at "the thing." Others cringed and began blessing themselves. "It is surely the devil," said the nun-cook.

A devil in the cell, a devil possessing the body of a bull—this was something the good nuns, even the most timid, knew how to deal with. They brought candles, a pot of holy water, and they knelt in a semicircle around the door. Then they began praying. They prayed as they had never prayed before. It was not often in these modern times that the devil showed himself so clearly; they meant to make the most of it. They prayed all night, exorcising the possessed animal and contaminated cell. They tossed blessed water through the cell window.

When General Braga finally agreed with Mrs. Melding that they should reveal themselves, it was too late. When they began shouting in Spanish, the nuns only prayed that much harder.

Old Vasco was immensely proud of his suit of armor. As he rocked out into the night on his way to the masquerade ball, he stopped in several places to show off to friends. It was ten o'clock when he finally arrived at the Inn of the Friars. This delay was a fortunate thing because for some time after he had departed, no one noted that he had forgotten his visor. It was Ignacio who discovered this.

"Vasco doesn't have his beak," the idol-maker shouted accusingly at Don Juan de la Basura.

The refuse collector shrugged disdainfully. "He doesn't need it," he countered. "That thing would only make him too heavy. It would be the last straw."

"Ayi, chingada!" Ignacio swore. "Without the cover, people will see his face." He shoved the visor at Don Juan. "Hurry over there and get it on him. There's no time to lose."

"Why don't you go?" Don Juan complained.

Ignacio spat furiously. "I can't go. I must get to my

house and fix up my kids for the morning Mass. They become angels at dawn. You understand."

"I'm not dressed for a gringo party," Don Juan objected.

"Go, man!" Ignacio shouted. "What's wrong with your dress? It's what you wear. Now go, and slip in there and put the visor on Old Vasco."

Ignacio pushed him toward the door.

The patios and the gardens at the Inn of the Friars had been decorated even more brilliantly than the general's villa. While the masqueraders danced under the moon, or flirted and traded wives in the narrow colonial corridors, the official costume committee, Mr. O'Murphy and Mr. Spire, wandered about, casually studying the potential prize winners. A third member of the committee, Captain Perlimplin, had failed to appear.

The good captain had not been himself for some days. Since he had found Father Juniper's basket of gringo loot, and had hidden it in the police station, he had been most uneasy. As the fiesta drew near his discomfort grew acute and he could not sleep. Finally, on this night, he happened to catch a glimpse of twelve embattled blackbirds guiding a bewildered pastor homeward. It was too much! Perlimplin decided that he didn't want to be a party to the trapping of Juniper, even if it cost him his job. The problem was one for the Church and not for the civil authorities. Moved by such thoughts, he took the basket of treasure from the police station, carrying it across to the church, then hid it in a recess beneath the pedestal upon which Santiago stood. Having passed the responsibility for guarding the treasure on to the saint, he breathed a deep sigh of relief.

Meanwhile, left with the task of judging the costumes at the ball, O'Murphy and Spire worried about the selection.

"It will require a nimbleness to make a decision this time," observed Mr. O'Murphy. "I can't understand, however, what has happened to the general and Mrs. Melding. 'T would be no trouble, were they here."

Mr. Spire took out his Westminster-chime watch and glanced at it. He let the chimes tinkle. "It's late," he said. "We can't put off the judging much longer. Poor Miss Goldengrove, she's so upset and angry. She suspects they've eloped."

"Ah, there's a fine handsome fellow there," O'Murphy pointed.

Both judges stared at the tall armored figure clanking fiercely through the patio. Mr. Spire nodded. "Don Quixote, I suppose," he said. "Really, a crashing good getup, but he's lost his jolly visor."

O'Murphy was about to suggest they vote for the knight, but suddenly his attention was caught by a figure in rags and patches, who ran after the Quixote and was brandishing a can opener and a beaked piece of metal. O'Murphy slapped his thigh with enthusiasm. "Now there's a costume!" he cried. "A peon! Authentic peasant garb, to be sure!"

The two judges exchanged glances and there was a meeting of minds. In the lively history of masquerades in Santiago de Gante, countless people had come as Napoleons, flappers, songs, Aztec emperors and gaudy ranchers, but this was the first time anyone had ever worn the everyday dress of the peon in the region.

Mr. Spire signaled to Herr Fablehaft for a fanfare. The Bavarian bandmaster nodded; he blew a happy toot on his whistle and spread his arms out above his musicians. "Ven I zay blow, ve blow!" he shouted. His arms slashed downward and the orchestra sounded the *diana*.

It was in this unexpected manner that Sir Juan of the Gar-
bage was awarded the first prize at the costume ball.

Don Juan was stunned at first. He dazedly clutched the
envelope, fat with ten crisp one-hundred peso bills. After
a certain number of drinks had been pressed upon him by
well-wishers, the significance of his good fortune began to
penetrate his mind. He was aware that Old Vasco was watching him, and he knew that Father Juniper, Policarpio and
Don Ignacio were expecting the thousand pesos. They might
resent it if he held the money too long.

He waited until a moment when Old Vasco's back was
turned. Then he fled. Ten minutes later, he was on the
night bus to Mexico City.

THE MOORS

When Old Vasco discovered that Don Juan de la Basura had absconded with the prize money, he felt that this loss was his responsibility.

"I should like to skewer that goat on my lance," he said furiously.

"Don't take it so to heart, old man," Policarpio soothed him. "It's a loss, but who would imagine they'd give him the prize?"

"Call the police," Zapopan shouted.

"What's the use," Policarpio replied. "They'd never catch him. Once a year Don Juan shaves that beard and clips his hair. This happens to be the time of the year. No one will recognize him."

"Does the padre know?" Vasco demanded.

"He's still asleep."

"It will be a blow to him."

Policarpio nodded. "I'll explain it to him. I'll wait until he awakens. He has to say the Mass that begins the fiesta. I'll let him sleep another few hours."

Because Don Juan had also run off with his American can

210

opener, there was no way, at this hour, of getting Old Vasco out of his armor. He was bent and soldered in snugly. Thus, Vasco, thinking vaguely that the gringo judges at the masquerade party might have realized their error, and might offer another prize, returned to the Inn of the Friars. When nothing like this occurred, he came back to the plaza and sat on an iron bench to brood disconsolately. In the semi-darkness, he was hardly aware of the life that began to stir in the plaza. Men and women were moving around him silently. At times a lonely rocket rose into the sky, a capsule ripening and bursting to announce the nearness of the celebrations.

An hour before dawn, Zapopan passed by and noticed the ex-bandit. Thinking Vasco was asleep, the bell ringer knocked noisily on the armor.

"Go away," Vasco said furiously. "I'm thinking."

"The fiesta begins soon," Zapopan replied.

When Zapopan left, the old man sank back into thought. He had found the inside of the armor wonderfully private. It was like a cave, and was conducive to thinking. But whatever thoughts he had about regaining the prize money were soon scattered, for even from within his cave he began to notice other changes in the plaza. Children armed with wooden swords were tiptoeing and scouting around the bushes, spying from behind the bandstand, and searching cautiously for the Moors who were reported to be approaching the town. Suddenly a contingent of men dressed as Christian soldiers headed toward the dark portals of the church.

The fiesta! Santiago's fiesta, Vasco thought! He heaved himself to his feet and hurried across the way into the pink parish house.

"Is the padre awake?" he asked Policarpio.

The bartender sat on the edge of the fountain in the rectory patio. He nodded somberly. "I've just managed to awaken him," he said. "It was a job."

Juniper stumbled into the patio and peered around in the darkness. Spying Old Vasco and the armor, he remembered the masquerade and the drinking bout. Somewhat dazedly, he asked, "Did we win?"

Both Policarpio and Old Vasco shook their heads.

"No?" Juniper asked.

"Someone else won," Policarpio replied. "It wasn't the general, either."

"Is this the day of the fiesta?" asked the pastor.

"In less than an hour it begins," Policarpio spoke sadly.

For a moment the priest stared at the two men. His head seemed to have some loose bolts in it that were shaking and grating. Gradually, riding above this hangover, came a distressing realization. The premonition he had had, that in the end he would be left alone with the problem of Santiago's rental, now struck him as coming true. "I'm afraid I have failed Santiago and the people of the parish," he said. "Now it's too late to do anything more. The general will want the saint back tomorrow. The only thing that might keep Santiago in the church after tomorrow would be a miracle. If Santiago or his angels could do something . . . But this is asking too much."

"A miracle? Like the general dropping dead?" Old Vasco asked.

"That would help," Policarpio observed.

The old ex-bandit looked about thoughtfully. "Perhaps if a machete fell upon him," he said.

"There was a time," mused Juniper, "when they say the two angels came down and—"

Policarpio interrupted him, saying, "I have been waiting to tell you something, padre."

"What is that?"

"The basket of gringo treasure has reappeared. It was found in the church, in the little recess under Santiago's pedestal."

A smile wreathed Father Juniper's face. "It's come back. How did this happen?"

Policarpio shrugged. Earlier in the morning Zapopan had discovered the hidden treasure and had brought the news to Policarpio. The barkeeper had his own idea how the basket of trinkets had gotten there, and it worried him. When he had gone to see for himself, he had noticed a policeman kneeling nearby, saying his prayers as though deeply intent upon a novena. A little later, when he had looked in again, the policeman was still there.

Not wanting to upset Juniper on so important a day, Policarpio thought it best that Father Juniper should take it for granted that, perhaps, Santiago had assumed control of the treasure. "I think we should let it alone," he warned the priest. "Maybe the saint has something in mind, and doesn't want it touched."

Father Juniper nodded in agreement. He was still puzzled and disturbed by the entire affair of the trinkets. There were times when he suspected himself of having stolen them without realizing it. But now, having them so mysteriously disappear, then reappear, put another light on the problem. There was something miraculous . . .

He smiled at Policarpio, saying, "This would seem to be a proof of—"

He had no chance to finish his comment, for a tremendous series of explosions shook the plaza and the rectory. Then a hundred rockets leaped up into the sky, alerting the valley. On the heels of the fireworks, there came a delirious clanging of bells from the green church. Even the smaller bells in

Father Mérida church and in other chapels took up the wrangling.

Juniper listened and frowned. *"El Temblor* isn't ringing," he said. "The little birds still do not fly."

"Nevertheless, it begins!" Vasco shouted.

Juniper took leave of his two friends and hurried next door to the sacristy. Several altar boys were waiting for him. They had laid out the finely embroidered new vestments which Monsignor Gaspar had had sent. Mother Monica was also present, along with Raimundo and Eulalia, Ignacio's two children who were dressed as Santiago's angels. The good nun was a little haggard after her ordeal with the devil. Only an hour ago she had discovered that the creature in her cell was none other than General Braga and Mrs. Melding, and an exceptionally fine bull's hide.

"The Moors are here," said little Raimundo, his eyes shining with the promise of the day. "They're in the plaza, behind the trees."

"And the Christians are in the church," added the girl. "There are *conchero* dancers, too."

Juniper had the two children run through the Latin oration he had taught them. Then he vested himself, and with a sigh, he followed the altar boys and the two angels through the doorway into the sanctuary of the church. For a second, he caught his breath over the change within the church. The long structure was gaudy with candlelight and torches, and there was a great deal of commotion near the statue of Santiago.

A half hour earlier, a chosen group of men led by Tzintzuntzan and Señor Villada had entered the church where, for a short while they had barred the doors to all women. They had quickly undressed and redressed the wooden saint. Now Santiago was elegantly garbed in his chamois riding suit. He wore leather bullet bandoleers crossed upon his chest, two silver pistols, silver spurs and a velvet maroon cape. On his head he had a handsome, big-brimmed sombrero with a horseshoe stitched with silver thread upon the crown.

In the narrow spaces between the saint's place and the pews, a group of *concheros,* that curious sect of half-Christian, half-Chichimeca Indian dancers, whirled tirelessly beneath the saint. They danced to the music of armadillo shell guitars, and they wore bright plumes, chamois loincloths and vivid satin capes. A troop of Christian soldiers stood behind them guarding the saint. They were a curious army, equipped with swords, lances, machetes and rare uniforms from a dozen lands.

During the Mass the dancing stopped, but the moment after Father Juniper had intoned the last Gospel, a bugler outside in the plaza sounded a clear and brilliant aria that echoed across the town. As the sound died there was a nervous stirring within the church. Juniper heard one of the altar boys whisper excitedly, "The Moors are in the churchyard!"

Suddenly there was an explosion of activity around the saint. Some Christian soldiers unceremoniously removed Santiago from his pedestal and seated him upon the dappled merry-go-round horse. The saint was strapped in place and given a shining sword. Then the horse and saint were lifted upon the shoulders of a dozen men who raced down the aisle toward the door. The remaining soldiers shouted battle cries and plunged after their wooden commander.

From the rooftops around the plaza, cannon crackers and rockets burst and hissed everywhere, signaling the beginning of the battle in the churchyard. Santiago and San Jocobo lunged about, galloping here and there, leading their shout-

ing, sword-slashing supporters. They fell upon the turbaned
Moors who had dared invade the atrium. Slowly, the Moors
were driven back across the dawn plaza. A number of canapé
eaters who were still in costume joined in on the battle. For
them, it was like another and better masquerade ball. Mr.
O'Murphy, still dressed as a cardinal, sided with Santiago.
He clutched Miss Goldengrove's arm, crying, " 'T is better
than any old masquerade!"

As the church emptied, except for one policeman who
seemed to be having trouble reaching the end of a prayer,
Father Juniper strolled toward Santiago's empty pedestal.
He looked behind it, into the recess, and saw the basket of
glittering trinkets. He smiled and murmured a little prayer
of thanksgiving. Then he went on to the church steps to
watch the battle outside.

From where he stood near the doorway, the plaza appeared
alive with color. Soldiers and Moors rushed back and forth
between the stalls and white cotton umbrellas which vendors
had set up. Moors paused in their struggle, to admire the
displays of toys, of strange foods, the frying *gusano* worms
crisp as cracklings, the deep-fried pork skin peppered with
chili. Now and then a Christian soldier would dig in his
pocket for money to buy a small good-luck figure of Santiago
upon San Jocobo.

"Embarrassingly barbaric, isn't it?" A familiar voice spoke
to Juniper.

The pastor glanced around; then he recognized Monsignor
Gaspar.

"You've come for the fiesta?" Juniper asked. "When did
you arrive?"

"Last night."

"Did Maria fix you a bed?"

"No. I arrived late, so I stopped at the hotel." The monsignor motioned toward the small traveler's hotel across the plaza. He did not take his eyes from the battle raging near the police station.

"I think you will enjoy the celebrations," Juniper said anxiously. "It lasts all day. This battle will go on until noon when the Moors are defeated. Then there will be a big confession. All the Moors confess just before the noon Victory Mass which Father Mérida will celebrate. In the afternoon there is another procession, and in the evening, the angels fly. I am very anxious to see that."

The monsignor nodded but did not smile. Unable to find General Braga, he had, upon arriving, finally located Captain Perlimplin. The captain had reluctantly given him more details about the crime wave in Santiago de Gante, and had shown him the cache of loot behind the statue of the saint. He had been somewhat relieved that the captain seemed anxious to withdraw from the affair, leaving it for the Church to handle. He had insisted, however, that Captain Perlimplin assign a policeman to watch over the stolen basket of trinkets.

It had all been quite shocking. It reinforced a suspicion that Gaspar had had all along about Juniper. The monsignor had always felt that Santiago de Gante was a difficult town, and that Father Juniper wasn't the man for it. He had argued with Bishop Sierra, pointing out that it had been a mistake, sending Juniper here. The plump priest had spent too much time in the United States where it was quite possible that Catholics were tainted by pagan and Protestant influences. Father Juniper's disobedience, his signing of a contract with the general for the rental of the wooden saint was an example of this.

Being a churchman, and versed in cannon law, Gaspar was not one to move hastily, however. He had informed

Captain Perlimplin that he would observe and question the pastor throughout the day, and on the following morning, he would make a decision. "We shall decide whether we shall institute civil or ecclesiastical proceedings against him," he said.

Now, glancing at Juniper with candid appraisal, Gaspar said, "I see that your vestments came. Have you made plans to pay for them?"

"It may take time," replied Juniper. "They're very expensive."

"Do you have funds?"

"No. Not yet," Juniper sighed evasively.

Gaspar pursed his lips diplomatically. "I should like to discuss your finances," he said. "Shall we have breakfast?"

When Father Juniper had devested himself, he went with the monsignor to the hotel dining room. They sat at a table facing upon the plaza so they could watch the activities below. After Gaspar had chased the last slippery morsel of papaya across his plate, he put down his fork and stared at the parish priest.

"Do you confess often?" he asked abruptly. "I mean your own confession?"

Juniper gave a faint scowl. *"Pues, sí,"* he murmured. "When I feel the need, I go to Padre Mérida."

The monsignor flexed his fingers. "When did you go last?" His fingertips remained poised, like marionettes.

"Two weeks ago."

"And you've nothing on your mind?"

The parish priest blushed faintly, recalling the drinking at the masquerade cocktail party. "There are one or two little things," he said ruefully.

Gaspar gave a satisfied cluck. "If you wish," he said. "I'll hear your confession while I'm here. My stole is upstairs."

Father Juniper shook his head gratefully. "Perhaps to-morrow," he said. "Always, when the men of the town confess, as the Moors will do this noon, there are thoughts that enter my mind. I should confess afterwards."

Gaspar's thin face clouded. "I'm afraid, padre," he said, "I must ask you not to administer the Sacrament of Confession today. I'll take your place. I've had certain alarming reports about you. Apparently you've gotten yourself into a mess over the wooden saint. You refused to take my advice. For example, the contract with General Braga."

"Contract?" Juniper looked up innocently.

"Is it true that you agreed to pay for the rental of the wooden saint?" The monsignor's voice was firm and searching.

Juniper nodded.

"An exorbitant fee," said the monsignor. "Now, apart from your disobedience, can the parish afford such an expense?"

"It is a lot, isn't it?"

"How do you intend to raise it, as well as to pay for the new vestments?"

Juniper scratched the halo fringe of hair on his head. "In little ways," he murmured.

"Would you be explicit?"

Father Juniper's glance slipped toward the windows. In the plaza below a ragged band of Moors raced past the church and sought refuge in a side street from the pursuing saint and his army. Meanwhile, in the center of the plaza both Herr Fablehaft's band and the *conchero* dancers vied with each other. The dancers executed their complicated pre-columbian steps in the increasing heat of the sun; the steady strumming of their instruments and the clacking of their

wooden-soled sandals filled the morning air with a monot-
onous, yet exciting, beat. At times, these sounds were
drowned out by an emotional Wagnerian blare from the
band.

Juniper's eyes returned to the monsignor's stern face and
he squirmed uneasily. He gave a dismal smile, saying,
"Money is hard to raise. It is something I can't explain now."

Gaspar drew his breath in sharply. "Would you condone
theft as a method?" he asked bluntly.

"Theft? Stealing?"

"A basket filled with American trinkets."

Father Juniper's face brightened. "Oh, the treasure," he
said. "You know about it?"

The monsignor nodded.

"It seemed lost for a while," said Juniper. "But now it's
in the church, hidden under Santiago's pedestal."

"How do you account for this affair?" Gaspar demanded
pointedly.

Juniper looked thoughtful. "I suppose Santiago put it
there for safekeeping," he said with utter innocence. "Really,
Santiago has full charge of the treasure. I don't know much
of what is happening."

"Santiago?" The monsignor stared at the priest, baffled.
"You mean the saint?"

"I sometimes think he started the whole thing," Juniper
replied. "If I were you, I wouldn't touch it until we know
what Santiago wants done with it."

For several minutes the monsignor seemed stunned. He
stared at the priest, wondering whether the man were living
in a dream world, or if he were being confusingly clever.

"You don't admit stealing the baubles?" he finally asked.

Juniper glanced toward the window. The staccato crackle

and burst of explosives rattled through the town. Now, it came from the hillside, up near the Old Bridge, where Santiago and his men had almost cornered the Moors.

"Did you steal?" Gaspar spoke sharply.

Juniper looked at him. "They just appeared," he replied simply.

"An impossibility."

"But it is something I had very little to do with. Santiago seemed to be—"

The monsignor's teeth came together with a click, and he raised his hand, silencing the priest. "I'll have you understand, padre, there are serious charges hanging over you. Charges that must be investigated. I beg you to think it over. Meanwhile, today you'll be permitted to lead the processions because it is expected. However, I'll hear the confessions at noon."

"There is a Benediction tonight, just before the angels fly."

"Mérida can give Benediction," Gaspar replied abruptly. "Tomorrow the statue of the saint will be returned to General Braga. And tomorrow, you'll appear before the bishop."

After breakfast, Juniper and Gaspar went out into the plaza. A steady flow of people eddied around them and under the shadow of the pale green church. There were the country Indians who had come days before to camp in the church atrium. They cooked on charcoal braziers, ate and dozed in the sun, or joined in the wonders of the fiesta.

The fiesta seemed to have no committee guiding it. Instead, it ran by itself. A stranger in Santiago de Gante never knew when or where a certain procession, a display of fireworks or an Indian dance would begin. These events just seemed to spring up automatically. The Santiagans, however, were never in doubt. They had a sense of timing born of centuries of hereditary fiesta-going. Everything was precise and clear to them, while for the canapé eaters and tourists, the events of the day were a vastly exciting, colorful chaos.

"I think I should like to take a nap for a little while," Juniper said apologetically.

As he went toward the rectory, the monsignor shook his head strangely. Then Gaspar listened to the band for a short while. Before an hour had passed, the monsignor could no longer resist the festivities, and he forgot his intention of keeping an eye on Father Juniper. He began following the Moor chasers about. The spontaneous vividness of these men in silk and satin pantaloons who tugged and carried the merry-go-round horse and wooden saint up and down narrow streets in pursuit of the heathens, had begun to infect him. Years ago he had studied in Rome and had seen fiestas there and in Naples. This one was better, he decided. These people had an amazing faith, even though it might have been slightly misdirected toward a wooden statue.

When the turbaned, scimitar-wielding Moors were finally trapped near the market and defeated, then were driven to the church where they were expected to confess their heathen ways, Gaspar had reached a point where stiffness bends. He was now eager to take part in the celebrations, and he hurried to take over Father Juniper's duties in the confessionals.

He let himself into the sacristy where Juniper, looking worried and uneasy, was training the two child-angels in their Latin speech.

"I'll borrow a cassock," Gaspar announced. "I brought my stole. Don't you think you should confess, before I go out?"

Juniper smiled somberly. "If I were to hear the Moors, then there would be something," he said. "But perhaps to-morrow."

"Tomorrow, then," Gaspar agreed.

Juniper inclined his head, but at the same time the thought ran through his mind that he would not confess to the monsignor on the morrow, either. How could he confess to some one who was so doubtful of Santiago's virtues and powers?

The monsignor slipped his stole around his neck and went into the church. He stared at the lines of fierce looking Moors waiting at the boxes, and with an indifferent shrug, he entered the first box. For Gaspar, the confessions proved to be more than he had bargained for. In his spare moments at the chancery office he had quietly amassed a set of religious speculations, some of them slightly on the side of heresies, which he intended sending to the Pope. Now, the hour and a half which he spent in the wooden confessional, listening to the complicated sins of the Moors, breathing in the odors of garlic, *pulque* and peppers, became both an ordeal and a revelation. He had never dreamed there could be so vast a variety of sins: sins wonderfully involved; sins daringly and richly embroidered. No grand duke nor dissipated duchess, no Roman roué nor Parisian prostitute had ever whispered so imaginative a catalogue of sins through the little screen. These were of such a quality so as even to pale his own collection of religious speculations. He began to wonder how anything that Juniper might tell him could equal any of these.

After the last of the Moors had mumbled their Confetiors and Acts of Contrition, Gaspar waited on, hoping there would be more. When it became apparent that he had come to the end, he stepped carefully out of the box. He had heard so many sins that he felt like a bucket on the verge of overflowing. Casting a speculative glance over the numerous children playing on the pews and in the church aisles, he wondered what they had on their minds.

FIESTA

The afternoon of Santiago Day was reserved for a triumphal procession through the streets. Much later in the day there would also be a bullfight, a cockfight, another band concert and dancers, but the procession was the most important.

The three o'clock sun blazed down upon the crowd milling before the church and out in the plaza as the Santiagans gathered to watch their saint and San Jocobo be placed upon the *carroza*. In the crowd, mingling with the shriven Moors, the Christians and churchmen, there were eager tourists with clicking cameras. Some of them incautiously tried to snap the little group of clergymen who were dressed in processional vestments. Whenever a camera was aimed at either Father Juniper, Father Mérida or Monsignor Gaspar, one of Santiago de Gante's policemen stepped up and forbade the picture. Somewhere in Mexico, an overly ambitious politician might come upon the photograph, and remembering that it was against the law for clergymen to wear vestments on public streets, he could cause trouble.

The saint's *carroza* was also taboo. This curiously boat-shaped float commemorated the fact that Santiago had on several occasions gone to sea. Upon its deck there was a superstructure resembling a Roman rotunda, while around this stood a low white picket fence remindful of the fences encircling historic cannons. Santiago and San Jocobo, one looking disdainfully fierce, and the other quite gay, occupied the deck of the float. Ignacio's two children also rode there as the saint's guests of honor. The little girl, Eulalia, appeared angelic in her long white dress to which cardboard wings were attached. Her brother, Raimundo, seemed blasé and annoyed. He was a bit of a business man, and usually, during the fiestas, he had a stand in the plaza where he sold baby swallows, which, when fried and eaten, marvelously restored the powers of speech to people who had lost their voices. Today, Raimundo was losing money.

While the procession was forming, Zapopan and other workmen were stretching two cables high above the plaza between the city hall roof and the church tower. It was the cable arrangement the child-angels would ride upon in the evening.

General Braga stared up, watching. He was dressed in the uniform and appropriate medals of a General of the Division. He was still a bit shaken from the ordeal in the nunnery— not so much because of what the nuns had done, but because being alone with the hawklike Mrs. Melding had been a revealing experience. He was considering abandoning his pursuit of poetesses for more vigorous women.

The general's attention swept over the crowd and settled upon Father Juniper and Monsignor Gaspar. Seeing the pastor gave him an uneasy turn because Juniper appeared so at home here in this tremendous and enthusiastic crowd. It was as if he had been leading Santiago processions all his life. Something more also affected the general. As he sat in his red roadster with Mrs. Melding, the people had cheered for him several times. This was a new experience for him. He began to toy with the idea that when Juniper was removed from the parish, he might dicker with Monsignor Gaspar about leaving the wooden saint in the hands of the Church. It would depend, precisely, on who replaced the priest.

General Braga was not the only one impressed by the fiesta. Snooping about in the crowd were two exceptional visitors who observed the festivities stiffly. One was a gringo Episcopalian bishop; the other was his wife, a plump woman in tweeds and walkover shoes. The bishop had come to Santiago de Gante as a tourist, but he was not beyond spying out useful information, particularly regarding saints.

"Look at them," Father Mérida pointed the Episcopalian out to Monsignor Gaspar. "There they are. They say he's a bishop—and he's married."

Gaspar didn't respond. Instead, he was staring at Santiago. His lips were puckered in a tight, dry smile that was half-grimace, for he was no longer sure that the saint was just a wooden statue. The long exciting day, and now the shimmering heat and the heaviness of the vestments, had done something to the monsignor. He had begun to sense the power of the saint over the imaginations of the people of Santiago de Gante.

As he looked up at the saint, he had the distinct impression that Santiago's boxlike face had changed expression. The saint was no longer the stern, soldierly Moor chaser. At this moment he seemed ever so slightly relaxed, as though he were having a good time. Gaspar reflected a moment on the vagaries of saints. This Santiago, for example, seemed as much a freebooter as Señor O'Murphy's Saint Patrick. He began to wonder how he had ever questioned the saint's importance.

"Look," Father Mérida said, nudging the monsignor. "There's the Episcopal bishop's wife."

Before Gaspar could get a close look, a couple of dozen men, dressed as pirates, put their shoulders under the long heavy poles extending outward from the bow and stern of the saint's float. They lifted it and staggered across the plaza.

Now the entire procession began to move. It extended out, caterpillar-like: the drummer and flutist, Temerio and Coconino, leading the way. They were followed by whirling *concheros,* by the clergy in their rich vestments, then by the saint's float, the official cars and the legions of Christians and Moors. Throughout the afternoon the procession would shuttle across the town, weaving back and forth among the pink- and rose-walled houses.

From the steps of the *Parlamento Inglés* Policarpio Flores viewed the crowd with awe as it streamed out of the plaza after the procession. In twenty years of Santiago fiestas, he had never seen one like this; the entire region had turned out for it, as well as half the tourists in Mexico. His bar had never before done such a wealth of business. But now, suddenly spying General Braga and Monsignor Gaspar, he frowned worriedly. Something must be done, he thought, something drastic to convince Braga and the monsignor that Santiago must remain in the church. Remembering the basket of gringo loot, still in the church, he realized that something must be done about that, too.

"It must happen now," he murmured resolutely.

A few minutes later, having retrieved Don Vasco and Ignacio from the procession, and calling Zapopan down from the church tower, Policarpio faced his friends in the back room of the *Parlamento.*

"The fiesta is keeping our padre, Braga, the monsignor and the police busy," he explained. "But it is useful for us to

remember there is that basket of loot in the church. It is
evidence that they might use against Juniper."

"Give me a pistol," Old Vasco said waspishly. "I'll remove
it from the church."

Policarpio shook his head. "Your idea is right," he said,
"but the method is wrong. Remember, a policeman is kneeling there, guarding it. If you seize it, you'll be in trouble as
well as our priest."

Ignacio wrinkled his volcanic face. "The padre seems to
think Santiago will help him," he said. Then he gave an ag-
nostic shrug. "I have never seen a priest get into so much
trouble, then expect miracles to get him out."

"We got him into this," Policarpio replied.

"We did?"

"If we hadn't driven Caldo out, he wouldn't be here."
Policarpio rose and began pacing the floor. After a bit, he
paused, adding, "And sometimes, I begin to think maybe
Santiago is behind all this."

Ignacio grunted dubiously. "If he is the brain, then let
him work it out."

"Yes, he could be the brain," Policarpio nodded. "But
there must be hands to do the work. It would be useful if we
gave a little push. Now, I have an idea." He glanced at his
friends and nodded sagely, saying, "There is much talent
among us. You, Ignacio, being an atheist, know a great deal
about religion. You, Don Vasco, can speak for banditry."
His glance rested upon Zapopan. "And you, being the sexton, have all the keys to the church."

A few minutes later, while the sound of firecrackers
marked the progress of the procession on the far side of town,
and the plaza was as deserted as a corner of the moon, Don
Ignacio slipped out of the *Parlamento Inglés* and went

around to the other side of the church where, with the aid
of a borrowed set of keys, he let himself into the church
sacristy. Here he hurriedly rummaged about until he found
a cassock that would fit his stocky frame. He draped himself
in it and put on a Roman collar. Then, carrying a large mis-
sal, as though he were reading it, he made his way into the
church and went directly to the confessional box near the
Santiago pedestal.

The policeman who was sitting in a pew, keeping an eye
on the pedestal, noticed the priest come in but gave it no
thought. A minute later he saw three men enter through the
main portals. He thought nothing of this, either, for the
men were dressed as Moors. They came up the side aisle.
One of them entered the confessional while the other two
waited.

The policeman shrugged, thinking that they were Moors
who had, during the battle earlier in the day, somehow gotten
involved in a saloon or two. They were now hastening to
be shriven so as to join the procession before it ended. Suddenly the policeman's interest was aroused. From the priest's
compartment of the confessional he heard loud comments.
It was the priest saying, "Oh my. Shameful!" And then,
"And you did it again? Shame, man!"

Suddenly the bearded Moor, his turban somewhat askew,
staggered from the box. He hurried rather stiffly to a pew in
the back of the church where he knelt and began praying
furiously. The policeman turned to watch, wondering what
manner of strange sins the man had committed.

A half-hour later, Zapopan came down from the church
tower and went next door to the *Parlamento Inglés*. He was
breathing heavily and there were still traces of charcoal dust
on his face, just enough to make people think he had been

one of the men in Santiago de Gante who had been elected
to play the part of a dark-skinned Moor for the day.

"The knickknacks?" Policarpio asked him.

"They're safely hidden up in the tower," Zapopan began
to shout.

Policarpio raised a hand, silencing him. "Good," he said.
"Now, we've time to think of some way to get rid of them."

25

ANGELS FLIGHT

Monsignor Gaspar had been unable to stand up under the pace of the procession. In the late afternoon he withdrew and returned to the hotel to freshen himself and to think over the problems that he must deal with.

Now, he stood on the balcony of his hotel room awaiting the return of the procession. The flushed and swollen sun had already gone down; a coolness had crept into the plaza. The music and movement below him was renewed. Beneath the glow of colored lights strung out from the bandstand and among the limes and laurels, the *serenata* or evening promenade had begun. Santiagan girls, ablaze with ornaments and Sunday finery, strolled in one direction around the square; the boys, teeth flashing and eyes questing in frank excitement, marched counter-clockwise.

Gaspar sniffed the evening air. The scent of laurels, limes and jasmine, and the faint acrid odor of Tzintzuntzan's gunpowder blended in a subtle heady perfume. It left him with a curious feeling of wonder, for in the air there was a half-abeyant, strange sense of the consummate, as though the miraculous hovered over Santiago de Gante like a faint bluish evening haze.

The monsignor glanced across toward the church and wondered if he should go again to examine the basket of stolen gringo treasure. It disconcerted and annoyed him that Juniper should admit the existence of the trinkets, yet refuse to assume any responsibility for them.

Suddenly, the monsignor stiffened to attention. Don Temerio and Don Coconino came fifing and drumming into the plaza from a side street. Behind them, moving and tipping awkwardly, came the saint's float and the procession. The *serenata* around the plaza abruptly disintegrated. People flowed toward and enveloped the *carroza* like metal filings drawn to a magnet. Only Santiago, San Jocobo and the weary angels were visible, bobbing above the heads of the crowd. The float moved toward the churchyard and came to rest near the skeletal shapes of the firework *castillos*.

Monsignor Gaspar withdrew from the balcony and hurried downstairs in order to make sure it would be Mérida who celebrated the Benediction in church. As he hurried across the square he bumped into General Braga who was again staring up at the cables overhead. The general glanced at him almost absent-mindedly, muttering, "When I had the fiesta at the inn, we never had real angels."

"These are not real," Gaspar corrected him. "They're children."

Braga nodded and sighed enviously.

"The evidence is still in the church?" Gaspar asked.

"I haven't looked," replied the general. "But Perlimplin says his man is still there. Until now, no one has been in the church except some Moors, to confess."

When the last *Laudate Dominum* had been sung and the church was still heavy with the pungency of incense, the smaller tower bells began to toll and the crowd poured out into the atrium and plaza. During the Benediction, Eulalia and Raimundo had knelt on each side of the altar. Now they were taken in hand by Mother Monica and another nun who rushed them to the convent to perform certain last duties so that there would be no accident over the crowd as had once happened during an angels' flight.

Meanwhile, up in the bell tower, Zapopan flexed his strong hands, preparing for the biggest bell ringing of the year. He felt a little depressed because *El Temblor* would not be rung, and yet the giant bell's inactivity was proving useful. Earlier in the afternoon he had carefully managed to hide the gringo treasure in its throat. The treasure had been put in a cloth bag which he had tied to the bell clapper. There had been some objections on the part of the young starlings living in the upside-down bell. They were beginning to fly now, and seemed to need all the room they could get within the bell.

"The stuff is in there," Zapopan shouted to Ignacio who had come up into the tower and was waiting to see that his children got off to a good start as angels. "You can ring the other bells, but not *El Temblor*. Remember."

Ignacio smiled and went to the railing to look down.

In the plaza below the crowd waited patiently. Tzintzuntzan had begun touching off fireworks. The ranchers and country people eyed them stolidly; the children and the canapé eaters in the crowd oohed and ahed, while the smaller children watched with eyes full of the gleam of initiates in a mystery. The band was playing something from *Carmen*. All the while, deep in the mass of onlookers, the feathered headdresses of the tireless *concheros* bobbed up and down.

Monsignor Gaspar followed Father Juniper outside and they stood on the church steps. Although a number of children came to kiss the padre's hand, the priest looked unhappy. It was as if the full realization of what might soon happen to him had finally penetrated his mind. This was especially evident when he glanced worriedly toward General Braga and Captain Perlimplin who stood with Señor O'Murphy.

The priest looked up toward the city-hall roof where a number of figures could be seen in silhouette. The girl-angel would be launched from that point, and to catch the scene, cameramen from a Mexico City television company had mounted their equipment on the rooftop.

Suddenly a series of rockets hissed into the night sky. Then a pin wheel broke loose and sailed wildly into the crowd while shouts and screams marked its erratic course. Here and there firecrackers exploded with foolish reports and colored flares danced among the trees in the plaza like nervous ghosts. The displays, one after the other became more breath-taking and frightening. In Santiago de Gante, as in all of Mexico, fireworks assumed an importance somewhere between a presidential election and religion. The fingers of dizzy green and red rockets climbed starward in a dozen directions and seemed to drag the earth up with them.

Fablehaft's band struck up the national anthem. Finally, the last of the *castillos*, a monumental structure, was ignited. Flame and smoke gushed forth, depicting the handsome figure of Santiago and his horse in shimmering red, green and white tracery. Then abruptly, the whole thing exploded, turning the night into a brilliant carnival of vivid streamers and colored planets.

While smoke shrouded the plaza and curled upward, floodlights mounted upon the rooftops around the square flashed on, bathing the filigree church towers in their glare. The bells in the tower loft began clanging and spinning, end over end.

Juniper could no longer resist the excitement. He turned

to Monsignor Gaspar, saying, "Now they'll be taking one of
the angels up to the church tower and the other over to the
city-hall roof. When the bells stop, they'll fly." He looked
toward the float and the figures of Santiago and San Jocobo.
"This is the part that I think Santiago enjoys most," he said.
"This, and chasing the Moors."

Even though the bells had not stopped their wrangling, a
great ahing rose from the crowd. A gringo woman near Father Juniper suddenly screamed, then fainted. At the same
time a swirl of black starlings and, with them, two white
doves, flew out of the laurels and whirled over the plaza.
For a flashing instant they were caught and pinned by the
glare of the lights.

"Angels!" someone shouted.

Juniper looked up. He knew what to expect: a boy-angel
trolleying out from the church tower, dangling from the
cable somewhat like limp wash; a girl-angel sailing from
the bunting decorated city-hall roof to meet him above the
plaza.

But suddenly Juniper's eyes widened. Something was
wrong! The angels weren't following the cables. Instead of
hanging and swaying limply, they flew through the swirling
fireworks smoke with grace, hovering lightly over the jammed
plaza like hummingbirds. The two angels seemed to be
carrying baskets larger than usual; and now, in place of
making the Latin oration as was the custom, they upended
their baskets.

There was another, sharper gasp from the crowd. In place
of the snowy flurry of tiny paper prayers, a shower of glittering objects seemed to pour from the baskets. The first thing
to plummet into the mass of people below was a gold-plated
corkscrew with a ruby set in it. Then came the rain of

cigarette lighters, ash trays and all manner of silver knick-knacks.

Suddenly the angels soared upward. They were surrounded by the flock of starlings which had flown around the church. Both the birds and the angels vanished.

Up in the church tower Zapopan paused in his task of ringing the medium bells. He caught a glimpse of the giant *El Temblor* slowly swinging end over end, and of Don Ignacio, nearby, arms flailing about his head as he tried to ward off a flight of chick starlings excitedly flying about his ears. Zapopan leaped toward the big bell, trying to halt its movement. Then he saw that the throat of the bell was empty.

Meanwhile there was a riot in the street below. Men and women scrambled for the precious objects that rained down upon them. General Braga recognized a silver stiletto as it struck the steps near him. He roared out to Captain Perlimplin, "The loot! It's the gringo loot! Round it up!"

Perlimplin scrambled after the knife, but before he could reach it, a ragged urchin had snatched it away and vanished into the crowd.

At the same time, Monsignor Gaspar turned toward Father Juniper, giving him a dazed, inquiring stare. "What is it, Junipero? What is it?" he asked.

Juniper looked up at the sky again. He was not quite sure, but he felt that he had witnessed something which filled him with awe. There were no angels now. They, and the birds, had simply vanished as though an invisible sponge had wiped them from the blackboard of the sky.

"Junipero! What's the meaning of it?" Gaspar's voice rose insistently.

The padre looked at his superior, and said softly, "There were angels! We saw them!"

"Of course, angels! I saw them!"

"They didn't use the cables."

The monsignor gulped enormously. "No cables?"

Father Juniper nodded. "None," he replied. Then, as if it were an afterthought, he scratched his tonsure wonderingly, adding, "I suppose they were real angels."

26

THE MIRACLE HUNTERS

Late in the afternoon of the following day a large black
limousine drew up in front of the pink rectory. Although the
sky was cloudless, the shopkeepers and townsmen watched
Monsignor Gaspar hurry outside with an open umbrella to
meet the car. They saw Bishop Sierra ease his large body
from the back seat and enter the parish house. Some minutes
afterward, a panel truck pulled up behind the limousine.
It was dark blue in color and had *Televisión Azteca* lettered
upon its sides. Men busily carried cameras, coils of electrical
cable and a motion-picture projector from the truck into the
rectory. Finally, General Braga's red roadster arrived. The
general and Captain Perlimplin hurried into the priest's
house.

Shortly before evening the projector was set up in the
patio of the rectory and the television company's technicians
were almost ready. To one side of the patio, the bishop, Monsignor Gaspar and Juniper sat together beneath the cloister
arches. The bishop, a big man with saurian eyes and a purse-
like mouth, was wearing the black cassock of a working priest.
Normally on an official or diocesan visit he would have come

attired in rochet and mozzetta, and there would have been a strictly observed ceremony at the church door. His visit today was different, however. There were rumors of a miracle.

Before his arrival, Bishop Sierra had received a long telephonic report. He had been given the details of Father Juniper's curious behavior, the attitudes and beliefs of the Santiagans regarding their saint, and a complete summary of the events during the fiesta. Since there was nothing more to add to this, and while waiting for the cameramen to thread the film that had been taken of the fiesta, the bishop discussed liturgical prayer and formal prayer with Monsignor Gaspar. During such talk his heavy-jowled face would light up for there was argument, indeed, as to exactly how a Benedictine abbot should sing a Pontifical High Mass on a double of the second class in the presence of a cardinal archbishop of the Ambrosian Rite.

Father Juniper listened politely, but it was all beyond him. Furthermore, he was troubled by the bishop's businesslike visit. Perhaps the bishop was one of those practical men who didn't understand saints, especially saints that you had to be somewhat lenient toward? Juniper found it easy to put himself in Santiago's place because his faith was simple and direct. Undoubtedly the saint had wanted to see his wooden likeness installed in the church. He had done some unusual things, perhaps even small miracles, to bring this about. But maybe he had gone too far with it? Father Juniper had visions of the bishop and God being angry with the saint.

While the bishop and Gaspar argued, while Juniper worried, Doña Maria was busily passing around clay cups of coffee. Though ordinarily she might have resented so many high churchmen sitting around in the rectory, today her attitude was different. Bishop Sierra had won her respect, partially because he was big and looked as though he enjoyed eating, and because he had accepted the crude cups and had not demanded china.

Standing a bit apart from the clergymen, General Braga and Captain Perlimplin waited uneasily. Perlimplin's glance kept straying nervously from the green parrot which eyed him with suspicious anger to the reed wastebasket resting upon a table near Bishop Sierra's elbow. The basket was the same one which had held the gringo treasure. The captain winced as he remembered the events of the previous night.

Immediately after the angels had jettisoned the treasure some of his policemen had tried to recover the knickknacks, but without success. The Santiagans had gotten away with everything, and now not a single person in town would admit knowing anything about the objects. A little later, when he had entered the church with General Braga, Father Juniper and the monsignor, he had found Corporal Taxco sitting in the pew near the saint's pedestal. In the recess behind the pedestal there had been nothing but that empty basket.

Corporal Taxco had sworn that he had been watching the pedestal faithfully. No one had even been close to it since early morning except a priest and several Moors who confessed in the afternoon. This had been somewhat confusing because there were no priests in town except Juniper and Mérida and Gaspar, and they had been in the procession.

Following the interview with the corporal, Monsignor Gaspar had looked into the empty basket, then had asked Father Juniper if he recognized it. The pastor had admitted it was his wastebasket.

"Then where are the jeweled knickknacks that were in it?" Gaspar had demanded. "You admitted, padre, that you had placed certain objects in it."

Juniper had given the basket a gentle, houndlike sniff.

"What things?" he had countered. "There's nothing in the basket. You can see."

"Find the children who were the angels," General Braga had suggested. "They should know how they got the things."

This was the part that had scared Perlimplin, and it had likewise begun to shake Monsignor Gaspar as well as General Braga. It was discovered that neither of Don Ignacio's children had even reached the city-hall roof and the church tower. "Little Eulalia's cardboard wings had come undone," Mother Monica had explained upon being questioned. "The two children were in the convent with me. We were delayed."

"Naturally, the children had nothing to do with it," Father Juniper had explained. "This time, it was angels."

"A miracle," Mother Monica had agreed.

Thus, the miracle had been suggested. At that point, Perlimplin had suggested it would be best to drop the whole affair, but Monsignor Gaspar wouldn't agree to it. He had telephoned long distance to the bishop. Then the television company had been asked to process the film of the fiesta and rush it back to Santiago de Gante.

"Lights, please."

The voice of the projectionist alerted the company in the patio. Maria ran to switch off the cloister lights. There was a whir of cogs and wheels in the projector; then a beam of light played upon the screen hung near the fountain and a picture of the fiesta crowd came into focus.

Captain Perlimplin crossed himself quickly and glanced toward the bishop.

Bishop Sierra fitted on a pair of thick-lensed glasses and leaned forward attentively. All this talk of miracles annoyed him somewhat, as it would annoy any busy man burdened by diocesan affairs. He had established a complete Curia modeled on the Roman: his chancery handled matters legal and disciplinarian—the bureau of missions, the marriage tribunal, the bureau of charities and the building program. But somehow, he had never allowed for a department of miracles. The thought of a miracle faintly upset him, not because he disbelieved, but because a town like Santiago de Gante might claim one. A troublesome parish was hardly the place for a miracle.

The picture on the screen showed the flickering lights and shadows upon the upturned faces of the people in the plaza during the fiesta. Then it caught the expressions of wonder and astonishment.

"Where are the angels?" asked the bishop.

All at once Monsignor Gaspar sat bolt upright. He gripped the bishop's arm and pointed at the screen. "Look!"

A part of the church belfry came into view upon the screen. It was like illuminated filigree against a dark sky. Suddenly there was a flight of birds; then in one corner of the velvet sky, where a hole seemed to have been poked through, an abrupt stream of glittering objects poured forth. The camera's eye trailed the falling knickknacks downward and offered a final shot of the riot in the plaza below. With this, the film ended.

Bishop Sierra turned his saurian glance upon Gaspar. "Angels?" he asked heavily.

"But we saw them last night," replied the monsignor.

General Braga moved his chair closer to the bishop. "I saw them, too," he said. "Definitely. Everyone in town saw them." He glared suspiciously at the television technicians. "Do you have the right film?"

The cameraman nodded. "Señor," he said. "I ran one of the cameras last night. I had angels in my viewer, if those were angels we saw. They should be on the film. I can't explain why they aren't."

"And those objects falling from the sky?" asked the bishop as the lights were turned on. He glanced toward Perlimplin. "A curious sight, indeed. What would you say they were?"

Captain Perlimplin coughed in embarrassment. "It would be hard to say," he replied.

Father Juniper flashed him a look of gratitude. It pleased him that Perlimplin was anxious to help, but he felt it was no longer necessary. There was a need for frankness now. On the previous evening, while being questioned, he had been evasive because he suspected that his friends, the Parliamentarians, might have taken the treasure from under the saint's pedestal. It had been a dangerous thing, even for friends to do. But this morning after Policarpio and Zapopan had blandly disclaimed any connection with the affair, he had begun to put another interpretation on it.

"The things you saw," he explained candidly to the bishop, "were the trinkets that got into my pockets. I think Santiago took them back so as to reward the people of the town who have been very faithful to him. Why else would he allow valuable objects to be scattered about so?"

As the priest was saying this, General Braga began nodding vigorously. Although he was not one to go in search of miracles, neither was he a man to deny them if they were properly presented. Some years ago when he had toyed with the idea of running for the presidency of the Republic, he had done what every candidate must do if he is to stand any chance at all in the elections—he had made a well-publicized pilgrimage to the Shrine of Guadalupe on the outskirts of Mexico City. Although he had finally withdrawn from politics, he had not forgotten The Virgin's shrine and the countless tourists and pilgrims who visited there. Now, he

thought, if The Virgin had initiated a miracle on the drab
hill at Tepeyac, why shouldn't Santiago do something in a
place as fine as Santiago de Gante? One shouldn't discourage
such things. Definitely. What if the authorities in the old
days had sent police to investigate and to arrest little Juan
Diego who had seen the Virgin of Guadalupe that first time?

He gave the bishop and Father Juniper a broad smile,
saying, "This affair of the angels flying. A miracle. Definitely. The other problem of the missing knickknacks is of
no importance."

The bishop frowned. "I saw no angels in the picture," he
said.

"But there were angels," replied Gaspar. "I can't explain,
but there were angels."

"It is very simple," Juniper put in. "It is just that angels
do not photograph well." He smiled vaguely. "It would be
troublesome if they were to be photographed; there are so
many angels flying about at all times, guardian angels and
special-messenger angels."

The bishop's mouth sagged slightly. He shook his head
slowly, murmuring, "Do you suggest this as a miracle?"

"That angels cannot be photographed is no miracle," Juniper smiled. "It is something God arranged a long time
ago because he knew there would be cameras. But when two
angels come to Santiago de Gante and fly during the fiesta
of our saint, this could be a miracle."

Bishop Sierra frowned with quiet deliberation. "Such a
phenomenon must be investigated," he said. "But with caution. It would mean that the wooden statue of Santiago must
remain in the church during the period of the study." He
paused, looking at General Braga. "I understand there is
some talk of a contract? Some problem regarding the possession of the wooden figure?"

The general's brows creased deeply. He thought of Juniper, of the angels and the saint. He had no intention of being outdone by them.

"The bishop speaks of the contract," Father Juniper put in.

Braga nodded. Then abruptly, he reached in his pocket and took out a folded paper. It was the contract that he and Juniper had signed. With his accustomed vigor he rose and strode to a niche where a vigil light burned. He touched the paper in the flame, and as it flared up, he lit his cigar with it.

Turning toward the others, he gave them an inextinguishable smile, saying, "Bother the contract! We've got a miracle. Definitely! The statue belongs to the church."

27

A THING LIKE CHEESE

In the high clerical language of a man like Monsignor Gaspar, a miracle is not merely a supernatural event beyond human power, that is to say, miraculum or τέρας; it must also possess the attributes of πυεύματι θεοῦ, meaning, God-given or divine. In addition it must have some overtones as a seal of divine truth, or a sign of divine intention. And then there is the matter of filing it in its proper pigeonhole; of tabbing it as a cosmical miracle, one of healing or cure, or some other variety.

Having had much practical experience with miracles, the Church is always cautious about them. It regards any new phenomenon of this kind as though it were a fissionable product that might blow up unexpectedly, or unleash an unpredictable chain reaction. For reasons such as these the Church likes to properly age its miracles and have them under control before accepting them officially.

Thus, for many years to come, Santiago de Gante would be without an official miracle, even though by the mere act of instituting the processes of an inquiry, the Church nodded its head slightly and kept a controlling finger in the pie.

However, as far as Father Juniper and his parishioners were concerned, there had been a miracle. Most Santiagans demanded no additional proofs because they knew their saint. They accepted the fact that heavenly angels had flown above their streets without awe or wonder. In Santiago de Gante, as almost anywhere in Mexico, such things can happen. A Santiagan is rarely startled if he sees a pink horse on the streets one day, then sees the exact same animal in another color on the following morning. In their way of thinking, miracles were just a little more complicated.

For a long time after the fiesta there were arguments, of course, as to exactly how the miracle had occurred, and whether it would do the town any good. The gringos who had seen it were a bit shy and uneasy when they spoke of it. Often their voices rose with notes of embarrassed uncertainty. One of them, Miss Goldengrove, had been so impressed, however, that she had let herself be baptized. But when any serious arguing was done, it usually occurred in The Vicarage of the *Parlamento Inglés*.

The Parliamentarians were, in a sense, insiders on the miracle. Unlike Gaspar, they attributed several assorted miracles to Santiago. Regarding the miracle of the jettisoned treasure there were some doubts. Each of them had played some part in it, and could account for his rôle, but no one knew who or what had set the big bell tolling, thus launching the treasure. Had it been Ignacio who had stood nearest the bell? He denied this bluntly. Or had it been the starling chicks? Or Santiago himself? Since none of them had ever told Father Juniper of the removal of the treasure to the church tower, only Juniper believed in the totality of that miracle—and no one would dream of disillusioning him.

But it was the other miracle, the angels' flight, which had

even shaken Don Ignacio, about which most of the discussions occurred.

One day, not too long after Santiago's fiesta, another miracle argument took place when Junipero, Policarpio, Old Vasco, Don Ignacio and the baker, Villada, had gathered for a late afternoon of dominoes.

"The miracle will bring many visitors to our town," Villada observed. "Santiago de Gante will become as holy as Lourdes."

Ignacio slapped the clay dust from his sleeve and looked up sharply. "It'll bring more tourists and gringos," he said flatly. "Will that be good?"

Old Vasco narrowed his eyes angrily at Ignacio who was mixing the dominoes. That morning he had laboriously carved himself a spare double-four which he had blackened and dotted. Now he awaited an opportunity to put it to use, and he resented the way Ignacio was watching him.

Policarpio pulled his own dominoes toward himself, then glanced at Ignacio. "It is useful to remember, Ignacio," he said sardonically, "the saint is now in the church and available for fiestas. General Braga has given him up. Furthermore, there is peace in town. *Caray!* The miracle is good for all of us. My *pulque* tastes much better. Haven't you noticed? And Tzintzuntzan has not had an explosion over in his place since the return of the saint. The miracle even helps you. You're selling more idols. I think it might be useful if you began making clay figures of Santiago and San Jocobo."

Ignacio grunted indifferently. "You watch," he observed darkly. "The thing of the angels, and of the treasure, were mistakes."

"A mistake?" Juniper looked up gently.

"Sure, padre. It's no good for the town. Right now neither

Braga nor the bishop mind because they're waiting. They
don't care if we have the saint. But when the real money
begins coming in, and after the Church declares the miracle
official, then there'll be trouble. Big commercial trouble."
The idol-maker rubbed the pitted, volcanic skin of his
cheeks, adding, "You'll see. The rich ones will want to build
a special shrine for Santiago. They won't let him go out to
chase Moors."

During this speech of Ignacio's, Old Vasco managed to
slip the counterfeit domino into his array. He leaned back
with a sigh, glanced toward the *pulque* vats where Juniper's
green parrot, El Furioso, was peering at his reflection in the
brew with unrequited fury. "If Caldo were here," the ex-
bandit observed, "the miracle would go sour. But with us
here, nothing can happen."

Ignacio snapped a domino down contemptuously. "I think
of a bombing that went wrong some time ago," he commented.

At this, Old Vasco spat angrily. He pushed back his chair
and grabbed for his machete. Both Policarpio and Villada
pulled the old man down before he could do violence. To
smooth the atmosphere, Policarpio turned toward Father Juniper and asked, "What do you think, padre? What do you
say about the miracle? You haven't really given an opinion
since it happened."

While the eyes of all the others turned toward him, the
pastor creased his brows. His pink cheeks reddened somewhat. It was as in the old days at the monastery when the
philosophic monks had put questions to him. He studied
his *pulque* jar and hiccuped gently. Actually, he had not
given much thought to the little miracles that seemed to dog
his footsteps. He was in the habit of just accepting such
wonders. But since the fiesta, and the flight of the angels

which had seemed to remove so many burdens from his
shoulders, he had thought deeply upon their miracle. It
had changed many things in the parish. Now the canapé
eaters, both Catholics and non-Catholics were coming to
church. Again, he was giving sermons both in Spanish and
English, and there was money in Doña Maria's stove-black-
ened treasury pot. But the thing that gave him most comfort
was that the bishop and Monsignor Gaspar were no longer
urging him to put chrome steel statues of saints in the pale
green church.

"Was the miracle good or bad?" Villada prompted the
priest.

Juniper smiled at his friends. He absent-mindedly
scratched his tonsure, seeming to tip the halo-like fringe of
hair precariously. "It is hard to say anything about so young
a miracle," he observed. "It's like with strong cheese. There
is the taste and the smell. In everything there is always a
little good and a little bad. One cannot do much about such
things."

"The saint should have thought up some other miracle,"
Ignacio replied stubbornly.

"What kind?" Villada asked.

"We don't order the saints around," Father Juniper put in.

"I know a miracle that would take him a long time to
accomplish, and it would be good," Villada announced.

"What would that be?" Juniper asked.

The baker smiled challengingly. "A simple thing," he said.
"Santiago could try converting Ignacio!"

Father Juniper glanced from Villada to the idol-maker.
He shook his head slightly. Ignacio was no longer a problem,
he was sure. Of late, he had had the feeling that the idol-
maker was coming closer to believing. It was only a matter
of time.

"I don't think Santiago should bother," Juniper said. "But there is something more important that needs attention."

Policarpio stared sharply at the priest and gulped uneasily. He remembered an evening visit he had had with the pastor.

One night, shortly after the bishop and Gaspar had left Santiago de Gante, Policarpio had run next door to the pink parish house with a loaf of amusing cheese and a jug of *pulque*. The gifts had been but an excuse to see the padre and re-examine him. In his anticlerical way, Policarpio had begun to worry about the *cura*. Now that the latter had a miracle on his hands, it might go to his head. He would need watching.

When he had rapped at Juniper's bedroom door after Maria had let him into the rectory, he had been startled by the priest's appearance. Juniper was barefooted. He had on dark broadcloth trousers and a heavy brown sleeveless vest, the sort that peons make by sewing together two coarse saddle blankets of wiry donkey hair. Policarpio had stared at the prickly shirt.

"I'm not disturbing you?" he asked. "I—I brought some cheese."

"I was praying a bit to Santiago," The padre smiled benignly.

"I'll come back another time," Policarpio stuttered apologetically. He was unable to wrench his eyes from the hair shirt.

"No. Don't go," Juniper insisted. "Let's share the cheese. Also, there is some advice I wish to ask of you. I'll put on a cassock and we'll sit in the patio."

"Do you always wear that shirt, padre?"

"This?" Juniper scratched himself through the bristly vest. "It is what I wear. The evenings have a chill."

Policarpio's jaw had sagged. He had never seen a living saint, but in his youth he had read about monks and saints who had made a practice of wearing hair shirts without noticeable discomfort.

A few minutes later he and Juniper sat in the rectory patio, sipping *pulque* and tasting cheese. The evening was nice. The play of water in the fountain made music around them, while above, the stars revolved and glittered in the Mexican sky. There was a smell of rosemary twigs burning, and once, from somewhere across the town, a burro brayed the time. Upon the roof-edge overlooking the patio twelve adult starlings were tucked in sleep, while beside them there were some smaller blackbirds who seemed to be serving a kind of guardsmen apprenticeship.

Staring at the priest, Policarpio was struck by the deep simplicity in his round face. Suddenly, he thought how ridiculous it was that anyone should suspect the padre of losing his head over a miracle, or that a man like Juniper needed anyone's advice. He smiled at the priest, asking, "What advice was it you wanted, padre?"

Father Juniper folded his plump hands over his bowl-shaped belly. "I have been thinking," he said. "Now that we have settled the trouble over the saint, shouldn't there be another project?"

Policarpio frowned. "What project, padre?"

"Do you think it would be expecting too much of our saint if I asked him for something again?"

"But what?" Policarpio edged forward on his chair uneasily.

"You know La Yegua, the Mare Lady who inhabits the gorge below the Old Bridge—" said the priest. "I wonder if

Santiago would help if I set out to exorcise her? Perhaps the bishop would like this, too?"

Policarpio sat back with a sigh of dismay. He gave Juniper a long careful scrutiny and shook his head slowly. There were some priests, he thought, who just never got over getting into trouble. They needed a saint to help them out.